MW00514059

# A PERFECT DEATH FOR HOLLYWOOD

# A PERFECT DEATH FOR HOLLYWOOD

RICHARD NEHRBASS

HarperCollinsPublishers

 For information address HarperCollins Publishers, 10 East 53rd Street, New York, NY 10022.

FIRST EDITION

*Designed by Cassandra J. Pappas*

---

Library of Congress Cataloging-in-Publication Data

Nehrbass, Richard
A perfect death for Hollywood / Richard Nehrbass.
p. cm.
ISBN 0-06-016636-3 (cloth)
I. Title.
PS3564.E2645P47 1991
813′.54—dc20 90-55968

---

91 92 93 94 95 CC/HC 10 9 8 7 6 5 4 3 2 1

*To my mother,*
*and the memory of my father*

# A PERFECT DEATH FOR HOLLYWOOD

I sat back in the chair, put my feet on the desk, and closed my eyes as the words swarmed around my head.

Davey Lipsett said, "It's not going to take that long, Vic. It's no big deal."

Allison Hutton said, "She's dead, and no one gives a damn!"

Davey twisted noisily in his chair and raised his shrill parrotlike voice. "Look, Vic, I'd consider this a favor. I'd consider it a favor, the studio would consider it a favor. You understand what I'm saying? The studio, goddamn it! I don't know what the big deal is. You're on retainer and we bring this to you and you give us this shit."

"The studio is *not* paying for this," Allison quickly put in. Not raising her voice but insistent, making her point, making sure I understood. "I'm paying for it. She was my friend. *I'm* paying!"

"So what's the *deal*?" Davey squealed. "Christ!"

I opened my eyes and peered over at Davey's round, sweaty face. "I don't want to do it, Davey. I'm too busy, I've got too many other things going. Besides, it's a police matter. Do it right, go to the cops."

"Vic, for Christ's sake, we're *asking*! This is important—"

"You've heard about it, haven't you?" Allison interrupted. "You've seen it on TV? And been reading about it?"

I stood up and walked over to the coffee machine and brought back a cup. As I sat down again I stared at her across the desk. Allison Hutton was an elegant, self-assured young woman with reddish-brown hair to her shoulders, pale baby-soft skin, and the largest, clearest, greenest eyes I'd ever seen. I took a sip of coffee and said, "The Hollywood Vampire," not trying to hide my sarcasm.

"Look, Vic, don't believe everything you hear on TV," Davey said quickly. "The girl was killed and dumped under the Hollywood sign. That's all; forget all that vampire crap."

"She was crucified," I reminded him.

"She was *tortured* to death," Allison said. Her voice went suddenly soft. "Someone drove nails through her wrists and ankles before killing her. Then he took her up in the hills and put her under the H of the sign. He laid her out naked on the ground, looking up at the stars."

"The TV guys love it, don't they?" Davey said with a disgusted shake of his head as he slumped back in his chair. "The Vampire Killer, crucifixions, a nude corpse. It's a fucking circus."

I started to shake my head again but Davey quickly interrupted.

"Look, Vic, I know you gotta reputation for not taking orders real good; someone told me that's why you quit the force. But we *pay* for your services! Christ, you wanna go back to lookin' for runaways? You want the good life, sometimes you gotta do things you don't necessarily want to do. Like help us find out why this poor girl's been killed."

I said to Allison, "According to the news she hasn't even been identified. How do you know it's your friend?"

She stared at me, her face completely without emotion. "I know!"

Again I shook my head. I could already see where this was heading: teenage girl, probably an illegal, probably a hooker from what the papers said, probably into dope and all the other assorted Hollywood vices, is picked up by a freak bent on violence. A sad young woman in a sad life that ended shortly and brutishly but not unexpectedly. I didn't want to do it. Not now, not ever. "Still not interested," I said to them both. "Go to the police. That's why they're there, Davey. They've probably got a dozen people working on it already."

Allison sat unmoving, watching me, but Davey's fat body bobbed nervously in the chair. "Not a chance, Vic . . ." He began to babble again but after a moment I unconsciously tuned him out and found myself staring at the elegant Allison, sitting quietly with her marvelous long legs crossed, just a flash of white thigh exposed along one side. She noticed me staring and granted me a small, unexpected smile. *Like a gift,* I thought. *Or a secret being shared between old friends.*

"*Vic . . .*" Davey was pleading, the words coming to me vaguely now. I had seen him speak for an hour and a half without notes at a premiere once when none of the announced stars showed up and the fans were ready to tear the theater down. Talking was Davey's business; he had been in PR at half a dozen studios over the years and had it down to an art form. Turn on the Davey Doll, people said, and he doesn't stop until you rip the batteries out. Unexpectedly

Allison broke in on him, bringing me back to reality. "What are those marks on the wall behind your head?"

"Bullet holes."

Davey was suddenly out of his chair, hovering over Allison like an anxious parent. "Hey, Allison, sugar, baby, why don't you go out in the waiting room a minute, read an old *National Geographic,* study up on Sri Lanka while I talk to Vic, here."

Allison turned suddenly on Davey, gave him an angry look, and opened her mouth to argue. But then she abruptly changed her mind and rose and slowly left the room, throwing me a final glance as I settled back in my chair again and waited for the explosion. The moment the door shut Davey's voice flared up.

"Jesus Christ, Vic! What the hell you doing this for? Take her on, it's no big thing. Why are you fighting me?"

I gazed at the flat, sweaty, fifty-year-old face across the desk with exasperation. "I told you why, Davey. I've got a theft investigation at the prop department at NBC. I've got a gambling ring soaking the crew at a location shoot in the Santa Monica Mountains that I'm going to have to farm out to someone else because I'm too busy to handle it. And I've got a thirteen-year-old daughter who wants to go on vacation. Besides, your friend's a whore."

He waved his arms wildly as if he were being attacked by a swarm of bees. "She's an *entertainer*! She used to work for the studio. Christ, she's not a streetwalker—she's on her own, she's got about a half dozen clients; they got her set up in an apartment on Sunset." His tone suddenly softened and he became almost dreamy. "Really something, though, isn't she? You ever seen anything that looks that fuckin' *good* before? Christ!"

"What does Annie think, Davey?"

"Come on, Vic! Cheap shot. Allison's a friend, a sorta colleague, she still works for the studio once in a while. I'm not dickin' her. Anyway, from what I hear you ain't leading no monastic life. What are you getting on me for?"

"Forget it," I said. "It was a stupid remark. But I'm not taking the case, Davey. I've got too many other things going."

Davey hit the arm of his chair with his fist. "You're going to Vegas to gamble and get drunk and lay around next to the pool for a week with a hangover. Right? Or you're going fishing! Jesus, that's it, isn't it? You're going goddamn *fishing*!"

"I'm going to Mexico, Davey. Next week when Tracy gets out of school. We're going to do a little traveling, *maybe* a little fishing, a little father–daughter bonding." I smiled at him and laced my fingers behind my head. "Quality time."

"Jesus, Vic, fucking Mexico's been there eighty million years. It'll be there next month. Tracy'll be there next month. And what do you mean telling Allison those are fucking *bullet holes* on the wall? They're nail holes, used to be a picture there, horses or something."

"A sports car. A Morgan."

"So, Jesus—"

"Forget it, Davey. I'm going to Mexico."

"Forget nothing, goddamn it. All right. I'll give you the straight skinny, you fuckin' hardass. You know Teddy Kotzwinkle?"

"Studio VP?"

"The one. And not just VP. Christ, we're all VPs. They think it don't look good if I'm a 'publicist' so they call it VP in charge of marketing. Same fuckin' thing. Teddy's an executive VP, though, and he holds our futures in his grubby little hands. And he's the guy who signs the check we send you for a retainer each month so you can make enough money to take off whenever you want to go fishing, for Christ's sake, in Mexico or Brazil or wherever you're always disappearing to. Teddy is one of the lovely Allison's special friends, if you get my drift, and he wants your personal attention on this case. Is this all clear to you now?"

I sighed and looked at him. I thought Davey and I were better friends than that.

"It begins to be," I said. "We call it blackmail."

"Look, this is all we want from you: You nose around a little, make Allison happy, talk to some people, try to find out who did in her friend. So you take two weeks and you don't dig up anything and you say, 'Gee, Allie, I busted my gonads and we got diddly-poop to show for it, I think we oughtta throw in the towel.' Two weeks, Vic; that's all we're asking."

"Let the police handle it, Davey. The guy who did this is a psychopath. That sort of thing is out of my line."

"Come *on,* Vic! The cops *are* working on it. Allie just wants a little more, the personal touch. And she can afford it. What's the problem?"

"Do you like fishing, Davey?"

"Vic! I don't even *eat* fish. I don't go near the ocean. I get seasick on the boat ride at Disneyland. Where is this conversation going?"

"Not ocean fishing. Fly fishing in little white-water trout streams in the spring runoff up in the Sierras."

"Vic, don't go getting nostalgic or anything. Okay? I'm a businessman, we're talking business here. Not fish."

"You stand hip deep in icy water for half a day, casting back and forth, back and forth with a stupid-looking little artificial fly you've tied on the end of your line, hoping for a strike. Skill and technique are important, of course, but you know what's most important?"

"Jesus, a moral! Is it hot in here or what? Can we open a window?"

"*Patience,* Davey. You've got to have patience, you've got to be calm and relaxed and learn to wait. That's why cops catch killers and PIs don't: The cops can afford to sit and wait for the bad guys to make a mistake because no one's paying a per diem and no one's making it into something personal. Your friend doesn't want to wait; it's something *very* personal to her, and she wants the killer caught yesterday. It doesn't work that way. It's never worked that way. Why don't we tell her the facts of life and save her some money and heartache? She'll be richer, and I'll go fishing, and a thirteen-year-old girl will be happy."

"Vic, Tracy's happy now. Every time I see her she's happy; she was *born* happy. But how happy is she going to be when her daddy can't take her to the orthodontist because his biggest account went south?"

I shook my head. "Threats, Davey."

"Truth, Vic. This girl here wants some help, some big people in town want you to be it. I'm just telling you. Not threats."

Davey tugged nervously at his tie, an intense and remarkably ugly combination of reds and oranges and yellows; he knew it was ugly and that people snickered at it, and he loved every minute of it. He once told me he had the largest collection of ugly ties in America. ("Not counting TV weather guys, of course.") It was all part of the PR shtick: People *expect* them to dress like idiots and know all the latest off-color jokes, as well as who's doing what to whom and who's on the way up—or out. And Davey did it as well as the best. Hell, he *was* the best. So why was I fighting him like this? I saw sweat marks curling down the arms of his shirt, and his face was losing its color. Teddy Kotzwinkle, a studio despot who ran his department like a 1920s-era mogul, was leaning hard. And he had the power to do it. Davey looked beaten as he sank back in his chair. He yanked out a handkerchief and wiped at the sweat on his brow.

Christ.

"Did you drive her here, Davey?"

His eyes leapt up at me, wary, not certain of my point. "Yeah—"

"I'll take her home." I pushed myself out of the chair and crossed over to the door and yanked it open, motioning Allison inside. "See you later, Davey. Say hello to Annie."

He scampered up and raced toward the door before I could change my mind. "Yeah! Hey, thanks, Vic. You won't regret it, I mean it, you really won't, I'll see to it. Hey, I'll see you later, sugar." He winked at Allison and scurried out of the office like a terrier darting from under its master's feet, and for an uneasy second I wondered if I'd just been had.

After the door shut Allison settled into her chair in the sudden silence of the office and stared coolly at me. "So how did he persuade you?"

"How does anything get done around here?" I said as I sat back down behind the desk.

"Money and friends. But why not, right? This is Hollywood." She wasn't smiling, but I sensed a note of triumph in her exquisite green eyes. I punched a button on the desk.

"Everything you say is being taped now." I announced the date and time of day and then sat back and said, "Shall we start somewhere original? Like near the beginning," and immediately felt like an idiot. When sarcasm crept into my voice like that it was a sure sign for me to back off; I was losing my objectivity to a childish irritation and I didn't like it. I had accepted the case, I told myself; now I might as well make the best of it.

"I want you to understand something first," Allison said. "*I'm* paying you. Not Davey, not the studio. You're working for me."

I switched off the tape and said, "But as a favor to the studio."

"Exactly." She looked at me without emotion, but confident, full of the assurance that came from usually getting her way. As I watched the calm expressionless face, the clear unblinking eyes, I thought, *There's something not quite real about her; she's too perfect, too untouchable.* Even the clothes she wore and the colors she had surrounded herself with seemed too pure and flawless, like a picture in a fashion magazine—something to look at but not touch.

I switched on the tape again, a tingle of uneasiness running like a spider along my spine. "What is it you want from me?"

"I want you to come with me to the morgue. I want to identify her and get her body sent home to her family for burial. In Mexico."

"Why do you need me? Call a cop. Or go down there yourself."

She bristled at me, and for the first time I saw some real emotion in her face. "I'm not going to the cops. They give me nothing but trouble, they—"

I gave her an impatient nod. "All right, we ID her. Then what?"

"Then you find out who killed her."

"As simple as that?"

"Look, Mr. Eton, I know cops, I know how they think. Another dead whore, shove it in a drawer. I want someone *looking.*"

"Normally I'd agree with you. But not this time. This is a media case, minicams at the sign, interviews with the chief, editorials in the papers, even *Daily Variety* covered it. The department's under scrutiny. They've got to produce."

"It's still a hooker killing. How much help do you think the cops are going to get on the street? Do you think if someone out there knows something or saw something they're going to run to the police with it? Davey said you used to be a cop. You know how they operate—one night they'll bring a truck and trailer in and arrest five or six dozen girls and their johns and dump them in jail until they make bail. The next night the same cops will pick up a couple of girls on Sunset and take them to one of the rooms they've got over at the King George for an all-nighter. *Nobody* on the streets talks to cops. If the bastard that did this is going to be caught, someone on the outside is going to have to do it."

I tried one final tack. "Davey told you my rates?"

"I can afford you." Looking me dead in the eye. No smile. Like two kids: Who blinks first?

*Let it go,* I warned myself again. *She's a client, treat her like one.* I gave a little sigh and took out my notebook. "Let's start with her name."

Allison sank back in her chair and her face relaxed. "Rosa Luzon."

And slowly, subtly, the nature of our relationship began to change. Allison Hutton, high-class call girl, assertive and self-assured, determined to have her way, became by degrees a sad young woman who only wanted to find the killer of her friend. As she sat in the chair and began to talk about Rosa, her body seemed to soften, her voice lost its aggressive edge, and the corners of her eyes began to redden as tears hung on their edges, waiting like a flood behind an improvised dam.

"We met a few months ago, right after Christmas. We

were at a party and got to talking. Someone told her that I worked for an escort service and she asked me about it. Her English wasn't very good—she was an illegal and her family was still down in Mexico somewhere. She wanted off the streets. Too dangerous, she said. I wasn't with the service anymore but I said I'd talk to Antony. That's Tony LaCost, he runs the agency. I thought Tony would love her: She was quite pretty—kind of pouty, with beautiful straight black hair, and a marvelous figure. And I sympathized with her—too many crazy people out on the streets. It's better working for someone else."

"Then why did you leave?" I asked.

She smiled limply but also, I thought, with a trace of pride, crossing her legs and staring over at me, her eyes glittering like diamonds. "I don't need them anymore. I've graduated. I'm even putting money away." She shrugged and gave me an innocent, almost little-girl look—that hint of youthful vulnerability her clients would find so beguiling. "I'm on a schedule: Allison's Plan for Financial Independence, I call it. In five years I'll be able to get out of the business for good and live off my investments. Real estate and such."

"And Rosa?"

"She went to work for Antony in February or March, I think. About a week later she came to see me at my apartment with a dozen red roses." Allison shook her head and smiled at me with a helpless look. "Can you believe that? She brought me *roses.* 'Roses from Rosa,' she said, and she was giggling like a little girl. She wanted to thank me for getting her off the street. The agency was so much safer, mostly tourists or businessmen, not the weirdos and creeps yelling at you from cars.

"She started coming by every few days or so to talk. I

guess she saw me as a big sister or something. She didn't seem to have any friends. Just me. It was an odd feeling, having someone ask my advice. Someone to help."

Her voice began to waver. "The last time I saw her was a week ago. She told me she had saved a thousand dollars and was sending it to her mother in Mexico. She was so *proud.* A thousand dollars! It meant so much—"

I sat back in my chair, thinking out loud, moving it around a little. "So if it is Rosa, she was probably killed by one of her clients from the agency. . . ."

Allison's eyes watered and instantly I realized that she had been thinking the same thing and that this was what lay behind her determination to find the girl's killer. Allison had gotten her friend—her only friend, for all I knew—the job that had ultimately cost her her life. And now she was blaming herself. I was supposed to rectify that, to cleanse Allison's muddied conscience. It was a role that made me uneasy. As I looked over at her she began to sob. "She *trusted* me! I was the only friend she had and she trusted me. And I thought I was helping her."

We talked for another half hour, Allison telling me what little more she knew about her friend. Rosa didn't have any skills, she said. She wasn't even sure Rosa had ever been to school. And with her poor English what chance did she have for work? Sex was all she knew, the only work she had ever had. But she was really a nice kid, Allison insisted: friendly, almost innocent in some ways—not hardened and callous like most prostitutes quickly became. Not the kind to rip off a guy's wallet or doctor his drinks. It all had a sort of faded storybook quality to it: the hooker with a heart of gold. Even too much of a cliché for cliché-happy Hollywood, I thought. But I believed it because I believed Allison, her gaze turning inward and her face tightening with the memory of Rosa and the thought of what someone had done to her.

And all the time some part of my brain was working, annoying me with questions. Why had I been fighting it so hard? Why had I been so abusive to Davey? Tracy and I had all summer to go on vacation. So why the resistance? The fact that Allison was a whore? I had worked for a lot worse than that before, even in the Department, I thought ruefully. The fact that I was being not very subtly blackmailed by a not very subtle studio executive whom I disliked intensely? Or the fact that I was just generally in a pissed-off mood? *Don't be an ass,* I told myself again. Like Davey said, sometimes you've got to do things you don't want to. That's the mark of a mature mind, right? And why risk turning off a major client? So I handed her a contract and she signed it and wrote out a check for five days' advance without even blinking. *Now,* I thought, *what do I say to Tracy?*

We took my Buick to the morgue in East L.A., where after a minute we were met at the neat-as-a-pin reception desk by Eddie Clayton, an assistant coroner I'd known vaguely from my days on the force. He was a blimpish, untidy man with a bulbous nose and sweat marks under his arms and tiny dark pig's eyes that flitted from Allison to me and then hungrily back to Allison. "Vic, hey, long time! You brought a beauty along from the studios, huh? Great! Wonderful! C'mon back to my office. We'll talk. Gee, this is super. . . ."

Waddling from side to side on thick tree-trunk legs, he led us down a long, bright, hospital-like corridor that reeked of noxious medicinal odors, waving his short fat arms and chattering nonstop.

"You must be doing pretty good, from what I hear. Working for the studios, hobnobbing with the swells, running around with all those cuties out at Paramount and Universal.

Christ almighty, pretty good for a guy who spent two years on Vice peering under toilet stalls looking for wienie waggers. I guess getting fired agrees with you, huh?"

"I wasn't fired, Eddie," I said patiently as we rounded a corner into another corridor. "I quit. Remember?" What we called a "mutually arrived-at decision." Meaning I got fed up with them about the time they had had it with me. So rather than wait for the inevitable I took my retirement out in cash and set up an office in Hollywood on Bronson just down from the Paramount gate and made myself known around the studios. At first I drummed up a lot of studio business because of my police contacts, then later more business because of my studio contacts. There was a certain symmetry about it all that pleased me. I also valued the idea of being my own boss and not taking orders any longer. Working for someone else was obviously not something I did well. But Davey's veiled threat from Kotzwinkle had begun to stir up ugly little notions of just how free I really was, and I still felt a vague unease as Allison and I finally settled ourselves in Clayton's tiny, Spartan county-of-L.A. office.

Clayton laboriously lowered his heavy body behind his metal government-issue desk and beamed at us eagerly. "So! What can we do for you? The studios want to do a TV show on the coroner's office, maybe get Jack Klugman to play me, call it *Assistant Coroner*?"

I smiled along with the joke. "I'm afraid not, Eddie." I introduced Allison and told him that she might have known the girl who had been left at the Hollywood sign. We just wanted to make a quick ID and get out, I added pleasantly.

Eddie Clayton looked at Allison with renewed interest, more professional than personal this time. "You knew the dead girl?" Like it was the last thing in the world he would have expected.

Allison nodded quietly, but I could see the tension edging back into her face. She didn't like it here and wanted to get it over with.

"You folks called downtown yet, talked to Homicide?"

"We want to look at the body first," I said. "Make sure it's her."

Clayton's round face became concerned. "Well, I'd like to let you view the remains, Vic, but I'm afraid I can't."

"What are you talking about, Eddie?"

"We already did the post. There's nothing left to ID. We get a body that's been treated like this we gotta go in and open it up right away. You know that. We don't open it up, we might lose something. We did the post as soon as it got here. Of course we got fingerprints on file and pictures. Christ, we must have a hundred pictures." He stood and went over to a metal file cabinet, pulled out a bulging manila folder, and flopped down again behind the desk. He held the file on his lap so we couldn't see what was inside and rummaged around until he found what he was looking for and handed it across to Allison. "This your friend?"

It was an eight-by-ten of the girl's face frozen in death. Allison stiffened and bit her lip and nodded silently.

Clayton frowned and suddenly the good ol' boy began to recede in the face of potentially consequential business; in its place we watched as the county bureaucrat, never far from the surface, emerged instinctively like a bear from a cave after a long hibernation. Eddie Clayton, Assistant Coroner II, County Pay Grade 13, had been in the job long enough to know that you don't screw up a major-media case like this. Department heads and administrators and other cover-your-ass civil servants in polyester suits and brown penny loafers were lying out there in the grass like anxious headhunters, just waiting for someone, *anyone,* to make a mistake. For most of them it provided the only real excitement in an otherwise terminally boring job. But Eddie Clayton was not about to please them by offering himself up as a human sacrifice. He stuck a pudgy hand in his desk and drew out a blank interview form and a blue Papermate pen. "Well, then, Miss Hutton. We can finally clear up the little mystery of the decedent's identification, can't we?"

For a long moment Allison remained silent, her eyes glued on the photograph but her mind elsewhere.

"Miss—"

Allison looked up abruptly and very softly said, "Rosa. Rosa Luzon." She spelled it for him. "She was from Mexico. She didn't have any relatives here. Or friends. Nothing."

"An illegal," Clayton murmured to himself, making a neat notation on the form, and added, "Address?"

Allison shook her head. "I don't know."

"You don't know her address?" He looked over at me and raised a pale eyebrow.

"I'm sorry. I don't even know where in Mexico she came from. Just her name."

"Ah." Clayton seemed distressed. "But she was a *friend* of yours?"

"We knew each other," Allison replied. "I don't know if that means she was a friend or not." Allison's instinctive distrust of authority was beginning to assert itself as Clayton pressed and—as she had done in my office—she began to draw a protective veil of aggressiveness around herself in response.

"Well . . ." he said, obviously uneasy at her noncooperation in the face of an official request from an assistant coroner of the county of Los Angeles, "maybe it's better if she's not a friend. For you, at least. Whoever killed her really did a job."

He handed me a half dozen color shots of Rosa's body. They were gruesome and horribly depressing: cold, documentary photographs of holes driven through the girl's wrists and ankles, bullet wounds in her torso, what appeared to be bite marks on her breasts. And the tattoo the newspapers had made such a commotion over: a small red tongue edging up the inside of her thigh, next to her vagina.

I handed the pictures back. "What did the autopsy turn up?"

"No can do, buddy," Clayton said firmly, putting the photos back in the folder and laying his hand protectively on top of it. "This one's sealed as tight as your Aunt Sally's dingus. You didn't even see those pictures. You wanna find out what we got, you see the D.A." He turned to Allison. "You don't happen to know what line of work your friend was in, do you?"

Allison shook her head.

"I think she might have been an actress," I said.

Clayton looked at me. "Actresses don't usually have tattoos like that, do they?"

I gave him Allison's phone number and address and told him to call Parker Center so they could send someone out to her apartment for a statement.

His official acts concluded, Clayton put his pen carefully back in his desk and became chummy again. "You only got a week if you're planning to work this case."

"What does that mean?"

"Two at the max. Look, I've been doing this for a lot of years; you get to see the patterns: Freeway Killer, Skid Row Slasher, Hillside Strangler. All the golden oldies. This here's number one in a line of many, my friend. You saw what he did to her. You don't kill someone like that because you don't like them. And she wasn't killed in the commission of a felony. And it sure as hell was no accident. The guy who did this did it because he *had* to. And he got away with it, didn't he? Another week or so and he'll have to do it again. Face it, it's going to be a long summer."

After dropping Allison off at her apartment on Sunset I drove over to Hollywood Station and, after parking in my old spot in the restricted lot in the rear, trotted up the stairs to the noisy second-floor squad room, where I found Rudy Cruz hunched over his desk, arguing softly into the phone. *Julie,* I thought, and felt an unaccountable little lift to my spirits as I sank onto the visitor's chair. Rudy glared at me over the littered desktop and covered the mouthpiece with his hand. "What the hell you want?"

I smiled at him. "Just like Welcome Wagon."

Rudy glared again, and I relaxed back in the chair and let the familiar sounds of the room engulf me: phones ringing, radios blaring, people shouting, sirens screaming outside as the shift changed and the equipment was tested, people pushing and twisting their way through the crowded room as if they had an important appointment somewhere else and were terrified of being late. It was hot and smelly and uncomfortable and, in some odd sort of way I couldn't understand, I still missed it, missed the day-to-day excitement of being a cop.

Across the desk I heard Rudy's voice suddenly go very low and very, very calm.

Oh-oh.

Rudy had been my *patrón*, my official mentor, what the department calls my "Godfather," the old boy they paired with the new kid to show him the ropes. He was only forty-three but already had twenty-one years on the force, with no intention of retiring to a "security" position at Bank of America or wherever; he was going out at sixty-five when they pushed him out. The only visible sign of encroaching age was the line of curly black hair beginning to recede around the temples. I told him it added character. He said it added skin.

His official "mentoring" had consisted of a total of three words which he repeated to me the first thing each morning like a ritual incantation as he sat down at his desk: *Make Something Happen.*

"Hank Stram used to say it while he was coaching the Kansas City Chiefs," he explained that first day, then added, "Coaching football is a lot like police work."

"How's that?"

"Because I say it is."

The Godfather.

"You can do all that Academy shit, too, if it makes you feel good—lab work, witness interviews, informants. And then sit around and wait for something to turn up. Or you can push a little, *make* something happen. I push."

Rudy Cruz had one of the highest apprehension rates in the city.

Even though we hadn't worked together in five years he was one of my best friends. We get together every week or so and in the summer we take his creaky old sailboat out to Catalina or up to Santa Barbara or take the kids down to Baja and do a little fishing. Tracy and his three kids get along fine, and Julie seems to like me as much as she likes any of Rudy's friends, even though she has convinced herself that I spend my time peering into bedroom windows and tracking down errant spouses.

Across the cluttered desk I heard him grunt in disbelief and twist his massive head toward the phone, staring intently into the receiver as if he could see Julie at the other end. Faintly I heard his low patient voice. ". . . what I *want* is for you to speak English. . . . English! Is that too much to ask?"

It must have been, because Julie hung up, and he held the receiver for a minute in a meaty fist before letting it dangle into the cradle and muttering, "*Jesus* . . ."

With his drooping black mustache and menacing growl, Rudy could turn the single word into a spine-tingling threat. He snatched at a ballpoint pen and began writing furiously on a form in front of him without looking at me. "What the hell do you want?"

"Good morning to you, too."

"Fuck the morning."

"Get in touch with your anger," I told him. "Reach inside and feel it."

"I'm *in* touch with it!" He put the pen down and looked over at me. "You know what it is? We can't talk to each other anymore. All the time she was a third-grade teacher we got along fine. Now suddenly she's an 'educational resource specialist' and she can't speak English. *Educational resource specialist!* Christ, it sounds like a disease. You know what she just told me? She's going out tonight to talk to economically disadvantaged community residents belonging to legally impacted groups about nontraditional modes of education delivery. I said, you mean you're going to talk to poor people about night school. I did not get upset. I just said, why don't you *say* it in . . . plain . . . fucking . . . *English*? And she starts screaming at me that I'm not sensitive. Fucking *sensitive*!"

"Hard to believe," I agreed.

Rudy sighed heavily and flopped his body back in his chair. "So what the hell are you doing here? I figured you'd be out at Scandia or Spago, hobnobbing with the swells."

I hadn't heard that odd term in probably twenty years and now I'd heard it twice in one day. "You been talking to Eddie Clayton at the freezer?"

"Cold Eddie? Yeah, Eddie mighta just called here. The girl at the sign, huh?"

I nodded.

"Doesn't sound like the sort of thing you do now. I'm surprised at you."

"I'm surprised, too."

Rudy scrutinized me a moment, reading the cues. "Lemme guess: You don't like your client."

"She's a whore."

"You never dealt with whores? So what's the big deal? We all sell ourselves one way or another."

"Philosophy becomes you."

Rudy's mustache twitched slightly, the closest he ever came to a smile. "You think so? I guess you're right, then—big-time *private eye* and all, I gotta figure you know what you're talking about."

"Thank you."

"Don't mention it. But it's still an odd one for you. Why you doing it?"

"I don't know." I sighed. "Just one of those things there's no explanation for."

"Like Wayne Newton. Okay. But it's not my case, you

know. Morales is handling it. Actually Spencer and Morales, the only legally sanctioned S and M team remaining here in Hollywood dicks."

"But you can read the file."

"You asking?"

I said yes and moved my chair aside as a burly patrolman manhandled a handcuffed black teenager down the aisle toward the holding cells.

Rudy came slowly to his feet and stretched and looked lazily around the large, noisy room and then back at me. "I understand police corruption has become particularly rampant this year. Declining standards everywhere you look. It's all very sad."

"So I hear," I said. "What do you see in your future?"

"A case of Stroh's. At least. And none of that 'lite' shit, either. I'm into calories." He sighed again, and his thick black eyebrows edged ominously upward as his mind suddenly reverted to the previous conversation. "You know what it is? An educational resource specialist—you know what the fuck it *is*?" He leaned his heavy body toward me over the desk and lowered his voice to a whisper as if he couldn't say the word aloud. "It's a fucking *librarian.*"

While Rudy went off to read through the case file I moved a pile of computer printouts aside and grabbed the *Daily News* from his desk. NO PROGRESS IN CRUCIFIXION KILLING a headline near the bottom of page one read. The reporter who wrote the story seemed incredulous that a killing could be unsolved a week after the body had been discovered, and I wondered if newspapers always assigned the dumbest reporters to the crime beat or if crime reporters ultimately find their brains turning to oatmeal after several years of daily exposure to brutality and tragedy. As I tossed the paper back on Rudy's desk a couple of detectives I used to work with stopped by to say hello. We chewed the fat for a while, and they filled me in on departmental scuttlebutt and stories about the brass; it was great to see them again and I realized the day-to-day camaraderie was another thing I missed since being on my own. As they wandered off, Detective Captain Oscar Reddig, a massive, black, 280-pound mountain of a man, emerged from his glassed-in office thirty feet away and surveyed the noisy confusion of the squad room like a deck officer on an aircraft carrier. When he saw me his eyes twitched slightly as if a long-dormant memory had just come alive, and he began to maneuver his way toward me through the crowded room, arriving a moment later like a vision from *GQ*—gray Pierre Cardin suit, maroon patterned Countess Mara tie, Gucci shoes made from obscure dead reptiles. He stared down at me from huge dark eyes.

"The fuck you doing here?"

Everyone happy to see me. Maybe I didn't miss it that much after all.

"I got tired of hobnobbing with the swells, thought I'd come in and harass the civil servants."

He understood immediately. "Yeah, that uptown shit can get old pretty quick to you simple folk. Our friend Rudy's not doing anything out of the ordinary for you, is he? Anything I should know about?"

"Rudy? Uh-uh."

His head shook ruefully back and forth as he stared at me. "You always were the articulate one, weren't you, Victor? You'll probably be running for mayor next year, the fancy way you got with words."

I'd known Oscar for maybe five or six years. One of the best cops as well as one of the most unashamedly ambitious people I'd ever met, he was going to be L.A.'s first black chief, he let it be known. For years he had been methodically laying the groundwork, making it impossible for city officialdom to ignore him: He dressed expensively and with undeniable taste. He went to concerts of the Philharmonic, where he applauded in all the right places. He subscribed to thirty-five quality magazines and collected contemporary pottery from New Mexico. He watched everything on PBS and deplored the commercialization of art. He wrote articles for *Criminology* and *Justice Review.* He was, in short, a man of parts. "And all of them work," he liked to remind me. A captain by forty, he had been promised an administrative job at Parker in another year; then, he hoped, chief. I was rooting for him. So were most of the cops at Hollywood Station. He was not only a good policeman but a good guy, if you could get past the wine-and-soufflé façade. I said, "Anything new with Hollywood dicks?"

Oscar grunted dismissively, hunching his heavy shoulders and letting his gaze wander momentarily around the large squad room. *His* squad room. "You should know there's always something new here in Hollywoodland, Victor. After all, we're 'the police force of the future,' as our chief reminds us constantly. Didn't you see him on the news last night, smiling and being sincere? The *po*-lice force of the future! Last week those nice folks at Parker even sent us a *management consultant* to help spruce things up around here and improve morale, make folks *feel good* about their job. He wanted to spend two weeks doing an 'attitude survey.' Tweedy little guy in glasses and wingtips and a real nice tie from K mart. I kicked his tight little butt outta here, told him if he wants to find out folks' *attitudes* he can go in the goddamn john and read the walls. It'd take him five minutes." He brushed some imaginary lint from the cuff of his hundred-dollar shirt and worked to keep a smile from his face.

"You're a fun guy, Oscar. I miss you."

"Well, we all miss you, too, young Victor—your silver-tongued wit and Ivy-League look and all. We lost you, and our polished and sophisticated image slipped a notch or two. Those *genuine* Levi's you're wearing or counterfeits from Hong Kong?"

I glanced down at my pants.

"You can still re-up, you really in the mood," he went on amiably. "You've only been out in the real world, what? Four or five years? They'd probably bring you back as a sergeant." He squinted down at me thoughtfully. "Seems like you sorta burned a bridge or two, though—"

"More like Sherman going through Georgia," I said, and smiled. "Just to make sure there was no retreat."

"Then maybe it's best y'all just stay put where you are," he suggested helpfully, and added, "How's that cute little MG of yours coming along?"

I allowed myself an inward sigh. "It's not an MG, Oscar. I told you: It's a Morgan." *And it needs a clutch,* I reminded myself silently. I'd been restoring the damn thing for ten years or so and finally had it almost completed. Either Oscar, who'd seen it twice, had a problem distinguishing it from an MG or just liked to needle me about it. But to a sports car buff an MG had roughly the same relation to a Morgan as I did to Sylvester Stallone.

"What's it going to be worth when it's done?"

"Don't be crass. It's not the money, it's the pride of ownership."

Oscar grunted as if he didn't believe me or as a matter of principle didn't believe anything a civilian said, and changed the subject again. "You been a mighty *busy* little beaver lately, haven't you? Heard you helped ID the girl on the hill this morning. Good work." He was watching my face closely now, seeking meaning in my eyes, listening to the tone of my voice.

I shrugged and kept my expression blank. Oscar was a cop again, I was a civilian, and the world reverted back to the black and white of the LAPD. "I didn't do much," I said. "I was just along for the ride."

He smiled, and his large face with its prematurely gray hair took on a benign favorite-uncle look. "We just let the press know she'd been ID'd. We kinda left you out of it, made it look like good professional police work turned up her name. You don't mind none, do you?"

"Hell, no. Take all the credit you want. I don't need my name in the papers."

"I got a team out talking to the Hutton girl now. You working for her?"

He knew I was, and I merely nodded.

"What do you think we're going to learn?"

"Probably nothing," I said. "She knew the victim. That's about it. She hadn't seen her in a week and got suspicious. I guess she saw my name in the phone book and gave me a call. She's a call girl, you know."

"Do tell."

"I'm sure your people ran her through the computer before they went out to see her. They know who she is and what she is. If I hear they leaned on her I'll have to get legal help. How's the ACLU sound to you?"

"Victor! You know we'd never compromise a murder investigation."

What a smile.

"That's what I'm counting on," I said.

His expression turned mildly concerned, and a single eyebrow edged up, a feat I've never seen anyone else able to accomplish; it was something I imagined him practicing for hours in front of a mirror. "You sure there's nothing you want to share with me?"

I said no, couldn't think of a thing, and Oscar nodded and grunted a good-bye and headed back toward his office, chairs moving quickly aside and people twisting out of his way in a parting of the human Red Sea of the squad room. A moment later Rudy dropped heavily into his swivel chair. "What'd Manmountain want?"

"I think he wanted me to compliment him on his threads."

"You didn't, did you?" He looked worried.

"No."

"Good boy."

He drew a piece of paper from his shirt pocket. "You want to write this down or commit it to your fading middle-aged memory?"

"Just talk," I said. "I'll remember."

He hunched over the desk, reading his scribbled notes. "Somebody wanted to make very certain the young lady in question was dead: three bullets in the rib cage, one of which pierced her heart, and any one of which would have done the job. But like I said, someone wanted to make sure. Or make a point. She was Latin, maybe eighteen years old. Traces of semen in her stomach, rectum, and vagina. Coke and heroin in her bloodstream but all of it recent—according to the report she was no junkie." Rudy glanced up from his page of notes. "Eighteen years old. Shitty way to go."

He shook his head as if clearing his mind and went on. "She had holes driven all the way through her wrists and ankles. From the size of the holes and the torn skin and broken bones, they figure she was nailed to something for three or four hours. Can you believe that? Three or four hours!" He looked over at me again, his gravelly voice disbelieving. "Fifteen years I've been in Homicide and I still can't comprehend it. Someone took a *hammer* and stood there and actually *drove nails* through her wrists and ankles."

He crumpled up the page of notes and tossed it in his wastebasket.

"The press was given all of this. What they don't know is that she had been washed clean with rubbing alcohol—her entire body had been very carefully gone over. The lab team couldn't find a single hair, a piece of fabric, makeup, tobacco, coke . . . nothing."

I let this odd bit of information sink in a moment, then asked, "What does Oscar think?"

"Oscar is not thinking; he's sweating. The line downtown is we've got another serial killer. You know how crazies like to go after hookers, and we figured this girl for a hooker from the beginning because of that curious little tattoo. Oscar does not *want* more bodies. Something like that can throw him off that express to Parker Center real fast. What Oscar *wants* is for this to be wrapped up. One body, one arrest, one conviction."

"What do you think?"

Rudy sat back in his chair and regarded me thoughtfully as the racket of the squad room continued around us. "I dunno, amigo. He *is* a nut, whoever he is, doing what he did to that girl. And taking her up to that damn sign and leaving her. He couldn't have been more public if he tied her to the Goodyear blimp. I just don't know—"

"A girl jumped from that sign once," I said, thinking back to a story my dad had told me years ago. "An actress or would-be actress, sometime back in the thirties. Her way to tell the Industry what a bunch of shits they were."

"Different scenario," Rudy said.

"But maybe the same message. What do you make of his

washing her body? I've never heard of someone doing that before. It must mean something." But what? It was the odd sort of fact that often gets in the way of an investigation by causing hours of fruitless work on something of little importance. Maybe best to forget it for now.

"Oscar's afraid it's some sort of ritual: blood rites and devil worship and all that Hollywood shit."

"Could be," I agreed. "Or maybe the killer was just being careful to destroy evidence. But who would be knowledgeable enough to be that careful about it except a doctor?"

I thought for a moment and added, "Or a cop."

Rudy's face went completely blank. "It would be best if you did not even *think* like that. Right now we are all treating this as a run-of-the-mill hooker killing—some john got pissed off at having to pay the girl or she bit his dick or something and he went crazy. Right now that's *all* it is. Don't make it into something it isn't."

Not wanting to call Allison from the squad room, I trotted down the narrow front stairway to the lobby and waited for one of the half dozen pay phones with a small crowd of bail bondsmen and pimps and distraught mothers until a middle-aged Chinese woman shouted something to whomever she was talking to and angrily slammed the receiver against the hook. I quickly grabbed the phone and dropped a quarter in the box. As I waited for Allison to answer, my eyes scanned the graffiti-covered walls: uncomplimentary comments concerning the police force of the future along with quickly jotted phone numbers for bail bondsmen and legal service clinics and immigration aid. An attorney named Al Scapio had gone so far as to tape his business card to the wall with the printed slogan, I CAN GET YOU OFF, under which someone else had written neatly in blue ink, "*So can I. Call Sheri at . . .*"

The phone rang several times before Allison finally

picked it up. The two detectives who had been questioning her had just left, she said. She sounded either tired or depressed. Probably both. It had been a rough day for her. "They weren't very nice. But I'm used to it. They said they'd probably be back."

"Did you give them Rosa's address?" I asked. I had to cover my free ear with my hand to hear because of the racket in the lobby. An angry fat man wearing a leather coat had seized the phone next to me and was sending up pillars of smoke and shouting to someone called Andre on the other end of the line.

"I don't know her address, Vic. I'm not sure they believed me but I really don't. Or her phone number. She was pretty secretive about her private life. She'd just show up out of the blue, usually in the afternoon, and we'd sit around and talk, mostly about her family back in Mexico. And getting into movies. She was a movie freak and wanted to be an actress. Who doesn't? I told her she'd have better luck breaking into Spanish-language films in Mexico, her English was so bad."

"Who would have her address?" I asked.

"Antony LaCost at the escort agency, I suppose." She gave me the number, then sighed and said, "You better let me call first and pave the way for you. He doesn't like strangers." There was a sudden lightening of her voice, and I could almost see her smile down the phone line. "Don't go over there with any preconceived notions, Vic. He's not what you expect."

I waited impatiently in the lobby, pacing up and down by the bank of phones. The Chinese woman had wandered back and was sitting on a bench nearby; her head hung against her chest and she was crying and twisting a handkerchief in her lap as everyone carefully avoided her. Kids shouted. Teenagers argued with their parents. A siren screamed outside, then another. People flowed through, in and out of the building. Finally after fifteen minutes I confiscated another phone and dialed the number Allison had given me. A young woman answered, very bright and cheery, and after a whispered conversation with someone, announced that it would be fine to come over right now before it got too late in the day. When she gave me an address on the ten thousand block of Wilshire in Beverly Hills I began to get an inkling of what Allison had meant: Antony LaCost was not going to be your typical pimp.

The building was called the Lafayette, a forty-story monument to postmodern eccentricity, with its busy-looking exterior of exposed granite, bas-relief geometric designs, and blunt eyebrowlike ledges above bronze-tinted windows. I left my two-year-old Buick in the underground lot and rode the plush silent elevator alone to the twenty-eighth floor. LaCost's apartment was halfway down the wide hallway. I pushed the bell and gazed up and down the corridor as I waited; it was empty and silent, just as the entry and the elevator had been. Unaccountably I began to feel uneasy; it was like a recurring nightmare I had had as a child of being trapped in a massive house with an infinite number of doors, and as I opened one after another there was nothing behind any of them. But then the apartment door swung open, and the illusion was instantly shattered as a striking young woman in a pale blue evening gown that matched her eyes appeared in front of me, smiling beautifully and sending funny little chills bumping along my spine. From the room behind, new-age music drifted softly out on waves of perfumed air, and I could catch fleeting glimpses of the glowing reds and yellows of neon wall art winking manically like the façade of a Las Vegas casino.

"Mr. Eton?"

I said yes and she smiled wonderfully again and pressed

her hands together as if tremendously pleased with her own prescience, and then she motioned me inside with a cute little curtsey. "Tony's outside with his garden. Please—"

After I stepped into the room and she shut the door behind me I stood for several interminable seconds and stared like a kid trapped suddenly in a carnival funhouse. The room—the whole apartment, evidently—was a mad high-tech playhouse of chrome and glass and bent polished pine and glowing tubular lamps and countless pieces of stereo and video equipment, each with rows of blinking yellow and green lights. Colors shouted from everywhere, demanding attention, the vivid childlike hues of a preschooler: bright reds and oranges and shiny wet-looking whites and harsh vibrant silvers. Massive framed Warhol prints were hung along one entire wall while another had been covered in a thick padded fabric etched with fine spidery highlights of blue and black and silver that quivered in the nervous light. Another wall was completely glass from floor to ceiling, and on the other side of it I could see a smallish man on the balcony fussing with a massive lavender watering can over a small, lush jungle of potted ferns. When he noticed me he put it down at once and moved his lips excitedly, but I was unable to hear him because of the window; then a glass panel slid open and he blew inside on a gust of hot air, quickly crossing the broad white sea of carpet and holding out a soft pale hand.

"So very glad to meet you, Mr. Eton. So *very* glad! Allison told us all about you, of course. Do you like it?" His high-pitched voice trilled with an almost uncontrolled excitement as he waved a frail arm proudly about the room and the art and the walls and evidently anything else within his compass. "It's just been redecorated! *Do* tell me you like it. I'd be crushed if you didn't."

"It's wonderful," I said with what I hoped was convincing earnestness, and I supposed it was in an odd Museum-of-Modern-Art sort of way; it certainly wasn't the sort of surroundings I would have associated with a pimp, even a high-class Wilshire Boulevard pimp. But Antony LaCost was not what I had expected, either: At least sixty years old, he had a wispy, wraithlike quality, as though his ghostlike image had been superimposed upon an artist's rendering of the room. He was about five feet four and had thin silver hair, a puffy babyish face, and a soft effusive voice that muffled and distorted his speech, as if his tongue had suddenly bloated and become too large for his tiny red mouth.

"Shall we go out on the balcony?" he asked, and glanced around brightly as though the answer lay hidden somewhere among the shiny gewgaws that surrounded us. "No, no, let's *not* go outside! Far too hot and sultry. Even my lovely ferns are sweating. We'll stay right here. Charlotte, do be a dear and bring us some iced tea, that's a good girl. Well, *sit,* Mr. Eton, sit, and we'll chat."

I lowered myself onto a hard white vinyl couch, as comfortable as a bus bench, while LaCost put his tiny body into a straight-backed director's chair across from me and crossed his short blond-haired legs. He was wearing trendy tan safari clothes—baggy shorts, epauletted shirt, knee socks, and leather sandals. All set for his next exciting adventure, I supposed.

"I'll get right to the point," I said. "What I want—"

"What you *want* is to find out everything I know about poor Rosa, Mr. Eton. And you shall, you shall!" He smiled and his old/young face positively overflowed with warmth and charm. Charlotte drifted back into the room bearing three tall glasses of iced tea like a slave in a seraglio, and placed them with ritual grace on a round glass table between us, then lowered herself onto the white-carpeted floor next to La-

Cost's chair, carefully smoothing her dress over her exquisite long legs.

LaCost took a sip of tea and smacked his thin pale lips as he put the glass down and drew up the delights of memory. "Dear, dear Rosa! She worked for me only since February, Mr. Eton—shall I call you Vic? Vic or Victor? I do so love that name: Victor, vanquisher, the one to whom all the spoils of life belong. *Vic?* Well, so be it!—dear Rosa worked for me only since February, as I imagine Allie told you, yet I grew to love her like a sister. But then I love all my girls like sisters, don't I, dear Charlotte? One reason my girls are so loyal to me is that I *do* treat them like sisters. No rough stuff, not even any sex. Well . . . almost never." He chuckled lightly to himself, passing a frail hand through his wispy hair.

"Whatever you might be thinking, Antony's not a pimp, Mr. Eton," Charlotte said with a smile as his hand moved carelessly down to caress her soft milky cheek. "He takes *care* of us. The girls who work for Antony have a very good life. We make excellent money and don't have any hassles. That's why Rosa was anxious to be a part of it."

LaCost broke in eagerly. "Let me explain how this little service of ours works. I have fourteen associates working with me, not including my lovely Charlotte here, whom I think of more as an *executive* of our firm. Except for those few very special guests to whom I allow the use of my apartment, we work exclusively in hotels.

"When a client calls and specifies his choice for an assignation, we first send over a young gentleman who works for us to collect the fee, the honorarium as it were. He's a rather brutish-looking boy I call Igor, but his real name is William. He then hands the client something in return to legitimize the transaction in the eyes of the law—a cigarette lighter, perhaps, or a nice fountain pen. Something tangible, you see.

Only later, perhaps ten or fifteen minutes, does the young lady appear. Since she's never actually handled any money there's simply no way she can be arrested for prostitution. And since the money's no longer physically present, there's no reason for the client to threaten her or beat her up to get it back. These ugly things do happen elsewhere, you know. But perhaps most importantly, instead of turning all her hard-earned income over to me, as they do on the street, we split fifty-fifty. It's a marvelous system all around. I even provide full medical coverage and paid vacations for my associates. Last year we went as a group to Rio; it was lovely, wasn't it, Charlotte? And I never lay a hand on the girls, do I, dear? Each of my young friends brings in an average of $500 a night. Some, like my marvelous Charlotte here and Allison—when she was with us—make much more, of course." He smiled at his companion, who was fingering the row of large pearls wound several times around her neck.

I was doing a little quick mental arithmetic. Fourteen girls at an average of $500 a night was a gross of $7,000 a day. In one year that was two and one-half million dollars, half of which went to the affable Antony. No wonder he was so damn happy.

"Was Rosa making that kind of money?" I asked.

LaCost shook his elegant head and reached again for his iced tea. "Alas, no. Rosa was not a full associate, I'm afraid. We used her only when she was specifically requested, which was lamentably infrequent. Rosa, you see, had a definite problem with English, and believe it or not, despite her rather remarkable looks and what I am told was an astonishing skill at her chosen trade, that little deficiency seriously reduced her value in the marketplace. Most of our customers are only partially interested in sex, you know. I'm sure you've heard this before, but it's quite true. What they really want is a companion, someone to talk to, to tell their problems to and commiserate with. Sex is only one part of it. An important part, I grant, but still a part. The rest is rather basic psychology. In fact, I've toyed with the idea of changing our name from Antony's Escorts to Hollywood Community Counseling." He chuckled softly at his little joke.

"How often did Rosa actually work for you, then?"

"Oh, my, we'd get a call once every two weeks or so, I imagine. Don't you think so, Charlotte? And then on nights where we'd be booked up we'd call and see if she was available. Usually she'd be out, though, working on her own. That, I suppose, is what got her killed. Picking up some odd creature off the street."

I said, "And she came to you through Allison?"

"Yes, of course," he cried. "A sort of job referral you might call it. I suppose Allison felt sorry for the poor girl. There's always been a touch of Mother Teresa altruism about Allison. Rosa actually fit in rather well here, I thought—something a little different, a little feral, for my clientele. You see, the secret of our success has been to emulate the successful automobile manufacturers. Rather than offer a single model to the public they provide a variety for whatever taste may exist. Well, then, I thought, I would, too! I've got quite a selection now: high-class fashion model, overly busty tall girls, bucolic apple-cheeked farm maidens, even, God forbid, an orange-haired punk rocker with tattooed arms for our Japanese friends."

*Antony LaCost, the General Motors of sex,* I thought to myself; commercialism had come even to the last of the cottage industries. He was probably already planning franchises and designing next year's new "models."

"When you took Rosa on," I said, glancing at them both, "did you ask her about her background? Is there anything about the people she knew or friends she had that you can tell me?"

LaCost laughed merrily and glanced at Charlotte, who smiled and stared demurely at the carpet, and I had the feeling I had committed some unforgivable faux pas.

"My dear boy, coming to me for possible employment was not exactly like applying for work at the telephone company. I did not make her fill out an application and I certainly did not check out her references. No indeed. We're much more pragmatic here. I had my young male assistant give her what you might call an employment test. He was quite pleased! It was on his recommendation that I hired her."

"And on my recommendation that you hired *him,*" Charlotte reminded him. LaCost laughed merrily again, eyes twinkling like stars, and Charlotte smiled beautifully, and even I began to feel infected by all this manic joy. I also became aware again of the fine subtle scent of perfume rising mysteriously from somewhere about me—from LaCost or Charlotte or perhaps even the furniture. It was all part of the milieu, I realized, the carefully constructed environment of a cultured house of ill repute. *This,* customers were supposed to think, was the epitome of high-class sex. *This* is what you've been dreaming about since puberty. It's here! And Antony LaCost was the master of it all, a fun guy with an engaging line of patter and expensive tastes and not to be compared to the jive-talking dudes in lime-colored suits and high-heeled boots parading their girls on Hollywood Boulevard. But LaCost was just as much a phony as they were, only with a bigger budget. And whatever his young "associates" thought of him, he was a pimp. And it was a goddamned way to make money.

In the next room the phone rang, an odd set of musical chimes that was evidently part of the flashy stereo system—a tune I knew vaguely but couldn't identify—and Charlotte drifted off to answer it, leaving ripples of perfume and excitement in the air. I watched her a moment, then turned reluctantly back to LaCost. "Can you tell me the last time Rosa actually worked for you?"

His soft pale eyes widened in mock surprise, and he made a dismissive gesture with his plump hand. "My dear, I could do much more than that if I wished. I could tell you the name her client used, how much he paid, what services quite precisely he required, any little *peculiarities* he may have had, even a complete description of what we rather unoriginally refer to here as his 'privates.' We like to know as much as possible about our clients, and it's all in my wonderful little computer in the next room.

"I *could* tell you this but I won't, of course. Our clients expect and deserve our complete discretion. But certainly you can find out when last she worked for us. I anticipated such a request and already checked. It was exactly one week before she was killed—May the ninth, quite early in the evening. The customer was one of my oldest and most discerning, a dear older fellow but rather unenergetic, certainly not the sort to chop her up."

Vaguely I could hear Charlotte on the phone twenty feet away, giggling, taking notes, a word now and then intelligible through LaCost's high-pitched chatter: the downtown Hilton . . . a very *tall* blonde . . . of *course* she will . . . ten P.M. . . .

I said to LaCost, "Your phone bell is a little odd-sounding, isn't it?" I still couldn't identify the tune, and it rankled like an unscratched itch.

He sat up very straight and looked at me with relish, his tiny white teeth flashing against the soft pink of his mouth. "Do you like it? I had it made up special for me. It's the Notre Dame fight song. It reminds me of those big saucy college boys pushing and groping at each other in the mud and snow. I do so love football."

Charlotte came over and sat again on the floor. "Tony is putting you on, Mr. Eton. He does that, has his little jokes with people."

"Don't be naughty, Charlotte," he lisped, and wagged his finger at her. "Football is my *life.*"

Charlotte said, "I doubt he's ever even *been* to a football game. He used to write scripts for the soaps, you know. He was quite successful."

"Really?" I looked at him in surprise. It didn't sound like a particularly useful preparation for a pimp-in-training. Or maybe it did.

"Oh, my, yes," LaCost said with a dismissive gesture. "Will Blake and Amanda be discovered by Amanda's psychopathic husband before Tiffany's abortion by the mysterious Dr. Caligaro is performed? Well, I gave it up because it was all very frustrating, as you can well imagine. The final straw was this wonderful little lesbian scene I had all worked out. I showed them *exactly* how to do it, even blocked out the shots for the dolts running things at the network. We'd have Estele's head shown from the rear, moving very slowly down Vicki's torso. When she got to the obvious place her head would begin to burrow back and forth like a furry little woodchuck and we'd hear all these little moaning sounds. But the whole thing would be shot from behind Estele, you see, only her head on camera, so we'd never really *see* anything. Very tasteful, I thought, very refined, very elegant. And quite sure to play in Peoria.

"Then this horrid little man who does 'continuity' at CBS said we couldn't actually show them in bed. We could only *infer.* Well, my dear, I just quit. Up and out the door. Luckily I had had the idea for this little service in mind already. I do so like the laissez-faire spirit of our town, don't you? May the best man, or whatever, emerge the wealthiest. I'm well on my way, as you can see. Charlotte, would you bring us Rosa's address? It *is* why Victor's here, after all, and I don't know where you keep these mundane things."

With soft catlike movements, Charlotte rose to her feet and padded quietly into another room, emerging a moment later with a business card on which had been written an address several miles away off lower Sunset in an area now mostly given over to illegal aliens who lived two or three families to a room. Below it Charlotte had written her own phone number also and neatly added *No charge!* and a little happy face.

LaCost smiled at me and seemed to consider our conversation at an end, his civic duty done. I slipped the address into my pocket. "What kind of girl was she?"

"Rosa? A *lovely* girl, but she would *have* to be to work for me. Just a little difficult to understand."

"Allison seemed to like her quite a bit."

"Well, Allison would, wouldn't she? Allison, too, is a jewel, Mr. Eton. We all think quite highly of her. I do so wish she would come back to us, but I'm always happy to see one of my associates prosper."

I was only half listening, as my attention had been caught by the wallpaper behind LaCost. What I had taken earlier to be etched highlights turned out on closer examination to be line drawings of nude men and women in athletic if sometimes fanciful positions. As the light reflected off the surface of the paper their bodies bobbed and shimmered magically. Charlotte smiled at me. "Amusing, isn't it? The decorator found it for us. It always amazes me what you can buy in this town."

I turned back to LaCost.

"Can you think of a reason someone would want to kill Rosa?"

He seemed surprised by the question, his voice rising. "Certainly not, particularly in that rather gruesome manner described in the papers. But then it does seem to fit the pathology of the sexually disturbed, doesn't it? That's why a little service like mine is so important—none of my clients would dare lay a hand on my girls. We know too much about them. And they *know* it—including the fact that their fingerprints are on the money they've handed over to our courier. Rather wise of us, don't you think? Even so, I can say my young associates would feel much better if this disturbed person were arrested. And the sooner the better. And speaking of sooner—" he came to his feet, thrust out a small delicate hand and smiled excitedly at me—"you will excuse us, won't you? Our day here is just beginning. And *so much* to do!"

By the time I left Antony LaCost's eerie whorehouse in the sky it was already five P.M. The daily layer of summer smog lay over the city like a brown army blanket, and I sat in the car with the windows up and air conditioner humming, listening to the Dodger game from Philadelphia and mulling over my next move. I could drive through Hollywood to Rosa's apartment—that would probably take an hour this time of day—and try to talk my way inside. Or I could head over to Allison's about a mile away on Sunset and tell her what I'd found out so far. I decided on Allison's.

She lived in a new security building called La Croix, a thirty-story cylinder of glass and pink stone and white iron balconies that towered over the nervous glitter of Sunset Boulevard. The small visitors' parking lot in the rear was crowded with the obligatory assortment of leased BMWs and Jaguars, so I pulled around to a side street and walked back to the entrance patio with its flowering bougainvillea and ferns and orchids and sultry tropical palms, all in the accepted L.A. tradition of Garden of Eden lushness. I pressed the button for Allison's apartment, and a moment later a disembodied voice said, "Vic?"

I said it was.

"Come on in."

She buzzed open the lobby door and I took the tiny mirrored elevator to the eleventh floor and walked to her apartment at the far end of the hall. The front door was ajar, and as I rapped on it she yelled, "Come on in. I'll be out in a minute."

I wandered in, shutting the door behind me, and looked around approvingly. The living room was everything Antony LaCost's was not: smallish and tastefully decorated in a low-key, elegant sort of way in shades of white and plum and gray. Allison's taste was surprisingly traditional, conservative even: antiques—genuine, I assumed—everywhere, and Persian rugs and original oil paintings in rich gold frames on the walls. I stood for a moment in the middle of it all with my feet sinking into the thick rose-colored carpet and sniffed at the pleasant and unmistakable scent of money. Not just money but charm, and an obvious taste for the stylish.

A moment later Allison destroyed the image by emerging from a doorway beyond wearing baggy pants and a T-shirt smeared with paint. She was barefoot and braless, and her breasts swung under the thin fabric of the shirt as she came into the room like a college kid who had been decorating her first apartment. When she smiled at me I realized that it was the first time I'd seen her smile, and the unexpectedness of it as well as the transformation to her face hit me like a blow: If Allison Hutton wasn't the most beautiful woman I had ever seen right now—baggy pants and all—she was damn close to it. She stared at me sheepishly, as if she had been caught doing something personally unsavory—reading romance novels or a sex manual, perhaps—and waved a hand in the air. "I'll be with you in a minute. I have to clean some brushes."

"Can't you hire someone else to do your painting?" I said without thinking as I stared at her disheveled state.

"What?" Her green eyes went large as she looked at me.

I began to feel flustered, still under the effect of that dazzling smile, and heard myself stammer stupidly. "It just seems out of character for the elegant Allison Hutton to be traipsing around with buckets of paint to save a few dollars."

She hesitated for a moment, confused, then laughed and said, "I'm not painting walls. *Pictures!*" And she pointed at the paintings hung around the room as she turned and disappeared again.

Pictures? I wandered over to the nearest wall and gazed at the half dozen paintings hanging there. She actually painted these? I was impressed. Most were street scenes: Paris in the rain, someplace in Italy, a small town nestled in the foothills of Southern California. Maybe a little trite, a little derivative, but well done; all very calm and serene, and almost otherworldly. They were also signed *Lebec.*

"I thought your name was Hutton," I said out loud.

"My *professional* name is Hutton," she shouted back from the room where she had disappeared. "My real name is Lebeck, with a *k.* I dropped the *k* so it would look French." She came back into the living room and smiled. "Do you like them?"

I liked them fine, I told her, and wandered over to a farm scene: Holland or Belgium, fields and dirt roads and a couple of indistinguishable figures in the distance.

Allison laughed as she saw me staring at it, and her voice

took on a grave, mocking quality. "But you don't know much about art. Right?"

"Wrong," I told her, still staring at the painting. "I don't know *anything* about art."

"Well, I'm not sure this really *is* art." She smiled as she gazed around at the walls. "It's therapy. Cheaper than a shrink and more effective. Believe me, I know." She flopped down on the couch and patted the seat next to her. "So tell me what I've got to show for purchasing your talents for a week. And what happens next."

I sat down next to Allison and repeated what Rudy had told me and what it all seemed to mean: Rosa had been raped, maybe; certainly sex had been a part of whatever ritualistic scene she had been through. It may have started as voluntary but it ended up as torture; of course, there was no way of telling if that was the killer's intent from the beginning. Sometimes things just get out of hand, as she undoubtedly knew. There had been drugs. And she had been shot. Three times.

Allison shook her head slowly, lapsing back into the melancholy of this morning. Quietly, she said, "And then he took her up in the hills and put her under the Hollywood sign. It wasn't something that happened on the spur of the moment, Vic. It wasn't something that just got out of hand. It was *planned.* There was a *reason* for that." Her eyes fixed silently on the floor, her body stiffened, and her voice suddenly sounded a million miles away. "On TV they said she had been very carefully laid out on her back under the H. There was a *reason* for that! It means something."

When I told her about the body being washed with alcohol, she just shook her head. And then, because I thought she had a right to know, I added, "They think she had been alive for three or four hours while she was being tortured. Maybe not conscious, but alive."

Allison's voice was soft, a whisper pulled from her soul. "*Jesus Christ!*" With an effort she kept the tears away and, after a moment, asked, "What did you learn from Tony?"

"That Rosa didn't actually work for him very often. The last time was a week before she'd been killed. Mostly it was a dead end. But I got Rosa's address. I'll check her place out tomorrow."

"So where does that leave us?" she asked. "Now what?" Her voice was taut and demanding, with a hint of suppressed violence tugging at the edges. It was hard to imagine that this was the same gamine-like creature who I'd seen with a handful of paintbrushes a few minutes earlier. And I thought to myself, *Now what, indeed?* Now common sense says we let it alone. From experience I knew that this was the sort of case that would turn up a multiplicity of leads—people calling television stations with ideas, turning in old enemies, psychos confessing to the police—"Catch me before I kill again." A thousand leads and a thousand dead ends. And one more person, working alone, wasn't going to be very productive. I tried to keep my tone reasonable.

"Let's think it out. Rosa was probably picked up by somebody who was looking for a victim. Some guy who can't get off without beating a girl up. Or being beaten up. He's probably been doing it for a long time but now he's a little further along; beating the girl up is no good anymore, he's got to torture her a little, see her bleed, listen to her scream. Maybe he was planning to kill her all along, maybe not. But he did kill her and drop her body. Why under the sign, I don't know, but if he's a crazy there doesn't have to *be* a reason. If everyone's right and he *is* a crazy and he got away with it once, he'll try it again. It'll get in his system. But next time he'll be a little riskier, maybe pick a girl up on a busy street so it increases his thrill. See what I'm saying? So far we've got nothing to go on. Rosa was picked up by a stranger and killed by a stranger and there's not a thing to lead us to whoever did it. So we wait, let him take some chances. Maybe someone sees a girl get in his car or he leaves a print or he's seen near where the body is discovered. There's nothing else we can do."

"Leave it to the cops," she replied tonelessly. "Let it happen again."

"I don't like it either, but we have to be realistic."

I could feel her body tense next to me, and she stared again at the same invisible point on the floor. Finally she lifted her head and held my gaze with eyes that didn't blink once. "Rosa came to me when I needed help, Vic. Remember I told you earlier that I was her only friend? Maybe that was true. But she was *my* only friend, too, the *only* one, and she was there when I needed help." Her voice became precise and intent, almost without intonation or emotion as she continued to look steadily at me. "Last March my sister was killed. Some punk walked into the store where she worked and shot her during a robbery. She was only thirty-eight years old, and this nineteen-year-old punk ended her life when she didn't hand over the money fast enough for him. Thirty-eight. Never married. She had raised me since our parents died when I was ten. Chris had been mother and sister and friend to me for thirteen years, and when she died I just fell apart. I slipped back into booze, cocaine, even heroin. If it hadn't been for Rosa I'd probably be dead today. I'm not being melodramatic, Vic. I'm telling you the truth. Rosa took me out of it, she visited me every day, talked to me, made me think of the future, made me think of the day when I could quit this goddamn life. She saved my *life,* Vic! She didn't give up on me, and I'm not giving up on her. I don't want *a* killer caught.

I want *her* killer caught." She stood up suddenly and gave me a small sad smile. "Come on, we're going to dinner."

She disappeared into a bedroom and emerged a moment later wearing a loose-knit top and slacks. "Your treat"—she smiled—"since I'm paying so outrageously for your services. We'll go to Tommaso's."

Which turned out to be an inexpensive Italian restaurant three blocks away. Allison wanted to walk, so I put some change in the meter and we set off straight down Sunset in the dry afternoon heat to a little brick-faced building with a stucco front done up in mock Italian style with columns and arches and potted geraniums near the sidewalk. The maître d', who turned out to be Tommaso, hugged Allison effusively and then led us to a discreetly quiet table in the rear, where dark young men in gold chains and open-necked shirts hovered discretely in the background, coming forward from time to time to fill water glasses or bring plates of bread and cheese and odd little vegetables that hadn't been allowed to reach maturity.

Allison took the opportunity to tell me the little more she knew about Rosa, what she hadn't told either me or the police. It hadn't seemed relevant before, she explained. But now she wanted me to know, to understand what her friend's life had been like, to understand what she had been through. Rosa had come from a village on the outskirts of Mexico City, where her mother still lived with her brothers and sisters in a tarpaper shack. It was an environment where she grew up quickly and developed the street smarts of the city urchin. But when she was twelve she had been raped and kidnapped by a family friend and taken to El Paso, where she was kept against her will in a bordello. The oldest girl there was only fourteen, some as young as eight. That was where she had been given that tattoo and forced to take part in films with other children. Finally she escaped and made her way to Hollywood—hooking her way west—where eventually Allison had met her. "Just a kid," she said, and stared at me across the table. "God, I feel so horrible for her."

"You can't blame yourself for what happened," I said, but it was obvious that Allison did just that, and that was at least partially why we were pressing ahead with this. I added, "Antony LaCost doesn't think she was killed by one of his customers. He said he hadn't used her much at all. I think it's a dead end." Maybe Allison could step back and view this whole situation more calmly if she believed, as everyone else did, that Rosa had met her killer on the streets rather than through the agency.

"Tony's nice," she said with a knowing smile. "But he also lies. He's not about to jeopardize that little gold mine of his just to solve the killing of a prostitute."

"Do you know different?"

She shook her head. "Rosa didn't tell me what she'd been up to. Believe it or not, we didn't sit around discussing our business lives. In fact, we never talked about them. I'm just saying you can't take what Tony says as the absolute truth."

"What are you suggesting, then?"

"That you get into that computer of his. That's where his secrets are. You can find out every client Rosa had, addresses, payments, everything."

I sat back in my chair and watched her. "And how am I supposed to do that?"

"Break into his apartment," she said, as if it were obvious.

"He lives near the top of a security building in an apartment with more locks than the Erie Canal."

A dark-eyed busboy appeared suddenly over Allison's

shoulder with a pitcher of water, but she smiled, waving him away, and his face visibly fell with disappointment. "All right, then," she said, "I'll try Charlotte. All she has to do is copy down the information and send it to me. She won't have to steal anything."

"Will she do it?"

Allison looked at me with exasperation. "I don't know. Tony's been good to her. She might not want to risk it. But it's our only choice at this point, isn't it?"

Allison signaled a waiter and ordered another bottle of wine, and after he brought it she told me why Rosa had been so anxious to get off the streets. "It's as if the whole world has gone crazy in just the last four or five years. It's too dangerous out there now. Not just herpes and AIDS but too many nuts with guns and chains and knives. They're out there by the millions. They want to beat you up or pour chocolate on your titties or let you wee-wee on their face. The only girls on the streets now are strung out on coke or kept by a pimp that won't let go. *Nobody* wants to work the streets. An escort service or massage parlor is safer."

"Or like you have," I said, and immediately wished I hadn't. That unfortunate note of disapproval had popped up again in my voice, and I wondered why I was provoking her like this.

Allison smiled, not quite warmly, and I could see candlelight from the table sparkle like jade in her large round eyes. "Or like I have. Three or four nights a week with some friends I trust, getting paid well for doing what I enjoy anyway. Why do I always feel you're judging me? How did you like the apartment, by the way?"

"It's beautiful," I said honestly, but I was also trying to atone for my own bad manners. I added, "It looks like you could open an antique shop."

She sat back in her chair and laughed. "I *have* an antique shop, in Pasadena. Antiques by Allison. I know, I know, it's corny, but that's what the trade likes, corny names like that, with the sound of middle America. It's doing okay. A friend of my sister's runs it. In fact, I'm thinking of opening another in Palm Springs." She bent forward, picked up the wine bottle, and filled our glasses. "Let's finish this and go for a walk. I have a week's worth of hostility to work off. As well as tonight's calories."

"Don't you have to work tonight?"

Just for a moment anger flickered in her eyes, then died out. She reached across the table and grasped my hand. "No, I don't have to *work* tonight, Victor, and yes, I *do* need to walk and I do wish we got along just a tad better, don't you? Let's go."

After saying good night to Tommaso we began to walk south of Sunset, into a residential neighborhood of eight-hundred-thousand-dollar homes. Literally, the slums of Beverly Hills—twenty-room stone-fronted mansions rising from behind vast manicured lawns and towering elms. And peopled by video producers and TV newscasters furious with the world because they hadn't worked their way into the hills yet and were still forced to associate with the hoi polloi.

As she walked next to me I could sense Allison's body moving against the thin fabric of her clothes; it was a suddenly and surprisingly erotic thought, and I decided I must have had too much to drink. Allison was a client, after all, as well as a hooker, and definitely not someone to get emotionally involved with. But when, a moment later, she slipped her hand into mine, I remained silent. There was nothing seductive in her behavior, however. She was serious about walking off her emotion: She took long, athletic steps that forced me to keep up as she plunged along the empty sidewalks, stopping only once to turn to me with a sudden intense look on her face, her hand grasping tightly at my forearm.

"Remember when I told you Rosa was the only real friend I had? Maybe she was the only friend I've *ever* had—the only person besides my sister who wasn't always after something. The only person who ever *gave* anything to me, even friendship. Maybe that's why she meant so much to me."

By the time we got to Sunset it was beginning to get dark. Back in Allison's apartment I stood in the middle of the living room while she strode nervously around pulling open drapes and flicking on lights; she was keyed up, still brooding on Rosa. Suddenly she turned to me, framed by the sliding glass door behind her.

"Do you remember when somebody was killing prostitutes in central L.A. a few years ago? He killed more than twenty before it finally ended. Why is it the crazies only kill prostitutes? You never hear about anybody killing accountants or lawyers, do you? Just prostitutes."

Maybe all that postprandial walking had done some good for her body, but it had done nothing to turn her mind from Rosa and death and guilt, and she seemed suddenly more depressed than ever. Even the faint aura of sexuality that usually surrounded her was missing now, replaced by the more common emotions of fear, hatred, revenge, and a sort of nameless disgust, disgust with the world, herself, me.

She threw me a sideways look and said, "Hold on," and disappeared into the bedroom beyond, and very faintly I heard the sound of mumbled voices as she played back her answering machine. I walked over to a window and looked down on Sunset and the lights of the cars below as they streaked through the darkness toward the ocean, or the hills to the north. When Allison returned she was wearing a filmy blue nightgown that did nothing to conceal what was under it. She wasn't smiling, and as she came up to me her voice was so small I almost didn't hear her. "Do you want to spend the night?"

I shook my head. "I'd better get home."

"Somebody waiting for you?"

"My daughter. She's thirteen. I don't like leaving her alone at night if I can help it."

She picked up my hand in hers and squeezed it and stared into my face. "I want you to stay, Vic. *Please.* Don't leave."

I looked into her eyes, green and deep and unfathomable, and began to feel uncomfortable. The emotion wasn't right. Had she so confused reality by years of pretense that she couldn't sense the swings in her own behavior, the manic ups and downs? Or was everything she did now an act: first the love child, then the budding entrepreneur, now the frightened young woman in desperate need of support and companionship? It made me uneasy, like being trapped in a room with a schizophrenic.

She was staring at me, and I heard the faint tremor in her voice, almost like fear. "Please, Vic—" and her body pressed against mine, her breasts and pelvis moving rhythmically. Her lips parted and her tongue darted into my mouth and the nightgown slipped to the floor. A moment later she led me into the bedroom without a word, but I heard her breathing heavily and her hand unconsciously gripped mine tightly, almost painfully.

As I stood in the room and stared at her, something seemed to move inside me, as if one of the buttresses of my self-esteem had just given way. I put my hands on her wrists and stepped back. For a moment I didn't speak, then softly I said, "Let me call my daughter."

Holding the receiver, I turned away from her, and felt a

spasm of guilt pounding in the back of my mind. But I forced the thoughts away, telling myself instead that Tracy was used to my working nights; it was just part of the job. She knew to go next door or upstairs to her girlfriend's if I wasn't coming home. Even so, a part of me continued to resist, asking if I really wanted to get mixed up with Allison Hutton.

Tracy wasn't home, so I left a message on the machine. Allison sat mutely on the bed, seeming to take no notice, as though she was used to hearing men make excuses. Later, however, she surprised me with her aggressiveness. There was something almost feral about the way she directed our love-making, as if there was some sort of frantic instinctual need that insisted upon fulfillment. She was wild and catlike and obviously practiced at giving pleasure. But none of it seemed quite right: I had the feeling I had become suddenly invisible to her, that I was the means to some undefined end. Like her long, athletic walk, I was there to work off tension or take her mind off Rosa and send her into a sphere of feeling rather than thought. And when finally an hour later she smiled and kissed me on the lips and rolled over to fall asleep, I felt as if something had almost happened between us, something had been just within our grasp. But at last it had slipped away. And as I sank finally into sleep, a tiny voice in the back of my mind came alive and whispered that I had just made a very big mistake.

I left Allison's as the sun was beginning to sneak up from behind the steep rocky mass of the Hollywood Hills, giving them a cold gray luminescence that matched my mood. There was a chill in the air, and I shivered as I walked to my car a block away and then drove down Sunset—eerily empty, with the night people already home and day people not yet up—to Vine and then turned right and followed it a mile down to

Melrose where Vine becomes Rossmore and Hollywood honky-tonk gives way reluctantly to 1920s elegance.

I parked under a leafy thirty-foot elm and stared down the quiet tree-lined street toward the golf course. The air was clear and clean, the sun just beginning to warm; no smog, no traffic, no noise. Even the joggers weren't up yet, disturbing the early morning peace. The only thing keeping this from becoming the Paradise of biblical promise, I thought as I let myself into the marble lobby and headed toward the elevators, was a trout stream bubbling through the middle of it all.

Rudy's wife Julie likes to tell me that I moved to the Rossmore area because of what she calls my "obsession" with old-time Hollywood, the tinseltown of stars and glamour and excitement. "It's all part of your excessive fantasy life, like the Morgan. You're trying to ignore the cold realities of the present by focusing on the flickering images of the past. Besides, it's a spooky old building, and Hollywood's no place for a kid."

Nuts, I told her. I live here because I *like* living here. In fact I'd wanted to live in this building since I was eight years old and my dad used to bring me down on family visits. Like most of my family he worked in the Industry, starting as a grip and working his way up to a set designer in the fifties and sixties; his younger brother was a studio electrician and assorted aunts and uncles and cousins worked as hairdressers and bit actors and commissary people. I still have an aunt in Wardrobe at Disney and a cousin in the prop department at CBS.

For years my folks would come down here every few weeks to visit an aging silent-screen actress and distant aunt with the lovely name of Monica DePaul, a frail ghostlike creature with white, white skin and long, silver hair who lived off Social Security and a tiny Screen Actors Guild pension.

While my parents were visiting, my brother and I would scurry off by ourselves and sneak into the large stone-faced apartment buildings that had been put up all along the street in the twenties by owners anxious to display their cosmopolitan tastes while appealing to the nouveau riche extravagance of the film community. To my excited preadolescent mind they all had an air of mystery and intrigue and belonged in old black and white Bela Lugosi movies, filmed against a backdrop of thunder and lightning.

The mysterious Monica DePaul lived in The Keep, a quirky Bavarian-looking building of battlements and turrets and monstrous snarling gargoyles and narrow corner staircases that twisted up dark towers with leaded windows. The hallways were wide and wainscoted and the floors marble, and mirrors and paintings hung everywhere. It was the perfect place for kids and adults with excessive fantasy lives, and when an apartment suddenly became available five years ago I snapped it up.

The hallways this early in the morning were as vacant and quiet as the street outside. I was about to put the key in my front door when the door next to mine squeaked open and Mrs. MacDonald, the eighty-two-year-old widow who had lived in the same apartment for more than forty years, stepped out in her bathrobe and cane and bent slowly to collect her morning *Times.*

"Why, Mr. Eton! How surprising to see you." Her gray eyes twinkled mischievously as she watched me. "It's *very* early, isn't it?"

"That it is," I agreed with an inward sigh. But I was trapped. I slipped the key back into my pocket and walked over to her door. Mrs. MacDonald was a retired schoolteacher, a garrulous and far-too-trusting soul whose husband had died some time back in the fifties. In her lucid periods she could be quite engaging but increasingly she seemed overcome with confusion. She had been mugged several times while walking to the supermarket on Melrose, and I had gotten into the habit of driving her there on Saturday mornings to do her weekly shopping. It was the only time she got outside anymore.

"Looking for *clues,* weren't you?" she asked with a sly smile, and I was relieved to see that it was one of her good days. "Or staking someone out all night? That *is* what it's called, I believe: staking someone out. Such an odd term; it reminds me of something one would do to Dracula."

She generally thought my line of work worth a dig or two, certainly not the proper way for an adult to spend his time. Why didn't I look into classes for occupational retraining? Or call those nice people at the DeVry school she was always seeing on television?

"Actually I was doing a little of both," I told her, going along with it. "Along with patting people down, rounding up suspects, and yelling, 'Freeze!' That's the part I like best."

She allowed herself a tiny smile. "So very good to know you're *out there.* Makes one feel so safe!" She waved with the newspaper and disappeared into her apartment, and I walked back to my own apartment, picked up the *Times,* and quietly let myself inside.

Wondering if Tracy was still upstairs, I crossed the living room and pushed through the swinging door to the kitchen. Tracy looked up incuriously from the table, where she was eating a bowl of Froot Loops, and shook her head. "Sneaking home late again, huh? I hope you have a good excuse this time."

I let the door swing shut behind me and sat down heavily at the table. "It's a little early for thirteen-year-olds to be up, isn't it?"

"Studying my spelling." She tapped a mimeographed sheet. "Want to give me a test later?"

"Sure. Let me get some coffee first." I stuck some water in the microwave and made a cup and settled back at the table.

Tracy turned her ten thousand freckles in my direction. "Were you really working or were your lady friends keeping you out all night?"

"Working," I said without looking at her, and tasted the coffee. It was still too hot, and I put it down.

Tracy said, "Prevarication."

"What?"

"It's one of my spelling words."

I blew on the coffee.

"I wish it was a lady friend."

"Don't start," I warned her. Tracy's mother had died in an automobile accident eight years ago, and it had been just the two of us since then. We had gotten along pretty well over the years, I always thought. Or "pretty well for Anglos," as Rudy liked to say, as if it were a situation worth noting. But lately Tracy had begun to act as if an unmarried father was a crime against nature, and the barbed comments were becoming more frequent. I blew on my coffee again, decided I was hungry and popped a frozen burrito in the microwave, glancing at the sports section while the food was being radiated. The Dodgers had won in the tenth at Philadelphia. Great. I said to Tracy, "Let's go down to Anaheim for the Angels game tonight. They're playing the Red Sox."

"Masochist."

I glanced over at her again.

"Another spelling word. Yeah, the Angels game sounds like fun."

"Think you've got time to run this morning?"

She glanced at the wall clock. "Sure. Let me get my shoes. If it *was* work keeping you out I hope it's something gruesome. I need some new stories for the sisters. It keeps their minds off homework."

I'd taken Tracy out of public school several years ago while I was still on the force and had seen us booking more and more kids every year. Suddenly it wasn't petty theft or runaways but drugs, prostitution, robbery, even two eleven-year-olds for murder. The public schools here, it was obvious, were out of control, probably more dangerous than Hollywood Boulevard at midnight. The Catholic schools, if nothing else, had some sense of discipline. Or so I hoped.

After Tracy finished her breakfast we drove to Hollywood High, where we joined a half dozen other runners on the quarter-mile track, still moist with early morning dew. Normally running relaxed me, freeing my mind and creating a sense of nothingness that let the accumulated anxiety flow like sweat from my body. But today my mind fixed inexorably on the picture that Eddie Clayton had shown me of Rosa crucified, and as I jogged slowly around the track I fell into a melancholy despair as I wondered what could possibly drive someone to do that to another human being.

After dropping Tracy off at school I went back to the apartment and rummaged around in the back of the closet, looking for the clothes I'd stashed five years earlier. They were still there: the tweed sports coat with the leather elbow patches; dark brown slacks; even the brown wingtips up on the shelf. Everything a little dusty, maybe, but none the worse for wear. After pulling them on, I glanced at myself in the mirror and smiled at the detective lieutenant smiling back. Hey! Not bad, huh? It was all coming back. Method acting: Dress the part and *be* the part. And I was it, I was *the man.*

Shortly before ten I pulled up across from Rosa's apartment building in an area just off Sunset near downtown. It was a part of the city that had been Latino for decades but now was probably half Chinese and Korean and Laotian: L.A.'s permanent dumping ground for its revolving underclass. The squat Spanish-style buildings, probably not much to look at when new, were now completely run down and covered with layer after layer of graffiti, black spray-painted gang markers that separated the races as effectively as concertina wire unrolled down the middle of the street. Roofs leaked, windows were covered with wood, and the plumbing didn't work, but the buildings were fertile little gold mines for their absentee owners because they quietly nailed up plywood partitions and rented to illegal immigrant families by the room. So a tiny apartment that should have brought in maybe $700 a month was suddenly worth $3,000, most of which was never reported and never taxed.

Despite all this it was a surprisingly cheery neighborhood during the day, the kind of place where the kids had dozens of friends and played in the streets in the shade of forty-foot palms or squirted each other with lawn hoses or took the bus to Dodger Stadium to cheer for their favorites. But at night it was as if a switch had been thrown, and families barred their doors as it turned into a no-man's-land of roving teenage gangs and crack sellers and spaced-out hookers working for the price of the next hit.

I stood a moment on the sidewalk, cracked and buckled in a dozen places from earthquakes and tree roots, and gazed around: a noisy soccer game at the tiny park across the street; half a dozen *cholos* sitting on a stoop in their shirtsleeves, watching me and drinking beer out of bottles, giving me the turf-crossing scowl they called "mad-dogging"; barefoot kids playing marbles and shouting in Spanish; an elderly unshaven Mexican with a bad limp pushing a white cart from which he sold fruit-flavored ices. I waited a moment for a patrol car to cruise slowly past, then crossed the street and walked up to the door that said OFFICE in sun-faded letters, and knocked. After a long moment the door was noisily yanked open as far as the chain lock would allow by a heavyset Mexican woman of about sixty with a tired, angry face; inside

I could see the television tuned to a Spanish-language soap opera and newspapers scattered across the floor. She glared at me with instant distrust and then twisted her head and yelled back into the apartment in Spanish, and I heard the sound of a window scraping open and a man grunting and huffing breathlessly, and all of a sudden I began to feel like an idiot. The well-planned detective's disguise hadn't worked; she thought I was "Migra"—the Green Gestapo from Immigration—and someone inside was disappearing. Quickly I tried to summon up an official tone. "*Policía!*" I said loudly. "No Immigration! No *Migra! Policía! Habla usted inglés?*"

She shook her head emphatically and grunted. "No, no." She gave the door a push at the same time but I held it with my foot and flashed my state investigator's card, again shouting, "*Policía,*" and hoped she wouldn't be suspicious that I didn't show her a badge.

She glared at me a long moment in silence from dark angry eyes, and I could see her shoulders begin to sag, her face slowly relax, as she began to sense that I wasn't here to check on immigration status. After she muttered something under her breath and I removed my foot, the door slammed shut, the chain lock was released, the door opened again, and she stepped into the hallway. But her mood hadn't altered and she shouted, "*No habla inglés,*" and waved at me dismissively as if I were a fly buzzing around her head.

"I'm looking for Rosa Luzon," I said in English, and pointed at the apartments down the hall.

She shrugged her shoulders and pretended not to know what I was talking about.

"*Rosa Luzon,*" I repeated, this time loudly, and when she shook her head again and shouted something in Spanish I decided I'd had enough. I crossed over to the nearest apartment and rapped angrily on the door. After a moment it was yanked open by a youngish, almost emaciated Latino in a sleeveless T-shirt and black slacks who looked at me quizzically. Marijuana smoke came floating out from inside along with the thin tinny sounds of 1950s rock 'n' roll; a girl of about sixteen drifted up behind him, touching him with her fingertips and peering over his sloped shoulder as he stepped across the threshold.

*"Policía!"* I said again, but when I reached for my ID card the woman behind me came up quickly, grabbing my arm and yelling, *"Treinta y tres,"* and pointing angrily upstairs, shouting again at me in Spanish and then at the young man, who quickly slipped back into his apartment and slammed the door, locking it behind him. Seconds later I heard the toilet flush.

I turned back to the manager. I couldn't remember the word for *key,* so I pulled the key case from my pocket and indicated I wanted to be let into Rosa's room. Mumbling under her breath again, the woman stormed into her apartment, coming out a minute later with a passkey on a large brass ring, and said something angrily to me as she pushed it into my hands.

How much easier this all would have been with Rudy along to translate, I thought as I mounted the decaying stairwell. But then maybe it wouldn't have made any difference, anyway: It wasn't that I was Anglo that she resented or that I couldn't speak her language, but the fact that I symbolized an authority she didn't recognize. Police, Immigration, social workers, health inspectors, landlords; it was always something, and she just wanted to be left alone. *Don't we all,* I thought with a sigh.

The narrow third-floor hallway was dark and deserted, but I could hear sounds everywhere as I came out of the stairwell—televisions, radios, people talking—the sounds coming through the thin walls as though they had been made of paper. The three light fixtures overhead were shattered, as if someone had used them for target practice, and the fire escape door at the far end of the hallway had been ripped from its hinges and stood propped against the wall; through the narrow rectangular opening I could see the thin green top of a palm tree outside, swaying softly in the early morning breeze like an animated wall hanging. Holding the large key ring so it wouldn't jingle, I made my way down to 33 and was about to unlock the door when an unshaven man in a straw cowboy hat that marked him from southern Mexico or Guatemala appeared suddenly from the stairway at the other end of the hall. He halted and looked at me for a long moment, his dark eyes wary and distrustful, and seemed on the verge of saying something when he changed his mind and turned away. I waited until he disappeared into an apartment before slipping the key into the lock and then, again glancing quickly up and down the hallway, let myself into Rosa's apartment and locked the door behind me.

Inside it was cool and dark, and I flipped on the bare overhead light and looked around: a single tiny room—far too small to subdivide—with an ancient upholstered couch that made into a bed sagging against one wall, and a small kitchen and even smaller bathroom off to the other side, all visible from the doorway. Not more than 150 square feet, I thought—a doll's house, claustrophobic as a closet. But what struck me most was the apartment's obsessive neatness: no silverware or dishes out of place in the kitchen, no food on the counter or newspapers on the floor or couch, none of the normal clutter of everyday life left behind when you leave home and expect to come back shortly. It was almost as though no one had actually lived here—a room in a museum: L.A. Urban Life, Late Twentieth Century. Or, I suddenly thought, someone had been here before me and carefully put everything away. If so, it hadn't been the police; they didn't have Rosa's address yet.

There had been a few brave but unsuccessful attempts to personalize the apartment, make it into something more than rented space: a badly worn Garfield doll resting on the couch, a black and white photograph of an older woman on the dresser in a cardboard frame; a black velvet Jesus hanging on a wall and staring down reproachfully at me with vivid dark blue eyes. If we define ourselves by our possessions, I thought, Rosa Luzon had been an orderly if somewhat wandering child of the church: God, cleanliness, and whoredom.

Voices were coming from everywhere, seeping through the walls and filling the tiny room: a man and woman on one side, arguing in Spanish; children and television cartoons on the other. A woman laughing. Footfalls from the apartment above. It was beginning to make me uneasy, and I checked again to make certain the door was locked, then walked into the tiny kitchen and quietly pulled open a drawer at random: cooking utensils and silverware neatly arranged in precise rows in a yellow plastic tray. In the single cupboard above the sink a dozen glasses, washed and dried and lined up like soldiers on parade. Even the refrigerator was as regimented as an army commissary, with soft drinks and other canned goods neatly arrayed on one side and perishables on the other. Somehow it was all very depressing.

Where to start? I wasn't even sure what the hell I was looking for—an appointment book, or names of customers, or maybe some indication of what Rosa had been doing the final days of her life. Not that I expected anything to turn up. Like anyone in her profession, Rosa would have lived in the shadows, purposely obliterating any trail; even Allison knew little about her, except her purported history in Mexico and

Texas, and I'd talked to enough hookers to sense that even that was suspect. Most of them were so conditioned to lying that they no longer recognized the truth. Even Allison, I thought. Why should Rosa be any different? Still, you never know when you toss a place; I had done it enough to realize that anything could turn up. Might as well start with the refrigerator and work around the room. *Do it right,* I told myself. *Be as methodical as Rosa.*

It took twenty minutes to check the kitchen, opening bottles and cans, pulling out drawers, peering under shelves and in the recesses of the ancient gas stove. Then came the bathroom, a tiny paint-blistered room with the remains of a medicine chest hanging above the toilet and a stall shower with no door. Inside the medicine chest was the random detritus of any young female life: a toothbrush and half-used tube of Crest, neatly squeezed from the bottom; the usual assortment of cologne and perfume bottles, mostly unopened; deodorant and hairspray. On top of the toilet tank a plastic traveling case held makeup and a hair drier and a half dozen more bottles of perfume. Feeling like I was back on the force, I carefully opened each container and checked for drugs, but there was nothing. When I took the top off the toilet tank and peered inside, I began to feel foolish: This wasn't Mata Hari or an international diamond smuggler I was investigating, for Christ's sake, but a young woman who ended up getting herself killed by a psycho. What did I expect she would be hiding?

The only room left was the living room/bedroom. In addition to the pull-out couch the only pieces of furniture were two upholstered chairs, a Formica coffee table, and a double chest of drawers. I quietly pulled the bed out and checked the sheets and under the mattress and inside the pillows. Nothing. The same with the top two drawers of the dresser. Then my heart stopped as someone pushed abruptly against the apartment door, rattling the handle and muttering in Spanish. Then loud angry knocks, a man shouting. I halted what I was doing and stood completely still, aware of my breathing as the man pounded on the door and shouted in Spanish again as if he expected an answer. I waited. Whoever he was, he was getting angrier. The man in the hallway? I wondered. After two more minutes of pounding and shouting he kicked the door and stomped off. To the manager's? No matter. Time to hurry. I turned back to the dresser and started rifling through the bottom drawer. Under a pile of expensive-looking pastel panties I came across an envelope that had been mailed from Mexico two months earlier. Inside there was a card. Even with my poor Spanish I could see that it was from Rosa's mother, a *quincianera* card: congratulations on reaching fifteen, that magic age for Mexican girls, an event usually celebrated with parties and receptions. Fifteen. . . . I felt a sick feeling in the pit of my stomach as I stared numbly at the card and tried to grasp what it meant: *Fifteen!* Rosa had been barely fifteen years old when someone had tortured her to death.

Underneath the envelope I found a receipt for a money order. One thousand dollars sent home to mama by her hardworking daughter. So she had told Allison the truth. I wondered how she had explained it to her mother. Look, Mom, I'm an actress! An American success.

In the other drawer I found a stack of Mexican comic books along with two dog-eared Spanish-language movie magazines, and a container of birth control pills. Comic books, movies, and sex, the sum total of Rosa's fifteen years on earth. I shoved everything back and stood for a moment and stared around the room to see where else she might have hidden something. *Hurry it up,* I told myself again, *before anyone else shows up.* The chairs seemed too obvious but I quickly checked anyway, dropping to my hands and knees and feeling around the seams and turning them upside down and checking the bottom. Nothing. And nothing taped under the coffee table. I stood up and looked around again and tried to make my mind focus: Something about the room was bothering me; something was missing or out of kilter. But what? I stared at the chipped, peeling walls, the single naked window, and the sad furniture as the muted voices from next door continued to surround me, and suddenly I realized what it was. Sex. There was no sense that this room had been used as Rosa's workplace, no aura in the air of a daily dozen tumbles on the worn-out sofa bed, of sad make-believe scenes of passion acted out on the satin sheets of a pay-for-play lover. Meaning that she had managed to separate her personal and work lives. When Rosa was on her own, which seemed to be most of the time, she joined the growing legion of whores to whom sex is not even a fantasy for sale anymore but a five-minute workout in the back of a van or car hastily pulled into an alley or driveway. Fast-food sex at bargain prices, and quantity more important than quality. Hurry up and get it over with; and by the time the john zips his pants the girl's struttin' her stuff on the street again, because if she doesn't her pimp will kick the shit out of her. But Rosa didn't have a pimp. Or so LaCost said. Rosa sent her money home, a good girl.

For a moment I stood without moving: looking, hearing the voices through the walls, and wondering what had happened to the man who had been pounding on the door; then my eyes hit on the framed black velvet painting of Christ on the wall done in metallic golds and silvers that caught the light from overhead and changed colors as I stared at it. The eyes were oddly hypnotic, a glazed sky blue, then green. I took it down and slipped the glass from the frame and two $500 bills fluttered to the floor. Rosa's hidey-hole. And the final residue of her life. *Jesus save us,* I thought, and slipped the bills back and rehung the picture. Let the police find it and send it to Rosa's mother along with their form-letter condolences. The apartment oppressed me, and I felt ghoulish fumbling around in this poor girl's past, learning things I didn't want to know about. I needed to escape, to get into the air.

On the way out I knocked again on the manager's door—a sharp, unfriendly, official-sounding rap—and returned the key and instructed her in English not to allow anyone in Rosa's apartment without proper identification, not knowing or caring if she understood: I was acting like a policeman was expected to act in this part of town, and in a day or so she wouldn't be able to identify or even remember me as a person, only as a symbol of the authority she had distrusted in El Salvador or Guatemala and still distrusted.

And then I drove back to my office. It wasn't even noon, but I didn't feel I could face anybody now, not even Allison. I was weighed down with the knowledge that Rosa had been barely fifteen, a child still. In fifteen years her life had begun, played out its course, and ended. Something was wrong with a society that permitted that to happen, and somehow I began to feel the guilt personally. Fifteen. I hadn't thought about it before, but I suddenly realized that I see them every day, a hundred Rosas, standing alone on street corners, wobbling uncomfortably in high heels and swinging their tiny sequined purses, acting grown up. Getting ready to die. Fifteen. Ninth graders. A year and a half older than Tracy.

Back in my office I quickly checked the phone machine for messages, then left my sports coat and tie on the couch and went out for a walk. *Work off the tension,* I told myself. *Like*

*Allison.* Except that I took it slow, wandering down Hollywood Boulevard past unshaven men slouched alone in doorways or propped against walls, my eyes riveted on the gold stars embedded like fossils in the wide litter-strewn sidewalk, names most people had never heard of mixed among the stars: Colleen Moore and David Selznick, Joseph Schenck and Joan Crawford, Mae Clarke and Cary Grant.

Laurie and I used to come down here before we were married and try to identify some of the more obscure names. Those we couldn't we wrote down and looked up later in the reference books she kept at home. "I'm going to know everything there is about Hollywood," she would say; it was part of her preparation to become a film critic. "A *serious* film critic," she would insist. "None of this 'thumbs up' stuff." She had just been hired by a small paper in the Valley and hadn't even written her first column yet when a drunk driver crashed broadside into her on Gower. But she would have been good at it: She loved the business, loved Hollywood.

The "real" Hollywood was dead, of course; it had died fifteen years ago, the old-timers like to say. Or twenty years ago. Or yesterday. It depended on how old you were. But *Hollywood,* the Hollywood of glamour and klieg lights and stars and premieres, was always somewhere back in the misty past, just as King Arthur's Camelot existed only in the past. The present, to most people, was sleaze and punks and traffic and teenage hookers and the men who kill them. Still, every year more and more tourists stood in front of the Chinese Theatre, giggling and slipping their shoes into John Wayne's or Barbara Stanwyck's or Errol Flynn's cement footprints. Then taking snapshots of each other and glancing around hopefully for a star. Still the same and yet so different. Because now the tourists were likely to be Japanese, huddled together in nervous little groups with a native guide while gangs of predatory teenagers crouched idly at the corner like wolves eyeing a flock of sheep, waiting for one unwary enough to wander down the street alone.

Near Highland I halted in the shade for a moment to watch a group of animal rights demonstrators chanting angry slogans in front of the offices of a game show that occasionally gave away fur coats. Their leader, an intense pale young man in thick horn-rimmed glasses, was being interviewed by a group of TV reporters. He didn't *care* if the coats were synthetic fur, he said angrily, and waved his arms; it was the principle of the thing. Across the street a man in a cowboy hat and fringed buckskin jacket held a sign advocating an increase in toxic waste and passed out handbills that said, SAY YES TO CONTAMINANTS.

All part of the show, everyone auditioning.

Without realizing it I had walked almost down to Fairfax, so I stopped in at Canter's for a roast beef on rye and a glass of wine. Taking a table in the rear, I sat alone, cooling off and listening to the babble of voices all around me—Polish, Yiddish, Hebrew, others I couldn't identify—dozens of aging men and women chattering with friends from the old country, patting each other on the shoulders, smiling, shouting, waving. And not a green-haired punk among them.

By the time I got back to the office it was half-past two and I was feeling a little more upbeat. After turning the air conditioner up I switched on an oldies station and sat at the desk to go through the pile of mail I had picked up earlier. Along with the usual bills there was a check from Bill Lieberman at Columbia as payment for having dug up some film equipment that had been stolen from a soundstage the month before. I called to ask what he had thought of my report. I had found the equipment in a camera shop in San Diego. The owner, an angry little man of about sixty with a bald head and bad teeth, had been uncooperative at first, but when I smiled at him and suggested that his legitimate suppliers would probably vanish overnight if the studios indicated their unhappiness with him, he began to become marginally more pleasant. The equipment had been sold to him by a thirtyish script editor whose father was a second-unit director at the studio. She had been bringing in stuff every month or so, he said, and he figured she had a nasty habit. "Like the song says: 'lines on her face, lines on her mirror.' She was into quick highs."

"Pretty tough to deal with," Bill told me on the phone. "We let her resign. All very quiet."

"Did you tell her father?"

"He's sixty-seven, he's got colon cancer, he does his job. No, we didn't tell him."

Bill was a nice guy in an industry not noted for nice guys. It was to Bill, in fact, that I owed the comfortable office setup here that I was so damn proud of. The original furnishings—the little I could afford when I first opened shop—had come from a thrift store on Santa Monica Boulevard. Five hundred dollars to do the whole office. When Tracy first saw it, just before I opened up, she scrunched up her nose like a nine-year-old interior decorator and said it looked like a Greyhound Bus waiting room. "Well, it's what I can *afford,*" I had told her a little testily. At least the location was good—the McKay Building on Bronson, just a hundred yards from the main Paramount gate. "Lots of important people walk by here," I had added hopefully. "Maybe we'll see Sean Penn or Mel Gibson."

The ground floor of the fifty-year-old building houses an ancient drugstore with a small sandwich shop wedged into a corner, and a used book store specializing in Hollywood memorabilia: books, scripts, authentic posters, Disney cels.

It's owned by Moses Handleman, a bearded forty-year-old ex-chemistry professor at UCLA and current full-time philosopher who always has a glass of wine handy for friends and old customers. When I get bored I go down to Moses's and we talk about the ups and downs of the Industry or whatever else is bothering us. On the upper floors there's an odd mélange of small professional offices, including a modeling agency, a fact I never consider without a touch of awe because it really *is* a modeling agency and not a front for prostitution. Even so, it provides some pleasant if brief encounters in the elevator. Directly beneath my third-floor office is an endodontist's—root canals and such—which lends an occasionally Gothic touch to the day as moans drift up like ether through the floor. All in all it's an eclectic group of tenants who get along fine and even have monthly building parties in alternating offices. Finding a place here was a bit of serendipitous good luck that I've never quite gotten over.

The initial decor lasted only a year or so. Then I did a particularly touchy job involving cocaine and a runaway actress for Lieberman and he'd dropped by one night for a congratulatory drink. He sat uncomfortably in a blond Danish-modern chair and hemmed and hawed and looked embarrassed and finally asked me if maybe I wanted him to send over a decorator from the studio. He thought maybe he could get me $10,000 worth of office furnishings off a set they were closing—executive desk, leather couch, pictures for the walls, that sort of thing. Maybe even a cute little refrigerator that looked like an end table and a swivel chair where Cybill Shepherd had rested her round and precious rump.

I said, hell, for $10,000 I'd watch the uncut *Heaven's Gate,* which was probably an exaggeration, but Bill seemed relieved; it must have been trying, doing business amid such unhip surroundings. A week later the decorator showed up, a steely-eyed, anorexic young woman with short black hair that stood straight up, thick pink glasses, and a clipboard pressed tightly to her breasts as if to protect them from my unworthy gaze.

"The first question is, what do you want your office to *say*?" she announced importantly as she stood in the middle of the room and stared around with a pained look. She turned to me with what was probably a well-intentioned enthusiasm. "When a client first walks in the door what sort of *statement* do you want your office to make?"

"I want it to growl. And belch."

"Mr. Eton, I certainly can't help if you don't cooperate." Exasperation flooded over her face, and her hands fell limply to her sides.

"Manly sounds," I explained. "That's what people expect from a dick."

*"Mr. Eton—"*

"A private detective."

"Ah. Well, maybe so-o-o-o," she agreed slowly, and little bells began to go off in her mind. "Manly!" She began to look excited; I had the feeling it was an alien emotion. "Leather and wood and a wine-colored carpet."

"Johannesburg Riesling?" I guessed.

"Certainly not!" Another pained look; was there no end to my poor taste? "Pinot Noir! Or a good California rosé."

It all arrived six weeks later. But the carpet had somehow become a Budweiser gold. Maybe it was best, I thought. A better sort of statement.

Tracy said it was rad. I think so, too.

Lieberman even had the art department do up an ad for the trades: "Victor Eton, Investigations . . . In the tradition of Chandler and Hammett . . . Transcends the simple conventions of the genre." I liked that part about transcending the genre. Sounded like fun.

At three o'clock I was making a cup of coffee at the hot plate and thinking of going down to Moses Handleman's when Rudy called. His voice sounded distant and fatigued, and I could hear a clamor of background noise, including angry shouts from more than one voice. "Things just got worse."

I wondered if he'd found out about my visit to Rosa's apartment already. But it wasn't that.

"You think you got it worked out, got it figured as a sexual thing, some guy getting off on cuttin' up hookers. Then this happens. Another body's been found at the Hollywood sign. Only this time it's a man. It looks like we got a serial killer, someone who likes to kill."

Christ.

"I'd better come down," I said finally.

"There is a lot of activity around here," Rudy went on. His voice was as matter-of-fact as always, but I could hear the unspoken message.

"You name it," I told him.

"It's like a war room when the battle's taking place a hundred miles away: a lot of tension because no one knows what the hell is going on. When they don't know they get uptight and then they start looking for someone to blame. You don't want to be around. Lee Wong's at five."

I said I'd be there.

Lee Wong's is a cop bar two blocks from the station house that eons ago had been owned by a Chinese family that had tried to operate a cabaret-style nightclub with food and drink and music. It seemed like a good idea: a little authentic Far Eastern entertainment for the increasing number of wealthy Asian tourists on the West Coast. But after a year or two they ran into a sudden rash of problems with city building and health and fire inspectors and after months of fighting a losing war sold out to Eddie Darcy, who had just retired from the force after thirty years as a beat cop. Eddie reopened two days later as a topless bar and never had a problem with the city. *Just luck,* he said with a blank look, and knocked wood.

It was five-thirty by the time I arrived and parked in the crowded asphalt lot out back. I nodded to the unarmed security guard checking IDs and wandered in behind a group of guys in denim jackets and cowboy boots. Rudy was already at a booth in the rear, nursing a draft. On the tiny stage, backlit by a cone of weak, smoky light, a topless dancer was bouncing to the loud repetitive beat of a heavy metal group; the bar and most of the booths were already crowded and a half dozen off-duty cops in the back room were playing pool and shouting at one another and lining up empty beer bottles on the floor next to the wall, trying to see how high the pyramid would reach by closing time. I smiled and waved at the dancer, stopped at the bar and asked to have a pitcher of Carta Blanca sent over, then slid into the booth.

Rudy drained his mug and wiped foam from his mustache with the back of his hand. "We should've figured it wouldn't stop with one. That seems to be the trend lately." He drew a small picture from his shirt pocket and slid it across the wooden table to me. A middle-aged man, hair unkempt, nude, eyes closed in death.

"What makes them so certain this is a serial killer? Maybe someone wanted two people dead—these particular two—and this is it."

Rudy leaned back against the cracked leather booth, a carved dragon from Lee Wong's previous incarnation still visible above his head. "The Human Behavior unit came up with a profile based on past experience. Everything points to a psychopath: young, male, probably white, in the Industry or close to it, frustrated, a loner, a failure. So he decides to get back at the Industry for not recognizing his talent. Starts killing people. Controlled rage, they called it: He knows what he's doing. He's planning it out. But two isn't enough; twenty wouldn't be enough. He'll go on until he's caught."

"That's why he picked the sign?" I asked. "He's in the Industry? It's a message?"

"He wants to throw a little terror in Hollywood. Desecrate its most famous symbol, screw the bosses. The Department buys it. Two murders are enough: They've got the sign staked out now. They're using two teams with night vision binoculars."

"Do *you* believe it?"

"Sometimes the shrinks are right. Sometimes they're not."

"And this time?" It didn't seem right to me, somehow; it was too melodramatic, too "Hollywood."

"Maybe they're on to something," he said. "This time he hit someone very much from the studios. Richard Wheeler. Ever hear of him?"

I shook my head.

"President of Westway Records."

I said I'd never heard of it, either.

"It's a subsidiary of Trans-International Studios. Wheeler was reported missing by his wife two days ago, and the body was discovered this morning."

"Same M.O.?" I asked.

Rudy nodded. "Except this one was under the first O of the sign. Second body, second letter. Makes you wonder. There's seven more letters in that sign. Body was naked. Holes through wrists and ankles. Shot in the stomach and chest. The M.E. figures he'd been dead eight hours or so by the time he was found."

"Killed someplace else?" I supposed.

"And carried over to the sign. *Carried,* not dragged. Must be a strong dude. Wheeler was a big man, two hundred and twenty pounds."

"Or there's two of them." That was more likely, I guessed; one person would have had trouble carrying a body of any size across that hillside. But what were the odds you would find two people with the same sort of uncontrolled hatred of the Hollywood community?

The dancer who had been onstage when I came in had finished her set and she slid into the booth holding the pitcher of beer I had ordered and three empty glasses. She was wearing a bikini bottom and a halter top and she smiled at us and filled the glasses. I said, "How've you been, Ellen?"

"Locking my doors at night is how I've been. Car doors, too. Even my four-year-old kid's scared now, with what they're saying on the radio about another serial killer."

Rudy said, "Oscar's afraid that if the commotion doesn't die down real quick, downtown will take the case out of his hands. They're already talking about a task force."

"Christ." I sighed. "That task force crap's for the press. They ought to let him do his job." But that was another cost, I supposed, of living in the ultimate media city: the main consideration in running any high-visibility investigation was how the press would view it, particularly TV.

Eddie Darcy, the beer-bellied proprietor, wandered over and shoved a bowl of cold popcorn on the table. "Why ain't you guys out taking fingerprints or looking for clues or something? Instead of sitting on yer asses gettin' soused while decent citizens are murdered in their beds."

Rudy said, "We decided to hobnob with the swells for a while."

Darcy grunted. "So what the hell you doing here?" He dabbed at the sweat on his forehead, then wiped his beefy hands on the apron around his waist.

I said, "Why don't you turn up the sound? I can still hear myself think."

"I turn the music down, people stop drinking. Don't ask me why. It's like the topless dancers. I don't have 'em and no one comes in here, but when I do, no one pays no attention. How do you like the new one?"

A tall, thin Asian girl with overlarge breasts was dancing

slowly on the stage, ignoring the music, her eyes glazed over as if she were mentally a million miles away.

"Claims she doesn't speak a word of English. I think she saw the sign outside and wandered in thinking this here's a fuckin' Chinese restaurant." Darcy shook his fat head. "Whole city's going gook; they ain't runnin' the 7-Elevens or Shell stations, they're over in the park eatin' the squirrels for lunch."

After Eddie waddled off, Ellen said, "She's Laotian. She's only been in the country a couple of years. She's a nice kid. She asked me what a 'Vampire Killer' was today. She heard it on the radio, some reporter claiming the bodies at the sign had had all their blood sucked out. It's not true, is it?"

"Jesus," Rudy said, and drained off his glass. "Do these guys make up this shit? Where the hell does it come from?"

I said, "It's not like this in the rest of the country. But this is where the studios are, so everyone's auditioning. They're not talking to *us;* they want a casting director at Universal or NBC to notice them. Maybe they'll get a game show. What's the story on Wheeler's wife? Has she any idea what happened?"

"According to her, Wheeler left work two days ago and never made it home. The next day she reported it. Morales was checking through missing persons photos this afternoon after the body was found and made the initial ID. He's out with the widow now. From what they know so far there's no reason to suppose Wheeler was acquainted with the dead girl. The wife claims never to have heard of her. Seems likely: These are Beverly Hills aristocrats we're talking about, movers and shakers, as Oscar likes to say. Not off-the-street hookers. Oscar said, why didn't the asshole drop the body in Beverly Hills where it belonged and keep it outta his territory."

"Anything in the files on Wheeler?"

"Not a thing. Self-made millionaire by the age of twenty-eight. But who isn't, right? Well-liked, or as well as anyone can be in show biz. As far as we can tell no history of dealing with prostitutes. But if you consider a hooker as part of the Industry, maybe we got a tie. Makes the Human Behavior guys look like they know what they're talking about."

"He left work in his own car?"

Rudy nodded. "Light blue Mercedes, one year old. It hasn't been found yet."

"What'd the lab turn up?"

Rudy shook his head and refilled his mug. "They're not done with the post yet; this'll take some time. They don't want any fuck-ups. But you gotta figure if it's not a psychotic like Human Behavior says, it's gotta be a sexual thing—the nude bodies, the torture. We'll know tomorrow if he'd been sexually molested."

I had been thinking about sexually motivated serial killers since Rudy had called earlier in the afternoon. I could remember probably a dozen, I said, but couldn't recall any who killed both men and women—it was always someone fixated on killing one sex or the other. Not both. It just didn't happen.

"That doesn't mean it *can't* happen," Rudy said. "Something new for the City of Angels. The perfect death for Hollywood."

"The nuts are out there," Ellen said, as if anyone needed convincing. "Believe me. I see them, especially here in Hollywood. They come in here and sit by the stage and stare at me and never blink. One beer in front of them all night, and I never see their hands. The crazies are here all right. It's like some giant reached down from heaven and picked up the whole state of California and shook it until all the nuts fell to the bottom here."

"I'll tell you what I think," Rudy said. "I think we got a guy out there who likes to kill people. I think he's havin' a little fun. I think he's out there laughing at us right now."

"I'll tell you what I think," Ellen said. "I think I'm leaving this stinking town and going back to Fresno."

The obvious next move was to nose around Trans-International Studios to see what I could dig up on Richard Wheeler. But I decided to wait until Monday. I wanted as much time as possible between me and the homicide team from Hollywood since Oscar Reddig wasn't going to like hearing about me butting into his investigation. Having a private investigator on the case was bad enough, from Oscar's point of view; having an ex-cop was worse. Having me was probably worst of all. Oscar wanted a quick arrest, no loose ends, no outsiders to muck things up or share the glory with. And onward to Parker Center.

So I put it all behind me for the weekend and took Tracy to Catalina to atone for our lost trip to Mexico. As we'd done every summer since her mother was killed, we took our packs and sleeping bags and hiked far back into the hills, camping finally within sight of a herd of buffalo, a distant echo of when the island had been used as a location for western films.

Saturday we spent exploring and rock climbing and at night we talked and played cards. Near midnight Tracy at last went to sleep and I stretched out on my back and stared up at the stars and found myself thinking about Allison. What makes someone like that become a whore? I wondered for the hundredth time. Maybe it was a stupid question. Where else was she going to make that much money that soon? Enough so she could invest in real estate and antiques and plan for a more legitimate future? Who the hell was I to tell her she was messing up her life? What were her alternatives—get a job as a clerk or telephone operator? Like Rosa, Allison was doing what she could do.

Still, I felt a tug of more than mild disapproval, that seed of residual Calvinism that lies dormant within most of us, I suppose, waiting to come alive in the proper circumstances. There was just something wrong with how Allison went through life defining the closest of all relationships in terms of buying and selling. It couldn't help but blunt whatever sensibilities she had. Human beings and human emotions became commodities, elements of fantasy: faked feelings, faked loves, and faked orgasms. It was all as spurious and unreal as children playing grown-up, I thought as I began to slip into sleep, and I was an idiot for not keeping a greater distance between us.

I was still brooding about Allison early Monday morning as I drove out to T-I. I'd done some work for them before, so I knew the studio setup. After signing in, I found my way to the third-floor rear, where Westway Records shared a small suite of offices with a half dozen other labels, all under the same management. I told the receptionist that I was a detective and hinted at my studio ties but left unclear just who I was working for. I wanted to speak to whoever was now running the record division, I told her.

She smiled uneasily and disappeared into the back, and I stood alone in the waiting room, looking around at the pictures on the walls. Westway was a rock label, and most of the groups pictured seemed to be trying to outdo each other in outrageousness: green and orange spiked hair, spaced-out vacuous looks, torn clothes. The odd thing about these obviously posed PR photos was that none of the singers seemed to be enjoying themselves—or was it just uncool to smile? Propped against one wall was a life-size cardboard cutout of a punk group called the Nazi Joy Boys, except they were all girls in flesh-colored skin-tight clothes and electric hair and tattoos of Nazi death heads on their arms.

After a few moments the receptionist returned, followed by a good-looking youngish man wearing an Italian double-breasted suit with an open-necked silk shirt. Gazing at me with curiosity, he quickly crossed the thick carpet, his long blond hair bouncing off his shoulders and his hand outstretched.

"Gerald Lampson," he announced in a clear, well-modulated voice. His head tilted to one side as his gray eyes peered into mine, trying to gauge just how I entered into the scheme of things, Hollywoodwise.

"Vic Eton. I'm here about Richard Wheeler."

"Of course, of course." There was a slight spasm of indecisiveness as he continued to stare at me for a moment before coming to a decision. "Well, then . . ." another pause, more decisions being silently made, "we can go to my office."

He led me down a short, paneled hallway to an office marked PRESIDENT and settled me into an upholstered chair before taking his place behind a heavy desk of dark polished wood that looked remarkably like the one in my office. In fact, all the furniture looked remarkably like the furniture in my office. Rock music—Whitney Houston, perhaps—was drifting softly from speakers artfully concealed somewhere in the ceiling and walls. Leaning across the desk, he eyed me curiously.

"Do you mind if I ask who exactly you're working for? You're not actually on the studio payroll, are you?"

"Not at the present," I said, and recognized that what I was seeing in Lampson's wary eyes was the typical Hollywood executive's latent paranoia when having to deal with anyone even vaguely connected with law enforcement. Their day-to-day life took place in a shadowy subterranean world of drugs and racketeering and price-fixing and pandering, and a host of other transgressions, both petty and deadly, that any aggressive D.A. might unexpectedly take an interest in. I tried to put him at ease. "At the moment I'm representing a relative of the first victim."

"The girl—" He nodded calmly: Things were becoming just a little less cloudy. "Then I suppose what you want to know is whether there's any connection between her and Richard Wheeler. But I don't understand why we have to go over it again. The police have already been here asking the same questions. Why not just go to them?" He tilted back in his chair and watched me.

"It would simplify things," I agreed with a nod. "But the police won't release their interview notes, so—"

"So we do it all again! Christ!" His chair rocked forward and his voice rose with unexpected emotion. "Bureaucratic idiocy! People who can't contribute anything useful sit in their offices and make sure the rest of us *follow the rules.* So we both end up wasting our time by going through the whole damn thing again. All right, all right! What is it you want to know about Richard?"

"How he ended up naked and dead under the Hollywood sign."

Lampson laughed shortly; he had placed me in the appropriate mental box and could now relax: I was not a threat; I was not a part of his world. "I'm sure you do," he said. "Let me tell you, I was more surprised than you'd ever be when I heard it on the radio. Richard Wheeler was not the type I would have expected to end up kinky-dead like that. Dead, maybe, but not kinky-dead. He just wasn't the sort. He was pretty conventional, in fact. For the entertainment industry, anyway. A businessman, a decision maker. Not an artist or even a fan, exactly. A bottom-line type."

"How did he happen to end up as a record company executive, then?" I asked.

"Because he was an intuitive genius," Lampson replied, waving his arm and only incidentally showing me his Rolex. "He knew what would *sell,* not what was good. I hope I do half as well."

"Your position here is . . ."

"I was divisional vice president until he died. Now I'm president. Moving up the corporate hierarchy, such as it is. There's not much of a ladder on the record side, though. Only seven of us actually work out of this office. We try—the studio tries—to keep this whole operation low-overhead. As you can tell from the furniture in here. It came from some studio VP's office last year. I can't wait to dump it." He glanced around contemptuously at the office and furnishings.

I resisted the impulse to follow his gaze. "I'd like to find out about Wheeler's last few days, if I could. What happened when he left Wednesday after work? Anything unusual? Did he say he was going somewhere? Did he seem upset?"

"No, not at all. He left about four, four-fifteen. Actually

we walked out to the parking lot together like we usually did. He waved good-bye and got in his car and I never saw him again. I just assumed at the time he was going home."

"And you?"

"Home, of course. I live at the Marina. You don't think I killed Richard, do you? That's a little melodramatic, Eton. It sounds like a quickie pitch for a movie of the week: Vice president lusts after the company president's job—or was it his wife? That would be almost as good. Hires a hit man from Detroit and has him *crucified* beneath the industry's most famous symbol, then immediately jumps into his vacated position. At home *and* at work. Try it out on Ted Turner; nobody else would be interested."

Lampson leaned back in his chair and regarded me with a satisfied smile; he wasn't going to let Richard Wheeler's grisly death interfere with enjoying himself and his own witty repartee. I smiled back, showing my appreciation for his sense of humor, and asked, "Had anything been upsetting Wheeler the past week or so of his life? Something here or at home?"

"Here? Of course. *Every* day upset Richard. Just as it upsets me. It would upset *any* rational person to have to deal with the airheads who make up our day. You think it's not going to weird you out, make you a little schizoid, make you cry a little to have to deal with these millionaire juvenile delinquents?"

"That's an odd attitude for a record executive, isn't it?"

"*Odd?* C'mon! I spend my life dealing with misfits! Either these damn MBAs the studio hires to count beans who come in here with their off-the-rack three-piece suits and say, 'Whatdaya mean, sixty-five bucks for lunch?' or some buzzbrain with an electric guitar and an IQ less than his shoe size telling me to tell the *studio* to go fuck itself because they won't hire a private plane to fly them and their groupies down to

Brazil for two weeks of wall-to-wall sex and dope in a beach-front condo. You get *used* to it, maybe, but that doesn't make it any easier. You see that picture out front of the Nazi Joy Boys? The lead singer is an acid freak whose real name is Rita Shranski. In a rational society she'd be locked up as a menace to the rest of us. Here she's a role model for twenty million adolescent girls and a masturbatory fantasy for twenty million adolescent boys. She'll gross fifteen million this year. Maybe more. It's a wonderful life."

"Meaning nothing unusual was bugging Wheeler?"

"Meaning exactly that. At work, anyway. At home, that's another story. I can't help you."

"He never talked about his wife?"

Lampson squirmed uneasily in his chair and ran his hand through his long blond hair. "Never. And I only met her a few times. At the parties and receptions we hold for the press so they can actually touch the sacred skin of the newest music idol. Richard was surprisingly good with the press; he seemed to even enjoy it. I wish I could. His wife detested the whole scene. Of course, Hollywood schlock was not new to her—she grew up with it. She's Ivan Ryan's daughter, you know."

"No, I didn't know," I said. "Ivan Ryan?"

Lampson gave a little smile, enjoying my surprise. "Old Ivan was one of the real giants in the movie industry in the forties and fifties when he was directing at Metro. If you remember your local history he married one of his favorite leading ladies, Thelma Barrett. They met when he was directing musicals. Thelma Barrett was Elizabeth Wheeler's mother. She died several years ago and old Ivan lives on in the same godawful Beverly Hills mansion—"

"Ivan Ryan is *alive*?" I asked.

"Hell, yeah. Surprised me when I first heard, too. It'd be

like finding out D. W. Griffith or Samuel Goldwyn was still alive and creaking around Hollywood. His estate's next to Pickfair, the old Mary Pickford–Douglas Fairbanks place, now owned by Pia Zadora, of all people."

Thelma Barrett and Ivan Ryan: They were names out of the past, like Buster Keaton or Tom Mix or Irving Thalberg, the names you saw on Hollywood Boulevard. I could remember my family talking about these people when I was a kid, especially my uncle at Metro who had worked as a sound technician on a number of Ryan films. Damn! I was impressed; it was almost like meeting your childhood heroes. Lampson had warmed to his story and went on.

"These old-timers don't associate with the younger people in town, particularly record industry executives. They probably think we're all Sicilian Mafiosi and carry a 'rod.' All of which means I can't tell you a lot about Wheeler's personal life. I just don't know."

"From what you did know," I asked, smiling, trying to keep him talking, "from working with him every day, going to receptions and so forth, what kind of person would you say he was?"

"Like I said, a bottom-line person. A businessman, a music industry giant. Here, let me show you." He came suddenly out of his chair and headed toward the door. "C'mon. See for yourself. . . ."

Walking rapidly, he led me down the short hall and into a large bare room, in the center of which were two canvas-sided containers on wheels, each about three feet deep and filled with what looked like thousands of letters and packages. There were three inexpensive molded plastic chairs in the center of the room and a shelf with a specially built tape player capable of holding six cassettes at once.

"Unsolicited junk. Not one in a thousand of these is

worth ten seconds of our time. Maybe one in twenty thousand will actually get a contract. We got a boy who comes in three days a week and listens to this shit. *Boy!* He's twenty-five, graduated from Cal Tech in physics but wants to get in the business." He gave me a look and rolled his eyes. "Wants to *rock 'n' roll.* So we pay him a hundred a week to listen. Or send it back without listening. It doesn't make any difference. I gave him a quota: Find us ten tapes max a week to listen to. So Wheeler and I come in here every Thursday at three o'-clock and give it maybe sixty seconds.

"But here's the thing. They all sound the same to me—rip-offs, you know? This year it's Bon Jovi and Guns 'N' Roses they're all ripping off. I can hardly tell one from another; I've got to rely on our scouts and A and R people. But Wheeler was a wizard; he could really pick 'em. I swear, we could've put him in here blindfolded and without a tape player and told him to reach in the pile and pull out a winner and he would have. He was unreal. Come on back to my office. This place depresses me."

Once again in his office Lampson flipped off the music and sat behind his desk. I said, "I'm still having a problem getting a handle on the guy. What kind of *person* was he? Did he drink? Do drugs? Prostitutes? You work with someone awhile, you pick these things up."

Lampson's expression hardened. He was beginning to get tired of all the questions. "Look, as far as I know he left here every night and went straight home. What he did when he got there is beyond me, of course. Maybe he dressed up in a bra and panties and whipped his butler with spandex suspenders. If you must know, we weren't really what you'd call close. We were business associates. That's all. I was *never* invited to his house."

Lampson's face tensed with the admission; obviously this

had been a sore spot with him, and he didn't like making it public: record company up-and-comer, with his very own Rolex, and never invited out to the moneyed estates of old-line Beverly Hills. Life was a bitch. Lampson was beginning to brood on it, and I could see his mood changing; I wasn't going to get much more out of him, so I tried the obvious. "Can you think of someone with a grudge against Wheeler, someone who might want him dead?"

He waved irritably, indicating the world in general. "Christ, try the phone book. Singers whose contracts we dropped, executives at companies who've lost a star to us, waiters in the commissary. This is Hollywood, Eton: Envy, hatred, and revenge are everywhere; they're part of the territory. You learn to live with it."

Suddenly he stood up, his irritation mounting. The meeting was over. "I've got a cover conference—" he began.

I came to my feet and handed him the picture of Rosa. "Have you ever seen her?"

He shrugged his shoulders and handed it back. "Nice-looking. Nice tits. Doesn't ring any bells, though. I've never seen her."

"She was a prostitute," I said.

"So?"

"Is there any reason Wheeler might have known her?"

"Like I said: Wheeler did not confide in me. He certainly didn't amuse me with stories of frolics in the sack with prostitutes."

"But the studio hires prostitutes," I said, and thought to myself, *by the busload.*

"C'mon, Eton. The studio hires *entertainers.* Including us at Westways. We will provide *any* service our valued artists require, legal or not. That is just good business, part of our 'total package of services.' We start getting sanctimonious and they split to another label. I repeat, I have never seen this girl. You are, at any rate, barking up the wrong tree here."

"How's that?"

He looked at me as if it should have been obvious to anyone with an IQ larger than his shoe size. "There is no *connection* between the death of that girl and Richard Wheeler. These are random killings and it's just the beginning. There's someone out there who kills because it's fun. Which means it's going to be a *very* long time until he's caught."

I went straight back to my apartment and called Rudy Cruz to see what the Department had on Gerald Lampson, but Rudy was down at Parker Center talking to someone from the D.A.'s office. I left a message and then called Allison. She seemed distracted and said she was busy and would talk to me tomorrow. Fine. I made a cup of coffee and trotted down to the garage I rent for the Morgan and began to work on the clutch.

I had given up doing most auto work years ago, but I enjoyed fiddling with the Morgan. It was something I did well and it gave me the same sort of satisfaction that working in Homicide used to—moving the pieces around until they fit. Making things work. You can't play with new cars like that, of course. But the Morgan was simplicity itself; no on-board computers, no sensors or fuel injectors or automatic transmission. Just grab a wrench and connect Part A to Part B, maybe bend things a little if they don't quite fit, muscle them around. Of course, sometimes you wait six months for Part B to arrive from the manufacturer, but that just heightened the appeal of owning one of the world's great sports cars. Or so I told myself. I was done with the clutch by four o'clock.

At dinner that night Tracy gave me the latest theory circulating at school.

"Rabbit MacPhearson says it's a black magic cult. He said he'd like to come over here and 'explore his thesis' with you."

"I think I'll pass," I said, and began to wonder how a thirteen-year-old boy came to be known as Rabbit. Better not ask.

"Good!" Tracy said triumphantly. "Rabbit's a dweeb. The girls at school call him Gross-Out MacPhearson because he's always mooning out the side of his brother's car."

I gave an inward sigh at the realization that this is what several thousand years of civilization have brought us to: thirteen-year-old boys sticking their bare asses out car windows.

"Sister Maxima said there were crimes just like this in fourteenth-century Flanders. Where's Flanders?"

"Sister *Maxima*? What kind of name is that?"

Tracy squinted at me. "You don't know where it is, either, huh? I'll have to get out the atlas. Anyway, the church took care of it then. Heretics, Sister Maxima said, unbelievers."

"Great, we'll start a new Inquisition, get the rack out and inflict a little pain." *Except in Hollywood,* I thought to myself, *people would stand in line to be next.*

"We're only trying to *help,*" Tracy went on with irritation. The killings had evidently become a major topic of conversation at St. Vivian's and she enjoyed some degree of celebrity status because of my involvement. I decided to steer the conversation to more comfortable ground. "How's the basketball game?"

Tracy squinted again and dug at her frijoles with her fork. "The pits. Miss Horosky quit coaching today, and I heard her tell Sister Urbana that she'd quit teaching altogether before trying to teach basketball to thirteen-year-old girls." She made a face, wide-eyed and incredulous. "Something about 'physiological and emotional changes.' I don't know why she's making such a big deal. We're the ones going through the changes. By the way, I got invited to a dance at the Y next week."

*What?* I felt a sudden odd sensation moving through my body like a drug. Something funny going on here.

*Relax,* I told myself. *Think. Don't say anything stupid.* . . . I chewed awhile and then swallowed; I've got the sequence down pretty well now.

After another long moment, I said, "Don't you think you're a little young for a dance at the Y?"

She gave me a look of forbearance, as if I were obviously untutored in the ways of the world. "It's an early teen dance. You *have* to be twelve to fourteen, and it's over at ten o'clock." She made a face to indicate that ten was an altogether unreasonable hour in a civilized society but she was prepared to make a sacrifice in deference to the adults who went to so much trouble for 'the kids.'

I was beginning to feel the first uncontrollable stirrings of panic, as if I had inadvertently swum out too far and suddenly couldn't get back to shore. Now what, for Christ's sake? I took a breath. "Is someone taking you? A boy, I mean."

"That's the way it works, Dad. A boy takes a girl." She looked at me impassively over her unfinished dinner.

It wasn't getting any better.

"He'll pick you up here and bring you back."

She nodded, staring at me, and then added helpfully, "In a car."

Ah. A car.

For a moment I poked at my food until I found a piece of meat and chewed it thoughtfully. Finally I said, "The boy. Someone I know?" Vaguely I began to sense that I didn't know *any* boys her age; Tracy's friends had all been girls. Hadn't they? Jesus!

"You don't know him, Dad. He's fourteen, a ninth grader. He goes to Bishop Amat now. When he graduates he's planning to go to UCLA and be an urban planner."

"A what?"

"I met him last year at a football game."

"Last year? You met him last year and never told me about him?"

"His name is Kenny Shay. I've mentioned him before."

Okay, she probably had. Anyway, the name *sounded* familiar. Kenny Shay—like something out of *The Bells of St. Mary's.* Father Kenny Shay, just over from Dublin. Still, it could have been worse: It could have been Rabbit MacPhearson. But Christ, fourteen years old?

"Uh . . . look, Tracy. If he's fourteen, how is he going to pick you up? He can't drive yet and—"

Tracy made a face again, a million freckles glaring at me from across the table, and suddenly she looked about nine years old. "His mom's taking us. That's the way it'll have to be for a couple of years or so."

*A couple of years?* This is crazy.

Tracy broke into my thoughts:

"You'll get to meet him tonight, Dad. We're going to St. Vivian's to study together in the Learning Assistance Lab."

I was beginning to feel sick. Heretics, Rabbit MacPhearson, Kenny Shay, dances, urban planners, Learning Assistance Lab. Why did everything suddenly seem so weird?

Rudy came over about an hour after dinner. I had been anxious to show him the Morgan; I had actually gotten it running—not just idling, but *running*—and I was feeling pretty cocky and wanted to zip him around the block and show him that the damn thing actually was capable of locomotion. Eton's Folly, huh? I'd show him, damn it: Look at me in my ten-thousand-dollar toy. But Rudy wasn't interested and he sat impatiently on the couch for ten minutes, drumming his fingers on his knee, until Tracy left with Kenny Shay, who, I had to admit to myself, seemed like a nice kid. Then without a word he took a half dozen three-by-five photos from his shirt pocket and dropped them on the coffee table. As I picked them up he disappeared into the kitchen.

The moment I glanced at the top photo I knew what it was and I felt as if someone had kicked me in the stomach.

Rudy came back from the kitchen with a bottle of Bud and sank onto the couch. "They killed the girl for a movie."

I flipped quickly through the photos. "*Holy Christ . . .*" Rosa nailed to a wall, mouth open, screaming; Rosa being raped; Rosa with bullet holes exploding in her chest.

Rudy's voice came to me distantly, like the slow, faint tolling of a funeral bell. "I saw the film downtown this afternoon with Morales. I didn't think it was possible, not a real one. I've seen probably a dozen phonies over the years; there's a market out there for them. They pretend to shoot the girl, put a little catsup on her, tell her to scream a lot. This one isn't phony."

I sat there for a moment listening but not listening, my mind going through a series of maneuvers to convince me that it wasn't true. From the kitchen I could hear the refrigerator cycle on. The television was tuned to the Dodger game, Vin Scully saying two on, two out. A tremor of disbelief went through my body: fifteen years old.

"Both Wheeler and Rosa?" I asked after a moment.

"Just Rosa." His voice wavered. "They tortured her and tortured her. Then they shot her."

The breath seemed to rush out of Rudy as he sat staring at the top of the coffee table. There was nothing new about snuff films; like he said, they had been a part of the mythology of Hollywood for years. Everyone claimed to have seen one or heard of one or had a friend who had seen one. But in fact none had ever turned up. Not a real one.

Rudy finished his beer and sank back on the couch. I went into the kitchen and brought out two more Buds, and he opened one and took a swig. "Vice has had it for more than a week and didn't know it. They busted a distributor out in North Hollywood. A cement factory." He shook his head. "You believe that? It really *was* a cement factory, trucks rumbling in and out all the time, rattling the building. Big business, building freeways and office buildings. But they also ran a mail order outfit, amateur crap, videos, mostly of kids. They had customers all over the world, according to their mailing lists. Vice confiscated so many different films that they just got around to this one yesterday."

I sat for a minute while the idea of someone committing murder for entertainment moved around in my mind. It seemed incomprehensible. Or was it? This was the New Hollywood: a decade of splatter films for the teen market. Maybe stylized screen deaths just weren't enough for a generation that had grown up with *Halloween III* and *Nightmare on Elm Street.*

And Rosa wanted to be an actress, Allison had said. Rosa wanted to be remembered, to be famous; a star.

"That seems to blow a hole in the serial killer theory," I said after a minute.

"Seems to," Rudy agreed.

Christ, it was hot.

I went over and pushed open a window to let in a breeze. Then I sat down again on the couch. "Any idea who made it?"

Rudy said, "They arrested the factory owner and two guys who work in the office. They claim they bought it off the street; some guy that knows about their little sideline walks in and asks them if they wanna buy a flick, a little S and M, blood on the titties. So they screened it right there, then gave him two thousand in cash. Vice says they're probably telling the truth—they don't seem to be in production."

"The guy?"

"Thirty-five or forty-five or fifty, white, maybe Italian. Maybe Mexican. Could even have been Japanese. They didn't look real close."

"Which leaves us where?"

Rudy shook his head. "Vice is working on production. They'll check out all the producers in the normal porno trade. Vice knows who they are, probably's on a first-name basis with most of them. They think this is an amateur job, though; none of the legitimate porno producers would take a chance with something this hot. Homicide's working the Wheeler angle—so far there's no connection. They don't seem to have known each other."

"Yeah—" The big-time record executive and the street-walker. Even now it didn't make sense. I put my feet on the coffee table and closed my eyes a minute and pondered. Everything I thought I had known about the case had suddenly vanished in the wake of those pictures. There was no serial killer. No sexual psychopath. Just someone who tortured and murdered for entertainment. For fun and money. And I was no closer than ever.

Rudy finished his beer and set the bottle down on the glass tabletop. "If you want to see the film, the D.A.'s having a closed screening at Parker for the press tomorrow. Downtown figures if we let the killers know we have the film it might stir the waters a little, make something happen. I put your name down in case you're interested. Ten A.M."

"I may as well," I said. I asked Rudy if they'd come up with Rosa's address yet, and he said they hadn't. When I gave it to him he looked at me without emotion and I said, "Tell Morales it was an anonymous tip."

"What are we going to find there?"

"That the girl someone tortured and killed for a movie was barely fifteen years old."

Just then the glass coffee table beneath our feet began to tremble, the couch rolled under us and every window in the building rattled and shook.

Rudy muttered, "Shit," and tried to stand, bracing himself against the couch. A vase on the bookcase behind us fell to the floor and shattered.

"Let's wait it out," I said, hearing my own voice tremble but staying on the couch, gripping the arm with my hand.

And suddenly it was over. Maybe twenty seconds total, I guessed. Outside we could hear people streaming into the hallway. Loud, happy, angry, scared voices. Car alarms going off everywhere.

"About a five-point-five," Rudy figured. Everyone's first words after a quake: Where is it on the Richter scale? He looked around the room and then back at me. "Kind of makes your day, doesn't it?"

*

The next morning I picked up a badge at the lobby reception desk at Parker and went up to the bleakly modern fourth-floor hearing room, where three dozen men and women were already sitting in folding chairs. A projector and screen were set up in front of the room, and Arthur Haskins from the D.A.'s office was standing with three of his youngish assistants next to the screen, halfway through a carefully detailed explanation of the nature of the search of the cement factory, its constitutional validity, and why it took so long to turn up the film after the place was raided. There were another twenty minutes of questions from the press before Haskins said he wanted to defer any further questions until after the film. After ensuring that the TV cameras had stopped filming, someone doused the lights and the projector was switched on.

No title, no credits.

But suddenly there was Rosa, young and beautiful and completely filling the screen, the quintessence of male fantasy sex as she writhed on satin sheets on a large round bed. That childlike face I'd seen in photos distorted in death stared up larger than life at the camera as she spread her thin coffee-colored legs and moaned seductively; then a hand-held camera moved in for a slow close-up of the tattoo near her vagina and she laughed out loud, a childish high-pitched giggle, and suddenly she seemed exactly what she was: a fifteen-year-old girl pretending to be grown up. A child about to die.

As the camera drew back another person entered the scene, a stocky, nude white man probably in his thirties but seen only from the rear and side, his face deliberately hidden in shadows. It was a simulated rape scene, and I felt a sick feeling move through me and wondered what kind of person would get his kicks watching something like this, from watching a woman being violently raped. The scene dragged out slowly for several minutes, Rosa pretending to struggle with the man as he held a knife to her throat while thrusting violently into her body. It was all very amateurish, obvious play-acting and fantasy, with no pretense to anything else. But then there was a change in the tone of the film. Two more men, faces hidden from the camera, had joined the action. Rosa had performed fellatio on all three, slowly and lovingly for the close-up camera, moaning all the time with pleasure and excitement, when one of the men suddenly grabbed her by the hair and forced her to the bed as the other two held her while the first man raped her anally. Rosa was screaming and struggling wildly, and her face had contorted in fear, and it didn't look like acting now.

As I watched the next few minutes of film, I knew we were all seeing something that would remain with us forever. No amount of effort would will away the horror we were witnessing or remove the sense of degradation we felt as we saw what human beings were capable of doing to one another. Everyone felt it, and they stirred uneasily in their chairs and tried to avert their eyes. But it was there in front of them; it had really happened.

The three men, their faces obscured now by black hoods, worked quickly, binding Rosa's feet with electrical cord as her shouts pierced the air; then another hooded man joined them, and the three of them held the girl while the new man tied each arm to a massive wooden cross attached to a wall and strapped another cord around the bottom end of the cross and her already bound feet. All the while Rosa screamed, the men working wordlessly until she was tightly bound to the cross.

Chairs scraped on the floor around me, people twisted uncomfortably, and the air was hot and still. I could feel perspiration begin to accumulate on my spine. On the screen three of the men suddenly yanked the black masks from their faces, revealing massive hairy asses' heads underneath. It was hideous. Rosa's face was covered in tears and sweat as she shook her head wildly back and forth. Then the fourth man dramatically ripped his hood away, exposing a monstrous blood-red devil's face, shiny and horrible and awash with perspiration. With deliberate slowness he approached Rosa with a hammer and two giant steel nails that gleamed in the light. Rosa passed out in fright.

The next few minutes, filmed probably over two or three hours, were filled with unspeakable horrors; periodically the filming had been halted to revive the girl, now delirious with terror and the loss of blood. Finally she could barely keep her eyes open; her body was slack and drenched in blood and her head hung listlessly on the side, eyes half shut. Then, as if she suddenly foresaw what was about to happen, her head snapped up, her eyes widened, her mouth stretched open, and she tried to scream, but nothing came out and the naked devil's head slowly raised a long-barreled revolver and pointed it from ten feet away at her heart. He slowly squeezed the trigger. And then again and again as blood and flesh flew from her body. The camera lingered on the scene for a full two minutes and then the film was over, flapping in the projector.

I thought I was going to be sick. For a long moment there wasn't a sound in the room. Then Haskins flipped on the lights and strode to the front of the room to say something. I walked out.

The phone was ringing when I got home; I flipped on the window air conditioner and picked it up as I sank down on the couch. It was Allison. She was sorry she wasn't able to see me last night but she had had a friend coming over and it was something she couldn't get out of. I told her not to worry about it. Great, she said, sounding buoyant; perhaps too buoyant, I thought to myself. More of Allison's mood swings. How long would this one last? I wondered as she continued on in her "up" voice: "Why don't we go somewhere today? Maybe drive down to Santa Monica and walk out on the pier, watch the old men fish and then have dinner someplace nearby."

I said I didn't think today would be the day for it, then added, "I have to talk to you. About Rosa."

I heard a slight intake of breath on the other end of the line and then silence. After a moment she asked, "Do you know something?"

"I'll come by later this afternoon. Four o'clock okay?"

For a few seconds she didn't answer; then she sighed, resigned to a coming sadness. Four o'clock was fine. I hung up and dialed directory assistance and asked for Richard Wheeler's number in Beverly Hills. On the way back from Parker Center I had decided that I had to talk to Wheeler's wife. Something tied Wheeler to Rosa—somehow their deaths were linked—but after viewing the snuff film I couldn't see how. All I knew for certain was that these were not random killings. The operator said there was no listing for Wheeler, which didn't surprise me: Half of L.A. hides behind the anonymity of an unlisted phone. I tried Gerald Lampson at the studio, but he was out and his secretary wouldn't give me Wheeler's number. Of course. Reluctantly, I called Rudy. Too many favors can strain the texture of even the closest relationship, and I didn't want to make things uncomfortable for him at work. But Rudy said sure, no problem, and got back to me with Elizabeth Wheeler's number ten minutes later. When I called she was reluctant to talk to me; she had already been through all this with the police, she said. There didn't seem any point in doing it again. But when I told her I was working for the family of the slain girl she gave way and agreed to see me at two o'clock. But it was clear she wasn't happy about it.

It took me ten minutes of hovering over one of those detailed city maps to find where Elizabeth Wheeler lived. Chacon Lane was a twisting two-lane road as high and remote in the hills of Beverly Hills as you can get, and her address seemed to put it at the very end. I marked the location with a red felt-tip pen and folded the map and put it in my shirt pocket. Even so, when I set off an hour later I managed to get lost for twenty minutes before finally stumbling across the road by accident. From there I just aimed the Buick uphill, following the hairpin twists and turns until the road terminated abruptly at a locked gate in a ten-foot-high chain-link fence that looked at least fifty years old.

I pulled off into a small gravel parking area overgrown with weeds and picked up the intercom next to the gate. As I waited for it to be answered I heard a nest of jays arguing loudly overhead and caught a glimpse of a coyote out of the corner of my eyes as it disappeared into the underbrush and pine trees, and I couldn't help drawing a contrast between life up here, literally above it all in the clear, smogless air, and the real world of pornographic films and teenage gangs and drugs and random killings down below in the flat gridlike streets of Hollywood.

The phone was finally answered, and after I explained who I was the gate buzzed open. I drove through, stopping to reclose the gate, and stood for a moment, looking around. I was in a small dirt clearing surrounded by forty-foot pines and thick dry underbrush on all sides. But the house was still nowhere in sight. I got back in the car and followed the private road as it twisted downhill and bumped around a corner and then suddenly there it was, spread out in front of me. For the past half hour I had unconsciously formed an impression of what it would look like. I had been dealing with Industry executives long enough to know their tastes: handsome but rather nondescript brick and stucco homes of two stories with an attached four-car garage, pool and pool house in the rear, palms and ferns and flowering bougainvillea everywhere. But I wasn't at all ready for this. The house stretched out in front of my eyes like a vision in one of old Ivan Ryan's fantasy films from the forties: a towering three-story stone mansion looking like a centuries-old French chateau, with a dozen chimneys and turrets and thick round towers, and a long brick driveway that swept majestically up to the broad stone steps in front. A carnival of red and yellow and green asters and marigolds and petunias and geometrically shaped bushes and trees fanned out from the house on each side while a long marble reflecting pool lay directly in front, duplicating the entire fairy-tale scene in its still, mirror-like water. It took my breath away, and for a long moment I just sat in the car and stared.

It was 1920 again, and movie moguls imported masons and artists and builders from Europe and stone from Mexico and furniture from all over the world and damned the cost as long as their dreams came true. I didn't realize these places existed anymore. But for some reason I couldn't help but feel delighted that they did. Fantasy was alive, wishes were fulfilled, and anyone could be a star.

A middle-aged Asian houseman stood frozen next to the front door, watching as I parked the car and came up the steps. "Mr. Eton?" He stared at me with dark emotionless eyes and in heavily accented English added, "Mrs. Wheeler is expecting you."

I followed as he led the way into a cathedral-like entrance hall of stone and marble and asked me to wait, disappearing behind heavy double doors that swung silently on oiled hinges. I dug my hands into my pockets and gazed up to the massive crystal chandelier suspended forty feet overhead and began to feel very small. *Like a child in church,* I thought to myself in the eerie silence, and expected at any moment to hear an organ playing, but instead heard footsteps tapping on the stone.

Elizabeth Wheeler came in by herself, an attractive woman in her mid- to late thirties, with shoulder-length brown hair and pale skin and soft blue eyes, wearing gray slacks and a blouse. From a distance she looked like a skinny teenager, but as she came closer I saw it was because of her slight build: She weighed probably less than a hundred pounds and couldn't have been over five feet tall. She didn't smile and only reluctantly offered her hand, introducing herself and then leading me into a nearby library, a large masculine room with tall, arched windows and floor-to-ceiling bookshelves and paneled walls. For a moment she seemed confused, as if she didn't know why either of us was there. Then she shook herself, and ran her hand through her hair.

"Can I get you something, Mr. Eton? Coffee?" She looked at me from red-lined eyes, and when I said no she directed me to a leather couch in the middle of the room, taking a seat opposite on its twin. It was obvious that she didn't want to see anyone, and I began to feel uncomfortable at forcing a visit on her so soon after her husband's death.

"Mrs. Wheeler, if this is going to be too difficult for you—"

"No, no. Please." She pulled a Kleenex from her slacks pocket, but instead of dabbing at her eyes she wadded it into a ball and held it tightly, like a child grasping onto a blanket. "But I'm still not quite sure why you're here. As I told you on the phone, I've talked to the police. Twice. I don't even know who exactly you're working for."

"I was hired by a friend of the young girl who was killed. Her name was Rosa Luzon. Does that mean anything to you? Do you think your husband might have known her? Perhaps through his work?"

She shook her head. "No, I'm sure Richard didn't. At least I've never heard it, not before this. . . ." She tensed and squeezed the Kleenex harder, and I saw tears coming into her eyes, but she looked at me determinedly and went ahead, as if expressing grief to a stranger was somehow unacceptable. "Richard didn't talk about his work much, but I think I would have remembered the name if he did."

"He didn't discuss his problems at the studio?" I asked.

It seemed odd that the frustrations of what Lampson described as a high-pressure job didn't find an outlet in dinner or pillow talk.

Mrs. Wheeler slowly shook her head but it was a moment before she answered, as if she were being asked to bare secrets that belonged only to the family. "It was an agreement we had to keep our work life separate from our family life. I'm a curator at the Museum of Natural History, and he had his life at the studio, but we consciously tried not to bring our work home with us. It's an occupational hazard in this town that ruins too many marriages, and we were determined that it wouldn't happen to us. Sometimes people would phone, of course, or Richard would have to go somewhere after dinner, but as much as possible home was for Megan and us. Megan is our thirteen-year-old daughter."

"Then you wouldn't know if something had been bothering your husband at work lately?"

"*Nothing* had been bothering Richard lately. I'm sure of it. I've never seen him so happy."

"What about last Wednesday? He seemed normal when he left for work?"

She nodded. "I left first. But, yes, he was fine."

"When did you begin to think something might be wrong?"

"Almost immediately. I got home just before six as usual. Richard always got home between five and five-thirty. When he still wasn't here by seven I called the studio office but no one answered. So I called Gerald Lampson at home, but he said Richard had left at four-thirty, as always. I called a few friends, but no one had seen him. By then I was certain something was wrong. At nine I called my father—"

"Ivan Ryan?"

She nodded. Her eyes moistened again and her face tensed at the recollection.

"Did your husband often stop off there?" I asked.

She looked at me, surprised. "No, almost never."

"Then why—"

"He's my *father*!" she said, and finally the tears came. She seized another Kleenex from her pocket and wiped her eyes. "He said there was no point in calling the police; they weren't going to do anything about someone who was only missing a few hours. But he phoned all the hospitals here and in Hollywood. The next morning I finally called the police and they said they couldn't do a thing until he had been missing twenty-four hours. That night an officer came out, and I filed a report. They found him the next day. . . ."

"And you can't think of any reason why he was killed?"

Elizabeth Wheeler came to her feet and looked at me with emotion. "Mr. Eton, Sergeant Morales was out here this morning. I know why that girl was killed and I can't imagine what it has to do with Richard—"

I asked, as gently as possible, "Your husband wouldn't have had any reason to become involved somehow with prostitutes?"

Her whole body seemed to tense in denial at what I was implying. "Of course not! If Richard had been interested in extramarital sex he certainly wouldn't have needed to pay for it. The studios are full of willing young women. I know what I'm talking about—I grew up in the studios." There was an edge of defiance in her voice, and she glared openly at me as if daring me to contradict her.

"But as part of his work," I went on evenly. "Maybe for one of his rock groups? A favor?"

Elizabeth sank back onto her seat, looking tinier than ever as the couch swallowed her up. She brushed some hair from her face and stared at me, a beautiful, angry, terribly distraught woman about to lose control. "You'll have to ask Gerald Lampson about that. I know nothing about what he did for his singers. I don't *want* to know."

"I'm sorry," I said, meaning it. I came to my feet. I was feeling disgusted with myself and I wanted suddenly to get out of there and leave her alone with her grief. In the back of my mind was the memory of Laurie's death, of the horrible emptiness I had felt for months followed by an almost inexpressible anger. Inexpressible because I didn't know where to direct it except inward.

Elizabeth stood up also and took a deep breath, glad to see me go. But before either of us could speak the door flew open and we were rushed in on by a young girl about Tracy's age who seemed not to notice my presence. She was wearing pajamas and she ran red-eyed to her mother, grasping her tightly by the waist and breaking into convulsive sobs. Elizabeth hugged her tightly to her body.

"This is my daughter, Megan," she said to me over the girl's head. "She stayed home from school today. This has been very difficult for her."

"Of course." I looked at the girl but she twisted wildly away as if the sight of me were repulsive and tightened her grip on her mother. I took a business card from my pocket and handed it to Elizabeth. "If you think of anything, please give me a call."

She didn't answer but led her daughter away as the houseman took me to the door.

I was twenty minutes early when I got to Allison's, but she greeted me with a smile and a kiss, wearing short shorts and a tattered T-shirt and holding a paintbrush like an ice-cream cone.

"Come into my *studio,*" she said with a laugh as if the word were too pretentious to be used seriously, and led me by the hand into the back room I'd never been in before and where she had a heavy wooden easel set up amid a clutter of art supplies. Unframed canvases in varying stages of completion leaned against the walls, and a stereo was playing a Beethoven quartet. The room smelled agreeably of linseed oil and paints and perfume. I walked over to the undraped windows and glanced out at the city lying mute a dozen floors below.

"North light." She shrugged and laughed apologetically.

As she began to clean her brushes I walked back to the

easel and stared at the almost finished painting she had been working on.

"I won't ask if you like it," she said. "Because you'll say you do. People always do, no matter what they really think. Anyway, I don't care if you like it or not. I don't care if *anyone* likes it. I paint for me."

Tacked onto the easel was an old photograph she'd been working from of the Garden of Allah, a Hollywood landmark long since torn down. She had turned the dreary black and white snapshot into a bright dreamy scene of flamingo pinks and tawny browns beneath the pale blue of a clear and cloudless sky. Beautiful and ethereal. Like Hollywood must have been, I thought, in the days before smog and gridlock.

"The Hollywood of glamour," she said as if reading my thoughts. "Not like it is now."

"Not like it is now," I agreed.

She led me back into the living room. "Hold on while I clean up. Make yourself a drink if you want."

I sank onto the couch and looked for something to read. There were half a dozen copies of *Art Forum* and *Architectural Digest* lying around, both of which were somewhere near the lower end of my personal list of things to read. A book on the end table: *Vanity Fair.* Christ, I remembered that from high school: The Book That Would Not End. Screw it. I decided to turn on the television and looked around for it, then realized with a shudder that there wasn't one. I had heard about such people before but had never actually met one. It was almost creepy. When I heard the shower running I decided to get a beer and walked into the kitchen. The large ultramodern refrigerator was stocked with obscure vegetables and fresh fruits and champagne and even tiny jars of caviar. But no Bud.

"Don't you know anybody who drinks beer?" I yelled

toward the bathroom, and then realized I probably should have phrased it more diplomatically.

"*What?*" The shower went off.

A moment later the door opened and she stood in the doorway vigorously drying off with a large terrycloth towel while water dripped to the carpet. "I couldn't hear you," she said, and bent to dry her legs and feet.

"No beer," I repeated with a shrug.

She stood naked, with the towel dangling from one hand, her green eyes staring at me incredulously. Then she began to laugh. "Well, *damn*! We better go out, then, hadn't we? Hold on." She disappeared into her bedroom, leaving a trail of water on the carpet.

The phone rang, and I could hear her through the open doorway, laughing. I began to wander around the living room, gazing at her pictures. Five minutes later she came out dressed in slacks and a white silk blouse. Very Beverly Hills housewifely, I thought, except that her large breasts were pressed against the thin fabric of the blouse in a way most Beverly Hills housewives would have considered unseemly, if not downright outrageous. I thought it looked just fine.

"We'll go back to Tommaso's," she said. "If we ask *real* nice I'm sure they'll find you a beer somewhere. Even if they have to send out."

Tommaso's had a comfortable feeling. I'd begun to like the way they did things: the waiter didn't tell us his name or recite a long list of daily specials, the salad forks were not chilled, nobody rudely accosted us with a giant pepper mill, and the wine list represented more or less what people drank and not what they fantasized about. Allison sat across from me in the small rear booth, our knees touching. We had pasta and salad and a pitcher of cold dark draft beer that made her wrinkle her nose in either distaste or unfamiliarity. "Live dangerously," I said as I refilled her glass.

We could talk about Rosa when we got back to her apartment, she decided. But not now. Now was a time to relax. So I took the opportunity to compliment her on her paintings, and she glanced at me with an amused expression. "Well, you can't have one, so don't ask. I keep *everything* I paint. If I ever do something I really like, then maybe I'll let it go. Maybe I'll try selling through my store in Pasadena. Right now I don't have enough confidence. I couldn't take the rejection of seeing my pictures hanging there week after week with those little colored price stickers on the frames. You don't collect art, do you?"

"I don't collect anything."

"Where do you have your money, then? The market?"

*My money?* I thought.

She was staring at me across the table, the faint candlelight from the table flickering in her large eyes.

"Well, I put most of my money into little ceramic footprints of the world's wildlife. They come each month from the Franklin Mint. Very lifelike."

"Tell me you're kidding."

"I'm kidding. What money I have goes into a Morgan."

"A '48 through '55?" she asked.

I looked at her a moment. "A '49." I felt a flutter of astonishment, or fear, as if the floor had just moved beneath my feet. *Nobody* knew what a Morgan was.

"It's got good upside potential but it's not liquid enough for someone in your position. You ought to sell and get into CDs."

"You can't drive a CD," I said, and then added, "Why do you always start sounding like Jay Gould?"

Her face colored and she sat back in her chair. "Bad

habit, huh? Sorry. I'm just into investments, I guess. It's sort of a hobby. But I'm planning ahead, too. I can't keep working like . . . this, not forever. Maybe five more years at the max. I want to be ready when my time comes because there won't be any warning. Or pension."

"In five more years," I said, "you'll probably be worth more than Ivan Ryan."

"The old-time director?" She laughed. "He isn't still around, is he? Ivan Ryan?"

She had repeated the name as if it weren't quite real, as I had first done.

"I'll tell you later," I said.

She gave me a look, then said, "I'm not going to like any of this, am I?"

"None of it."

On the way back to her place she made me stop at a liquor store. She went in by herself and came out a few minutes later holding a paper bag folded over at the top as if she didn't want anyone to see what it was. "Two six-packs of Bud," she whispered confidentially. "I don't want to be accused of being a bad hostess again."

Back in her apartment she pulled open the living room drapes so we could watch the sun go down over the hills. Then she switched on a soft rock station, handed me a bottle of Bud without a glass, and sat on the couch, close but not touching. She looked as if she had been steeling herself all night to ask, and her body stiffened as she finally got to it. "All right, tell me about Rosa."

When I told her about the film a chill seemed to pass through her body. "Oh, Christ," she whispered. Her eyes lost their focus as she stared at the floor.

"I want to ask you some questions," I said carefully, "that might help me. There're a few things I need to know."

I felt as if I were walking on eggs as I began to probe the working life of a whore.

"Have you ever seen a snuff film?"

Her head shook slowly from side to side, and I wasn't certain she had heard me. Then she looked up and held my gaze, her eyes pleading. "Don't tell me about it, Vic. Please, I don't want to hear—"

I understood, I said. I wished to heaven I'd never seen it either. But now, as I tried to keep my head clear, to think carefully about my questions to Allison, my subconscious flipped on the projector at Parker Center and images began to fill my mind: Rosa screaming, Rosa pleading, Rosa seeing her life slip away as the gun was aimed.

I said, "You said she didn't talk much about herself."

Allison nodded. "Not much. Mostly she talked about her family, her mother and sisters."

"Did you know she was barely fifteen?"

"Oh, God, no!" She looked abruptly up at me, her eyes darkened with misery. "Are you sure?"

I nodded and waited while Allison sat very still on the couch. I wanted to find out what she knew about the porno industry. Living in Hollywood, she had to have had some exposure to it—if not firsthand, she would have heard things: people in the business, films being shot, that sort of thing. But any question at all about her working life was like waving a red flag: Instantly the defensiveness and hostility and anger would well up in a torrent. I decided to go at it obliquely.

"You said Rosa wanted to be an actress."

She nodded her head.

"Do you think she had been in a porno film before?"

Allison nodded, thinking. "She told me she made five hundred dollars once for two days' work. It was out in the Valley somewhere at someone's house. She was more like an extra, I guess, another body in an orgy scene. I told her to forget it if she ever really wanted to get into the business. Once you're typed as a porno actress you'll never cross over into legitimate films. I thought she believed me. But I guess it's hard to say no when someone says movies."

"Did she tell you anything about that film—who produced it, the title, anything?"

Allison stood up and walked over to the windows; it was almost dark outside now, and the lights of houses in the hills were switching on like fireflies in the distance. She shook her head, slowly, sadly, staring at me from across the silent room. "I don't think it was a professional film, from the way she talked about it. It wasn't even really filmed; they just videotaped it. She never even saw a print when it was done. It sounded to me like mail-order junk, sixty minutes for $29.95."

"What if I wanted to talk to someone in the city about porno? What if I had an idea for a film or wanted someone to process something too hot for legitimate labs?"

She came back and sat down next to me, her body shaking, her voice almost inaudible. "Christ, Vic, hold me. I feel like I'm coming apart."

She curled into my body, not seductively, not out of some shared emotion, but like a child that suddenly needs protection. Her whole body was trembling as if she couldn't get warm. After a moment, though, she pushed abruptly away from me and fled into the bathroom. When she came back she had a Kleenex in her hand and she sat at the far end of the couch, staring toward the windows. Her voice was faint. "I have a . . . friend . . . in the business. He's a producer at Universal, legitimate films only. But he was telling me about porno films a few months ago. The big studios aren't interested, he said. Not because of public opinion but because of profit. The market's not that big for hard-core pornography. The only way you can make any money is to keep your costs to practically nothing. The studios have too much overhead to charge off on each film to be able to do that, especially since you have to use union people on both sides of the cameras. Porno films are usually shot in a week and only the stars make even as much as a thousand dollars. Studios just can't work that way. He said most of the real dirt, the low end of the sleaze market, is handled by a company on Edgemont just off Sunset, that large purple building that says MUSIC RECORDING in giant letters. It's a front, he said. Mostly they process porno films, sometimes even shoot there."

"Do you think that's who Rosa was working for?"

She shook her head. "I don't know, Vic. I don't think so. Rosa said her film was videotaped. What about the snuff film?"

"It was film. But I suppose it could be transferred from one to the other."

Allison said, "I don't think anyone in the business would risk a snuff film. There's too many safer ways of making money."

"Unless there's no one around to talk except those who made it, those who'd go to jail if they did talk. That would keep everyone pretty quiet. Rosa was the only girl in the movie. Rosa and four men guilty of murder. A tight little group."

"Then where does that other victim fit in, the record company executive?"

I sighed. It was the same question I had been asking myself. "He worked at Trans-International Studios," I said, free-associating. "They make movies—"

"Not a chance, Vic. Don't even think it. Not a major studio with a snuff film."

"Maybe he decided to branch out on his own."

"Then why was *he* tortured and killed in the same way Rosa was? He's not going to turn up on a snuff film, Vic. Only men like that sort of thing. And they don't get their kicks watching other men get killed; it's got to be women, young women."

Allison sat quietly for a moment on the couch, staring at some point of inner vision. Idly she glanced at her watch and it shook her abruptly out of her mood. She came quickly to her feet.

"I'm sorry, Vic. I didn't realize how late it was." She looked at me apologetically. "You're going to have to go."

I got up and glanced at my own watch. Almost eight o'clock. Someone coming over. Allison gave me a quick kiss, pressing her body against mine, her voice trembling with emotion. "God, I wish you could stay."

*What do I wish?* I thought, looking at her. She was already composing herself, wiping away the tears and putting on her "working" face. *What's real?* I wondered. What goes on in the mind of someone who can switch from grief to seductiveness in the time it takes to glance at a watch? And that little voice in the back of my mind came alive again and said, *Let it go. She's a hooker; she's a client. That's all she is.*

I got home at half past eight. Rudy Cruz was eating tacos and enchiladas in the kitchen with Tracy. The small room was hot and stuffy and smelled of cheese and refried beans and guacamole.

"She makes better Mexican food than I do," Rudy said, and winked at Tracy. "Anyway, Julie called me at work and said she wasn't going to be home for dinner; she's out opening windows of opportunity."

Tracy was sitting at the table with a Diet 7-Up.

"Did you already eat?" I asked her.

"I'm not hungry. Anyway, I was getting a little fat."

"*Fat?*" Tracy had the lean, emaciated build of a Russian gymnast.

Rudy looked at me, his dark face calm behind his massive black mustache. "You don't understand because you've only got one kid. I've been through all this. It will not stop for ten years. Don't expect any of it to make any sense."

"Thanks."

He looked at me helpfully. "You wanna talk to Julie? Get a little help with parenting? Maybe they'll form a support group for you, help you with your role modeling."

Tracy said, "I'm going to watch TV."

As she left, Rudy said, "See you later, kiddo. And remember what I told you," and she smiled and disappeared into the living room and I could hear MTV through the swinging door.

I said, "What did you tell her?"

Rudy looked at me and swallowed the remainder of his taco. "Never go out with a guy named Rabbit."

I rummaged around in the refrigerator and pulled out a beer and sat down at the table. As I did, Rudy took an envelope out of his inside sports coat pocket and handed it across the table. Inside were Xerox copies of the lab report on Wheeler. "Read and burn. Anyone finds out what I did for you and it's my ass."

I read through the report slowly. Wheeler had been shot five times with a .38, all in the torso, the bullets entering horizontally and exiting his back. Very close range, less than five feet. There were holes driven all the way through his wrists and ankles, but much neater and cleaner than last time, none of the tearing of the flesh or bones that Rosa had shown.

"Practice makes perfect," Rudy explained.

Large amounts of cocaine and scotch in his system. Hadn't eaten in several hours. No sign of sexual abuse. The body had been cleaned but not obsessively this time and not with alcohol. He'd been dead for at least sixteen hours before his body had been discovered.

"Which would make it—?"

"Midnight to two A.M."

Wheeler's clothes had been found a day later by some kids in a field twenty miles away on the Palos Verdes Peninsula. Slacks and socks from an expensive Rodeo Drive boutique, white boxer shorts from Sears, handmade English shoes. All bloodied and stuffed in a plastic trash bag and probably thrown from a car.

"No shirt," I said.

"We noticed," Rudy replied.

"Not much to go on, is there?"

"That's why downtown doesn't like it; it's making them antsy. They decided to form a 'Hollywood Sign Task Force.' Oscar's still officially in charge, but they brought in a captain named Blalock from Ramparts to run the unit. He reports directly to Parker Center. Shitty deal for Oscar. I don't know if I'll be able to get you reports anymore."

I wondered about that. Two killings and they yank it away from the captain in charge. It didn't sound right. Unless there was something going on I didn't know about.

I put the papers back on the table. "What do you know about the porno business?"

Rudy gave me his don't-ask look. "I never worked Vice. I never *want* to work Vice."

"Who can I talk to?"

"The President's Commission on Pornography. The FBI. Any thirteen-year-old boy."

I waited.

He sighed. "I'll see if Organized Crime downtown will talk to you. Will that make you happy?"

"It'll help."

Rudy stood up and stretched and patted his full stomach. "Burn those papers. I gotta go parent. How's the Morgan coming along?"

"I think I'll sell it and get into CDs."

Rudy nodded. "Good move. More liquid for a guy like you."

I guess I don't quite understand why you're *here,*" the first man was saying. He was thirtyish, styled black hair, Rodeo Drive clothes, and the perfect, dazzling smile of all eager young Hollywood executives. His name was Alan Rezotti, and he claimed to be the owner of the recording studio on Edgemont Allison had told me about and where we were now seated. Another man was hunched over a control panel, flipping switches and staring through the glass at a rock group setting up equipment and tuning instruments while passing a joint back and forth.

"I'm planning to make a film," I said above the noise from the studio. "Me and some friends are putting up the money. We've already hired the actors: three girls, two guys, just amateurs but good body parts. We're all amateurs; we need a little help on the production side. And a place to film."

Rezotti shook his head. "You've obviously never done anything like this before."

I smiled and gave him a little shrug. "Me and my friends, we're mainly collectors. I must gotta thousand videos myself, good stuff, lots of pink, lots of close-ups. I buy and trade from all over the world, especially Denmark. They know how to do things there, they got no laws, age laws and shit like that. See, me and my friends, we figure why let the other guy get paid all the time? Let some dudes write *us* a check once in a while, right? So we got a script, got some horny actors, got equipment, and got money. Now all we need is a little help, technical shit."

The man at the control panel was still staring out at the rock group; he pulled some switches down and the control room went suddenly quiet as he turned his head and looked at me. "What Mr. Rezotti said was, how come you're *here*?" He was a large, muscle-bound, dark-complexioned man of about forty or forty-five, boulder-headed with tight-knit gray hair growing like moss on top, neat little mustache below a thick nose. He had none of the slick veneer of the other man: a middle-aged punk with a Jersey accent, not trying to be anything else, and I thought, *We have the whole evolutionary line here, the Alpha and Omega of mobdom*—the smooth, elegant young executive and the aging primal hood together in the same room as if this were an illustrated lecture on the history of American crime.

I squirmed enough to show my discomfort, show them I wasn't someone to worry about. Just another jerk trying to make a few bucks. "Well, what I heard was, I heard you wanna make a little porno, and you wanna keep it quiet, you come here. That's what I heard—" I looked from face to face, as if seeking confirmation, and shrugged uneasily.

"Who the hell tol' you that?" the older man demanded.

He had swiveled all the way around in his chair and was staring at me and chewing gum with a loud smacking sound. There was a small scar on his forehead, another on his cheek, and an ugly one amid a welter of dead tissue under his left eye. He must have been a pro fighter once to collect all that. But not a contender, or I'd remember him. Maybe a professional sparring partner. Sort of what he was doing now. Unlike his well-dressed partner, he was wearing brown work pants and a tight T-shirt designed to show his muscles. He was also wearing expensive brown leather cowboy boots with two-inch heels, probably to keep his knuckles from dragging on the floor.

"I don't think they want their names used," I said, looking at them both. "Guys."

"The fuck you talking about? What guys?"

"Cement guys," I said. "Vendors."

The two men exchanged a look. They were beginning to become aware of danger in some primitive sort of way, cavemen around a campfire pricking up their ears as enemies advanced through the brush. The older man said, "I think maybe something happened to them." Like he was testing me.

"I heard. They went away for a while. No big deal. You're in business, you take chances. I'm willing to take a chance."

"What confuses me about all of this," Rezotti said patiently, "is why you're making such a big deal about pornography. It's legal. Don't you read the papers? The Supreme Court says it's okay. Freedom of speech and all that crap. Why all the mystery?"

I squirmed again, looked at the floor, then back to them. "Yeah, well, what we like, my friends and me, the kinda films we like, you can't just buy this stuff at the K Mart. The girls we're using . . . actually, they're kinda young, you know. Ten, eleven, like that." I swallowed heavily and went on. "We got 'em in Tijuana and we gotta get 'em back before the end of the week or pay the house another thousand bucks."

Rezotti crossed his legs, smoothing the creases in his expensive slacks and thinking. "What kind of work do you do?" he asked finally, and smiled in an amiable sort of way.

"I'm an urban planner."

"I think you ought to stick to planning, friend. You see that big sign out front: MUSIC RECORDING?"

"I saw it."

"That's what we do here. Music. We've got three studios. We rent to rock bands. They come in here and make a demo tape and send it to the record companies. Which promptly dump it in the trash because they've got a zillion tapes a week coming in. But everyone wants to be a star so they come in here anyway and rent the space and equipment."

*Record companies.* I hadn't made the connection before.

I said, "You guys work with Westway, companies like that?"

The name didn't faze them. "We don't work with *any* record companies," Rezotti said calmly. "The kids come in here and come out a few hours later with a master. It's up to them to dupe it and send it out. The point I'm making is, we don't make films. We haven't got the room, for Christ's sake. Look at that studio out there. You think you could make a *movie* out there?"

"It doesn't take much room," I said, walking over to the glass and peering out at the ragged rock band, still trying to get set up. I could see the reflection of the two men in the glass as I added, "We just need a bed and a backdrop. Maybe a cross on the wall."

I turned around and stared at them, but their faces were

impassive. The large man hit a switch and the sounds from the studio filled the small room again.

Rezotti stood up and smiled reasonably. "Sorry we can't help you."

"My cement buddies said a girl died here a few weeks ago. For a film."

Just for an instant a flicker of emotion crossed Rezotti's unlined face. He stood still for a long moment and closed his eyes, his arms hanging loosely at his sides, then said, "Martin, will you show our friend out, please?"

As Rezotti silently left the room the large man turned the sound up so loud he had to raise his voice to me. "You had to go and fuck up, didn't you?"

"Is your name really Martin?" I asked.

He stood up and moved toward me. He was thirty pounds bigger than I was but also probably ten years older. He moved like a boxer, twisting from his hips, jerking his head and shoulders. But he was slow and had taken too many punches. He swaggered over and stood looking down at me. "Someone's been giving you some bad information, young fella. We do not film porno here. We don't film *nothing* here. We do music."

"Me and my buddies," I said, looking up at his bulk, "we just want to make a little money, won't take but two days, Christ, film a little in-and-out—"

His large hand clamped down on my shoulder and squeezed painfully. His voice was as calm as a mountain lake. "Look at my face and try to follow this. We are going to walk outside. You and me. We're going to walk through the studio and all the way outside. When we get to the parking lot you are going to get into your car and drive away like a good boy. You will never come back. I know you understand because you are an intelligent fellow. You will drive away and never come back."

I let him drag me up, making my body go slack. Then I hit him in the solar plexus, and when his hands instinctively dropped I clinched my fists together and hit him with an upward thrust against the jaw. He sank to the floor, eyes bulging, and rolled over on his stomach in pain. I stepped back and pushed with my foot on his back and he flattened out like day-old linguine.

"*What the hell?*" He moaned painfully and started to get up, but I pressed heavily again with my shoe. "Uh-uh."

He twisted his head and stared at me with a surprised look.

"You should have been ready," I said. "You should have moved in from the back, grabbing my wrist and twisting me up by the arm. You step in front of somebody like that and you're looking for trouble. You're lucky I didn't hit you in the nuts."

"I figured you for an urban planner."

"We work out," I said. "It's part of the job."

I drove to my office on Bronson and flipped on the answering machine as soon as I got inside. A message from Rudy Cruz to call him at the station. A message from Allison. An attorney in Beverly Hills I'd worked for a few times wanted me to try to track down a stolen yacht that had probably been taken to Mexico, where all the other stolen yachts ended up. Somebody raising money for the university that had expelled me thirteen years ago when I changed my major from English lit to American hedonism. I called Rudy. He sounded tired.

"Organized Crime does not want to talk to you. They do not particularly want to talk to me. At least as long as the press is dogging us. But I leaned a little, and they said maybe. But not here. Be at Lee Wong's at six. Seems like I'm all the time doing you favors, doesn't it?"

I went over to the hot plate and made a cup of instant coffee and brought it back to the desk, then leaned back in my big padded chair, the one with Cybill Shepherd's precious rump marks; I stretched my feet out on the desktop and closed my eyes and tried to move the pieces around a little, see how they fit. *Reason it out,* I told myself. Somehow it all made sense. Just need to work on it a minute.

Beautiful, young, sexy Rosa Luzon. Slowly tortured to death for a snuff film.

A week later Richard Wheeler met the same fate.

But for a snuff film? Not likely, unless the porno market had taken a sudden shift in direction. No, the middle-aged and very unsexy record industry hotshot and multimillionaire was killed for some other reason. But both victims were killed by the same person. Or people. For some reason whoever wanted Rosa dead also wanted Wheeler dead. And they wanted him to suffer slowly and painfully, exactly like Rosa had suffered. Which meant something tied Wheeler to Rosa. *Something.* Even if Elizabeth Wheeler didn't believe it.

Elizabeth Wheeler . . .

It was hard to believe that Richard Wheeler would be dicking around with prostitutes with that to come home to every night. Exquisite, tiny, sensual body, fashion-model face, rich as Croesus. No, Wheeler wasn't seeing Rosa. It just didn't fit.

*Elizabeth Wheeler.*

And Megan, still distraught, days after her dad's death. Was that normal? Tracy had only been five when her mother died, so I didn't have anything to compare it to. But the

Wheelers had been a very tight-knit family, Elizabeth said. They worked at making it work; not something you saw much around here.

I wondered how old Elizabeth Wheeler could be. Thirty-five, something like that. With the soft, unblemished skin of a twenty-year-old and the trim, athletic look of someone who cared about herself, cared enough to stay in shape, cared what people thought. What a life they must have had up there in that land of turrets and gardeners and walled estates. What a fantasy of a life.

Elizabeth Wheeler . . .

And why the Hollywood sign?

Christ! This was going nowhere. I needed that information from Organized Crime before I could hope to make any sense out of what I had so far, and I wasn't going to see Rudy for hours. Maybe I should take the Morgan out, get my mind off Rosa for a while. The Morgan had been running okay up and down the alley the past few days and I might as well take it down to Motor Vehicles and get it reregistered. Then I'd only have to get it painted. What would that cost? Two hundred, maybe. Ten years I'd been working on that damn car and I was this close to completion. And the damndest thing was, I wasn't sure how I felt about it. It was like having a kid that suddenly grew up when you weren't watching. *Now what?* Why didn't I get that rush of elation that you always feel after finishing a long, drawn-out job? What I was really worried about, I supposed, was what useless hobby would I turn to now? What hole would I find to throw money into?

But goddamn, I loved that car.

By the time Rudy wandered into Lee Wong's I'd half finished a pitcher of Carta Blanca, so he brought over another pitcher and set it between us with a thud. "Julie's been after me to try vegetarianism. Give it a week, she said; you'll like it. I said, okay, tonight's a good night to start, since she's at her channeling seminar. When I was a kid a Channel Master was a television antenna, now it's a twenty-five-hundred-year-old Greek slave named Arktus. So we start tonight, vegetarianism, you and me—the hops, grains, and malts of Mexico. We'll do it like research, start with Carta Blanca. Then Dos Equis. Next comes Corona, then Bohemia, Chihuahua, and Hussongs. When we're done we'll evaluate: color, flavor, bouquet, nutritional content."

"What about Tecate?" I asked.

"Thank you. We'll send out."

"Who's going to drive us home?"

Rudy nodded his dark head toward the parking lot. "Captain Reddig. He's sitting outside right now in the car, waiting. He likes you."

Ellen slid into the booth beside me, just before going onstage. She was wearing a bikini bottom and high heels and a dab of Giorgio that mingled uneasily in the warm air with the stink of stale smoke and beer. "I'll drive you home, Vic. The married guy can take care of himself." She took my mug and downed a full ten ounces without a breath and left quickly for the stage as the music came on, loud as usual, and I wondered if there was ever a time I really liked it like this. Maybe so. Maybe this is what age does to you. One of the things.

Rudy spread his arms out on the back of the booth and looked at me speculatively. "So'd you spend the day hobnobbing with the swells again?"

"Can't afford it. It costs two thousand to get a car painted now. And it's legal." When I had mentioned my earlier estimate of two hundred dollars to the paint shop manager he had had to sit down, he was laughing so hard.

Then he straightened up and said he didn't do humor.

Rudy squinted under bushy eyebrows. "You call Earl Scheib?"

"It's got to be authentic. It's a sort of curdled-cream color from the forties. They make it by grinding up hundred-dollar bills in white paint."

Eddie Darcy waddled over and plopped down two frozen burritos he had warmed up in the microwave. "I hate to see people drink on an empty stomach. You owe me four bucks. Pay me when you stagger out."

Rudy said, "There better not be any meat in those burritos. We're vegetarians."

"You kidding? There's no meat in my turkey sandwiches." He waddled back to the bar and bumped up the sound again.

"Organized Crime," Rudy said, "has a suite of offices at Parker like out of the Biltmore. Thick red carpets on the floor, real wooden desks, polished so you can see your face in them. They even have a conference room with paneling and paintings on the wall. Not prints—paintings!"

"Crime pays."

"So I hear." He checked his watch. "We're going to have a visitor from downtown in a few minutes. A guy named Vince Holgrin. You know him?"

"I don't think so."

"He's a lieutenant at Organized Crime. He wanted to know why you're so interested in their little specialty. I said you're writing a term paper. He said you're going to owe him on this one."

"What do I give him?"

"Tell him about the chair."

Twenty minutes later Rudy pointed out Holgrin, standing at a booth near the door talking to a smallish, dark-complexioned man with oily swept-back hair and a neat little 1940s David Niven mustache. A moment later he came back to our booth and slid in next to Rudy. "Did you see that chickenshit little asshole I was talking to? Name's Otto Bounds. I arrested him three or four years ago, I was working Motors. He's standing on Sunset, pissing in the street. I arrested him for indecent exposure, which in his case was true in more ways than one. He tells the judge he's a performance artist and I messed up his act and what he's done is protected by the First Amendment. It's guerrilla art, disabusing us of our bourgeois pretensions. Up with the revolution and down with toilets. The judge lets him go and gives me a lecture on the Constitution. Now he's producing videos on how not to commit a crime: *How Not to Set Up an Investment Scam, How Not to Rob Convenience Stores.* He's a fucking millionaire. First Amendment Otto, he calls himself. He told me maybe he'd hire me to narrate one he's planning to do called *How Not to Smuggle Illegals from Mexico.* I got two years left to retirement. I said maybe then. But maybe I'll lay him out in the street and run over him in my car instead."

He polished off half a mug of beer in one gulp and stuck his hand across the table. "I'm Holgrin."

I introduced myself. Holgrin was a big man, maybe six-three, two hundred and forty pounds, broad-shouldered and thick-necked, about forty-five years old, with widespread blue eyes and gray hair cut with boot-camp precision. There was an air of quizzical confusion to his face, as if he were perpetually surprised by the oddities of daily life. He looked around the crowded bar and finished off his beer.

"I hate this place. Can't fucking think in here. Downtown we go to a sushi bar in Little Tokyo, nice and quiet, little

Japanese girls slinking around in kimonos and bare feet. Nice and quiet. Rudy says you wanna know about porno and organized crime. The captain's name is J. J. O'Reilly, third-generation Irish cop, thirty-three years in the department. But every time someone starts asking us about what we know he gets antsy, thinks they're working for the mob or are some kind of management expert trying to close his unit down. I figured it's better we meet away from the office."

I told him I was working on the Hollywood sign case, and he looked surprised again but said, "Yeah, Rudy told me. I still don't see how we're involved."

"The girl was killed for a porno film. I figured you could tell me about the business, how it's tied to organized crime in L.A."

He filled his beer mug from the pitcher and shook his head. "I saw the film. Amateur hour, strictly from the cheap seats; not what the pros do. Besides, there's no point in the big boys getting involved in something like that. They make too much money on legal porno."

"How much?"

"How *much*? Christ, who knows? Serious money, multiple millions. It's number two, after drugs. First drugs, then porno, then gambling, then racketeering, prostitution, et cetera, et cetera, et cetera. We don't do drugs or vice in our unit, mostly business-related crap. But porno's a money machine, all right. I mean, they ain't exactly using union crews, are they? Make a flick for ten grand and bring in maybe two to five million. The studios can't make a trailer for under fifty grand."

"How much porno *isn't* Mafia-related?"

Holgrin had been taking a long guzzle of beer. He put the mug down on the table and eyed me sharply.

"Look, we don't call it the *Mafia.* The word does not exist downtown. There are Italians in L.A.; not many, but some, and they vote, sometimes two or three times each. We have no ethnic crime at all in Los Angeles. You understand? To answer your question, some porno is made free of what we term *organized crime.* Some. Not much. Mostly video shit."

Rudy said, "How do they control it? From out here or back in New York?"

"From here. A scumbag named Vincente Scali. He's an under-boss, he keeps his dark little eye on things here in lotus land. Decisions are made by families back east, New York and New Jersey. They don't turn that music down I'm going to put a bullet in the fuckin' amplifier."

"Scali," I said to Rudy. "Why do I know that name?"

Holgrin polished off his beer. "He's a slime ball, been here maybe twenty years and running a so-called *boutique* on Rodeo as a front—overpriced clothes for the rich and creepy."

I was trying to make my mind work, trying to remember where I had heard that name before while rock music continued to blare around us and people shouted and video games rang and buzzed electronically. Suddenly I had it. "Scali. Vincente Scali—"

"A.k.a. Tony Sal, a.k.a. Tough Tony—"

"That's the name of the place where Wheeler bought his suits," I said to Rudy. "It was in the crime report—the slacks they found in that bag came from 'Scali' in Beverly Hills."

Rudy sat back in the booth, looking at me. "Interesting."

"Damn right it is," I said. I felt a surge of excitement. It wasn't much but it was something. More than that, it was the first real lead I had had.

Holgrin didn't seem impressed. "So your record industry friend had a bad tailor. Or mob connections. It wouldn't be the first time, would it?"

But it meant something. I knew it.

Rudy said to Holgrin, "What about the address I gave you?"

"Yeah, the recording studio. That took a little digging." Holgrin stuck his hand in his shirt pocket and retrieved a piece of paper. "The building's owned by a completely legitimate real estate investment firm called Rexenbar Properties. It is leased, however, to an 'associate' of our pal Tough Tony by the name of—"

"Alan Rezotti," I said.

"You take all the fun out of my startling revelations when you do that. Why'd you ask, if you know? It took half a day to dig up this shit. Yeah, Alan Rezotti, a.k.a. Al the Wop."

"The film *was* made there! I'm sure of it!" I said to Rudy.

It was beginning to fit together, and I felt a sudden rush of adrenaline, a quickening of my pulse. The pieces were starting to come together.

Rudy finished off his glass and refilled it from the pitcher, shaking his head, thinking about it, fighting it a little. "I dunno, Vic. Films are usually made on soundstages. Even porno films. Stages or homes up in the hills with pools and views of the fantasy life."

"They made the film," I said, but I was only half listening; there had been a brief moment of silence over the speakers before the next record came on, and I suddenly became aware again of the voices all around me and the people and the smells and heat and smoke in the room. I began to feel anxious. I wanted to get out of there and talk to Vincente Scali or get back to that recording studio. I wanted something to happen.

Holgrin's voice came grating from across the table. "Scali's all cash. No credit, no walk-in business. It takes something like twenty-five or thirty grand to open an account, and if you don't spend at least that much every year they drop you. And get this: You got to have an appointment to go there. You believe that pansy-assed shit? You gotta have an *appointment* to let the slimy creep rip you off. The fuckin' Beverly Hills crowd loves him."

"Is it profitable?" I asked.

"It's a front! He doesn't fuckin' *care* if it's profitable. It's a tidy little laundry for all the quarters from videos and jukeboxes and the money from gambling and dope and whatever else his dirty fingers are stuck in. But the man himself, Tony Sal, he's a dollbaby, he's fuckin' cleaner than Gumby—no record, no arrests. He's got people to go to jail for him; they get out a few years later, they get a cushy job in one of the companies. He just sits back and counts the money."

"And kills fifteen-year-old girls for fun."

"You'll never prove it. Never! Scali doesn't *do* jail."

"Something else to think on," Rudy said. Next to Holgrin's, Rudy's voice sounded soft and smooth, the voice of reason. "This afternoon Morales found out Richard Wheeler was being talked up for lieutenant governor by the downtown business crowd, namely Artemus Willing Bartlett."

"The oil man?" *Aging oil man* would have been a better description; he must have been close to ninety.

Rudy nodded. "Bright young all-American entrepreneur takes his meager savings and starts his own little record company, which he sells a few years later to a major studio for several million dollars and thereupon decides to turn his obvious managerial talents to public service."

"Curiouser and curiouser," I said. Politics? What the hell did that mean?

"And very peculiar no one we talked to mentioned it. Morales learned it when a reporter from the *Times* called him to find out how the investigation was going." Rudy turned to Holgrin. "You fellows heard anything about it?"

"Christ, no. Wheeler and Bartlett ain't our concern. Scali is. We got nothing in Scali's file about Bartlett, though. If we did I'd remember it, name like that, always on the fuckin' TV hobbling along with his walker and talkin' to world leaders. Looks like he's been brain dead for twenty years. So what do you guys got for me?"

"Internal Affairs at Parker," I said.

He looked interested.

"You been there?"

"Yeah, who hasn't? They pulled me in once for using my piece 'precipitously.' I said, precipitously, shit! Some doped-out nineteen-year-old aimed a fuckin' .357 at me and yelled, 'Die, fucker!' so I winged him. Didn't even kill the sucker, just ruined his sex life for a while. Then last year they call me in and asked me how the hell I can afford to buy a new Porsche on my salary. I'm sitting there sweating like a stuffed pig and I hadn't done shit wrong. Yeah, I been there. A bunch of assholes."

"You feel a little weird in the interrogation room?" Rudy asked.

"Weird? Shit, I wanted to confess to starting the Chicago Fire. I think there's something they're pumping into the air there."

Rudy said, "It's the chair."

Holgrin looked confused.

"The chair in the interrogation room," I explained. "The two front legs are an inch shorter than the rear legs. It makes you feel uncomfortable but you don't know why. Makes you antsy and you start squirming around—and all these guys are sitting there comfortably, nice-looking Italian suits, not a wrinkle or sweat mark, smiling, staring at you and asking questions. It doesn't take long before you start *feeling* guilty."

Holgrin's face turned disbelieving, then angry. "Them fuckers . . ."

Ellen's stint onstage had ended and she came over and sat down next to me again. A thin sheen of sweat covered her full breasts, and her nipples glistened like .38 shells in the weak overhead light. Holgrin stared at her and muttered, "Jesus . . ."

Ellen shook her head at me. "You better slow down on the beer, Vic. I don't get off for four more hours. I don't want you passing out on me."

"I'm driving you home?" My memory seemed a bit cloudy, but something didn't sound right. I thought I was talking to Scali tonight. Or was Ellen driving *me* home? What was going on here?

"You're my protection from the Hollywood Sign Vampire. That's what the geek on Channel Seven is calling the killer now. Bloodsucking." She made a face and snuggled into my body. "Sounds ominous, doesn't it?"

"Somehow you never struck me as the type that needed protection."

She sat back in the booth with an expression of helplessness. "You look at me and you see a hundred and five pounds of coiled steel ready to strike, but deep down inside I'm sensitive, weak, and vulnerable."

Holgrin's eyes were riveted on Ellen's breasts; he had a surprised look on his face.

"I'll have to call Tracy," I said.

Ellen smiled. "I called her already. She said it's just fine with her, we can stay out all night if we want. She'll stay with a neighbor. But she thinks we ought to get married. Sounds like a plan. What do you think?"

I heard Holgrin say, "Jesus . . ."

Rudy poured some more beer and shook his head and said, "Curiouser and curiouser."

Darcy turned up the sound again.

The day started late at Ellen's very tiny, very neat Spanish-style apartment on Las Palmas, with coffee and toast and a funny little thing she did with eggs and sausage and salsa. Unlike me she was a determinedly cheery riser, singing to herself and kidding loudly with her four-year-old daughter as they ate in front of Woody Woodpecker on TV. I wasn't in much of a mood for this persistent gaiety and went to the bathroom and rummaged around in the medicine chest for two aspirin before sitting heavily at the kitchen table.

After breakfast Ellen squinted at me across the table. "I shoulda asked if you wanted your eggs hard-boiled."

I looked at her to see if she was smiling.

She added, "Detective style," but when I didn't respond she said, "You don't look real good in the morning. You know that?"

"The wages of sin."

"I'm going to my club to work out. Want to come along?"

I rubbed my neck, trying to restore circulation before rigor mortis set in. "Isn't that dancing you do every night enough? You've got to work out, too?" I had a disturbing image of the sleek and slender Ellen straining at the Nautilus machine, sweat dripping off her tensed body as she worked on her pecs.

"You remember that big prime rib you bought me last night?"

"Sure." Prime rib? Lee Wong's doesn't *serve* prime rib.

"Those calories weren't on my diet. So I've got to work them off now. That and that damn chocolate mousse you insisted on buying. I don't know how you can eat that stuff. I don't actually work out at the club. I swim, then sauna. Big old steamy room full of naked sweaty ladies lying about their sex life. You'd love it. Maybe a workout would make you more human."

I glared at her and took another sip of coffee.

"I guess that means no. After the club I'll be heading over to L.A. State."

"You're going to school, too?" *The world was full of surprises,* I thought to myself. Why hadn't she mentioned school before?

"Sure. You think I'm going to be dancing nude when I'm fifty? I'm studying fashion design; I want to go into manufacturing. Swimsuits, blouses, like that."

Ellen and Allison. Everyone had a plan, getting ready for the Golden Years.

"I'll drop you at your office, if you want. Your car's still at Lee Wong's, since you couldn't drive last night. Or walk. Or much else. By the way, what are those little marks on your lower back?"

"Bullet wounds."

"They look just like the scars my daughter got from chicken pox."

"Really?"

She stopped by a preschool to drop off her daughter, then cut over to Bronson and dumped me in front of the office.

As I closed the car door she smiled brightly through the open window, big brown eyes stretched wide, cheeks bunched up, an unexpected little wrinkle bisecting her brow. "Funny how these things work out, huh? I mean, who would have thought Rudy was an ordained *minister*? And able to perform *marriages*!"

Before I could ask what the hell that meant she had squeezed her aging Fiat back into the midmorning traffic, heading toward Sunset, and I turned toward the McKay Building and the prospect of a depressing day.

I wanted to go to a dark place and be very quiet but instead found myself in the lobby, as miserably hot as usual and mobbed with models and dental patients and would-be actors. I squeezed into the packed elevator just as the doors closed and stood pressed up next to an impossibly busty young blonde who was wearing nothing but a purple leotard stretched over her ample torso. After a moment of more or less uneasy silence I decided, *What the hell,* and took a wild guess. "Miss September."

She looked up at me suddenly as if I were psychic and giggled and "oohed" and said, "Miss *March*! But how did you *know*? That was two whole *years* ago."

"I have a good memory for faces," I explained as the doors parted and she "oohed" again in awe of my powers.

My office seemed refreshingly quiet and cool. Just what I needed. I scooped up the pile of mail on the floor and dropped it on the desktop, unplugged the phone, and turned the stereo to a classical music station, adjusting the volume down. I walked back out to the darkened waiting room and plopped on the couch and closed my eyes. I wanted to relax and try to work through what Rudy and Holgrin had told me last night. Two more pieces of the puzzle. That they both involved Richard Wheeler and not Rosa was something I would have to ponder later.

First.

Richard Wheeler, our big-time Hollywood executive, was somehow mixed up with Vincente Scali, local Mafia boss, porno king, and drug seller. Richard Wheeler and the Sicilian scumbag.

Second.

Wheeler was also involved with the traditionally squeaky-clean political movers and shakers downtown, the kind of people who could pick a complete unknown and turn him suddenly into governor or maybe even something more, in time. The sort of people who don't cavort with the Vincente Scalis of the world.

Wheeler the hood and Wheeler the hero.

The information about Scali came from Organized Crime, a group not given to flights of fancy. So I had to accept it. Wheeler and Scali. Wheeler . . . and Artemus Willing Bartlett.

But where was the *proof* of Wheeler's involvement with Vincente Scali? Other than the fact that Wheeler was a customer of Scali's boutique?

*Vincente Scali . . .*

Richard Wheeler bought his clothes at Scali's place in Beverly Hills. If "Scali" was like most Rodeo Drive boutiques it drew the bulk of its business from rock stars and Middle Eastern sheikhs and ball players—the ridiculously rich and insecure who yearned to be seen and noticed and talked about. Not business executives, most of whom, like Wheeler, led lives of luxurious but generally inconspicuous consumption. So why did he shop where only the determinedly trendy are normally seen?

It was interesting that Organized Crime had nothing in their files at all on Richard Wheeler; they didn't even know who he was.

But he bought his clothes from Scali.

I wondered where fifteen-year-old Rosa could have afforded to buy her clothes.

Wheeler and the politicos. Running for lieutenant governor. That was damn odd, coming out of a nonpolitical history like that. Of course, it had happened before in California, when Mike Curb had followed the same route. But no one had even hinted that there was a political bone in Wheeler's body. Gerald Lampson conceivably might not have known, but if Wheeler *was* interested in such a change to his lifestyle certainly his wife would have been aware of it. Didn't these people talk to each other? Last night Rudy had said maybe it just slipped her mind.

*Elizabeth Wheeler* . . .

Small hands and small tapered fingers, soft, soft skin, huge blue eyes that made my heart feel as if the bottom had just dropped out of an elevator. An ethereal, otherworldly quality about her, like the dream sequence in an old MGM musical, that seemed to be pulling at me, drawing me, sucking me in. . . .

Why the hell hadn't *anyone* mentioned Richard Wheeler's first tentative steps into politics? How close *was* he to Vincente Scali?

Why not ask?

I went back into the office, plugged in the phone, and

called directory assistance, then dialed "Scali" in Beverly Hills.

The phone was answered by a young woman with a soft, sexy voice. Could I possibly see Mr. Scali? About his friend, the unfortunate Richard Wheeler . . . it wouldn't take long. After being put on hold for ten minutes—the inevitable Beverly Hills harpsichord music on the line—it was arranged. Mr. Scali could give me at most ten minutes at four o'clock, precisely. Did I need the address? Was I familiar with Beverly Hills? I told her I'd figure it out.

Elizabeth Wheeler's number was on the Rolodex. The houseman answered and again I was put on hold—no music this time, just the dead silence of an electric connection. I rubbed my neck until the houseman came back on the line. Yes, Mrs. Wheeler would see me once more. But the reluctance was obvious in his voice. How was one o'clock? Fine, I said.

I left shortly after noon, first walking back to Lee Wong's to retrieve my car, then heading into the hills, finding the house with ease this time. The chain-link gate had been left unlatched, and I pulled through and around to the massive stone mansion, parking behind an older silver Mercedes sedan while the houseman observed me silently from the steps.

Elizabeth Wheeler met me in the library. I was beginning to feel uncomfortable at having to intrude again upon her grief like this; if anyone had badgered me with questions after Laurie's death I think I would have killed them. She sat stiffly on the couch as before and I sat across from her, wondering how to begin my questioning. She seemed to have forgotten that I was there, her eyes fixed at some spot over my shoulder, and I glanced over to see a family portrait in the bookcase:

Richard, Elizabeth, a baby giggling between them as they each dangled it by a hand. Happy times. She saw me looking at it and said, "Next month would have been our fourteenth anniversary. Everybody thought it was odd back then, because I was the one going to college while he worked. Even my mother thought it should be the opposite. Richard was a song plugger. He went from station to station all over the West Coast, trying to get the DJs to play certain records. Remember payola? Richard did it straight, no payoffs. But he was learning all the time, and watching and listening. He'd stop in some place like San Bernardino and ask the DJs about local groups, bar bands and the like. Then he started signing them to contracts. That's where Westways came from—West Coast bands, West Coast rock. I went to school all that time, except for a year when Megan was born."

"How long was it before he sold the company to T-I?"

"Eight years." Her face brightened with pride as she thought about it. "He sold to T-I because independents were having a hard time getting shelf space in the record stores. The wholesalers make it difficult for them, put pressure on the retailers not to carry their labels or to put them out of sight. So he sold out to get T-I's clout behind him. They gave him a management contract—he ran the company like it was his own and they stayed out of it as long as Westways made money."

"Which it did?"

"Yes, of course. In some years it was probably the only part of T-I that was profitable." Her eyes went back to the picture. "Megan was only two when that picture was taken. . . ."

"I hope she's feeling better," I said, remembering my last visit.

"My daughter's away. The atmosphere of this house—"

She shivered. "It was better for her to get away for a few days," she explained.

"I'm sure it must be difficult," I said. "My own daughter was much younger when her mother died, but it's terrible at any age. Maybe worst of all now when they need adults so much."

Elizabeth looked across at me from the couch, her voice hardening a little. "Mr. Eton, you must excuse my rudeness, but I don't understand why you're here. Have you learned something? Can you tell me something about Richard's death?"

"Mrs. Wheeler, why didn't you tell me about your husband's interest in politics?"

Her face looked surprised, then resigned. "What purpose would there have been? Richard was thinking about running for lieutenant governor. It was all still very exploratory. It certainly has nothing to do with his death."

"He hadn't made up his mind to run?"

She gave me an impatient look and spread her hands. "I suppose he really had, even though he hadn't admitted it to himself yet. But they—these party bigwigs he'd been talking to—they appealed to his vanity, and it was hard to say no. I understood: He had taken the record company as far as he conceivably could. And there wasn't much chance to go anywhere on the film side of T-I. He needed a new challenge. Politics was there, something to do."

"But you didn't approve?"

She curled up on the couch and slowly shook her head. "I didn't know what to think. But it probably would have meant splitting up our family for part of the year. Or moving to Sacramento. Both Megan and I would've preferred to live here. She has her friends and school, of course, and I have my job. I don't know what we would have done. We hadn't gotten to that point yet."

"Who were these people?" I asked. "The ones asking your husband to run."

"Businessmen from Los Angeles. Artemus Willing Bartlett was the main person involved, I understand. They were all corporate executives from the financial district. Richard said they all belonged to the Californian, a downtown business club; he lunched there a few times. He always laughed and called them power lunches—'wingtips and regimental ties.' But he was impressed, no doubt about it. They were all presidents and board chairmen and people like that."

"How about Vincent or Vincente Scali?"

She thought a moment and shook her head. "I don't think I recall the name. Richard called it the WASP nest, all very Anglo and very male. I still don't see the point of all these questions. He certainly wasn't killed because of politics."

I heard a scraping noise off to the side, and a loud throaty voice boomed into the room, "There *is* no point, my dear."

I turned and saw an aged, almost emaciated man staring at us from a wheelchair just inside the doorway. That explained the Mercedes out front, I thought. I wondered how long he had been sitting there listening.

A muscular young attendant in nurse's whites pushed the wheelchair into the large room, and the old man seemed to age dramatically the closer he came. His skin was wrinkled and dry and pale, the sparse hair on top of his large head wispy and white, his face thin and hollow. Only his eyes seemed healthy, large musky ovals staring intently out of dark sunken sockets, a racial reminder of the distant Russian steppes.

"My father," Elizabeth said with what sounded like resignation. "Ivan Ryan."

"*Ryazanov!*" the old man boomed without taking his gaze from me. "Ivan Denesovitch Ryazanov! A grievous mistake, giving that up. My *birthright,* since reclaimed. Didn't want to give it up in the first place, you know." He had been pushed to within three feet of me and he stared with an almost mesmerizing forcefulness into my eyes as if he could read my thoughts. "But *they* all gave up their born names and insisted that I change, too. 'Anglicize' it, they called it, the fools! Taking away a man's birthright was what I called it, but they made me do it. *Forced me!* I was only a young man at the time; didn't have the *balls* to fight them. But they can't do anything about it now, can they? They're all dead, and I sit here in front of you continuing to live and breathe and smoke fine Havana cigars."

A navy blue blanket was draped over the old man's useless legs, but otherwise he was dressed almost formally in a dark blue suit and white shirt and maroon tie. He looked sickly, and his body trembled slightly from time to time, but his voice was loud and demanding, accustomed to giving orders, and his eyes startlingly clear. I wondered how old he was. At least eighty-five, I guessed; his gnarled hands were clutching a dark furry muff and rubbing it softly when suddenly two bright green eyes flashed like candles and the furry ball hunched its back and snarled.

"My marvelous little Lenin," the old man said, enjoying my surprise. "Using the confusion of the moment to sneak in under the eyes of the authorities and then suddenly attacking. I once saw Lenin, you know. In 1920, in Dzerzhinsky Square in Moscow. I was just a child when he whisked by in a black Mercedes with some other party muckety-mucks. He had taken everything away from my family, of course. *Everything!*

We had once been quite comfortably middle class; my father taught at the university. But suddenly we were as poor as church mice, and still I thought Lenin was the greatest man who ever lived. I thought he was greater than Jesus Christ." He laughed loudly and shot a quick glance at his daughter, who hadn't moved since he entered the room. The young attendant stared blankly into space as if he were deaf.

"At any rate," the old man went on as the cat leapt suddenly to the floor, "I am pleased to meet you, Mr. Eton." His voice was normal now, and I wondered if the booming bravado had been an act; despite his infirmities he appeared to be as mentally alert as anyone I had ever met, and his dark eyes sparkled knowingly. "I was right, wasn't I? You have no motive for Richard's death so you have decided to fish around in the murk of his background. Unfortunately you're fishing with an unbaited hook."

"It's unlikely his death was a motiveless crime—" I began, but the old man cut me off.

"No vampires? No bloodsucking bats? Life imitating art, perhaps. I made a few of those hideous films in the fifties. But in those days it was all fantasy; we knew then that human beings were not capable of such degradations."

"Someone was," I said.

"*Now,* yes! See what is happening to us. Today the idea hardly shocks us. It has only a mild titillation value to the six o'clock news crews who can joke about it in front of millions, but in my time we would not have considered it as even remotely possible off the screen." He pointed a bony, accusatory finger in my direction. "This has been the promise of American civilization: bringing us to the point where the torture death of a young woman and young man are meaningless except for the amusement of the masses. We are in rat's alley—"

Ryan stopped and coughed loudly and then asked, "Are you familiar with the works of T. S. Eliot? He was a man of my generation, the generation right after the great war. I've had a good deal of time lately to study his poetry. *Four Quartets* especially contains much of interest to an old man like myself, a good deal of reflecting on the broken promises of old age. But it's *The Waste Land* that speaks to the Hollywood of your generation. That filthy wasteland of a city down there with its teenage gangs and pornography and drugs and nightly violence that no longer upsets anybody because we are conditioned to it, and we are a part of it because we allow it to go on. And you think that because Richard was a part of the Industry that controls the city he is tainted by it, too. He must have 'gangster' connections, you presume, to have become so successful, particularly in the record business. Am I right?"

The old man was trying to rattle me, put me on the defensive. "I was asking your daughter about Richard Wheeler's political ambitions," I reminded him. "I hope you're not going to tell me that California politics is run by 'the syndicate,' because I saw the movie; George Raft was gunned down on Vine Street, and virtue again triumphed."

"One of my better films." Ryan chuckled good-naturedly. "Except that I seem to recall that it was Gower and not Vine." His face had lost its aggressiveness and he relaxed back in his chair. "Are you a film buff?"

"Of a sort," I admitted. "Mostly 'B' films, the old Saturday morning serials and westerns. Randolph Scott, Joel McCrea, that sort of thing. I don't much go to movies anymore."

"Is that so?" The old man was obviously pleased. "You must come by my place sometime to see my collection of classics. I have a whole library of Republic westerns and serials, virtually everything they turned out. On *film*, too, with a projector and a screen; not the video junk people watch today. I heard you mention your daughter earlier. Bring her along, too. Or we could even use Elizabeth's projection room here in the basement." He glanced quickly at his daughter and then back at me and again grinned triumphantly. "I *was* right, of course. The police have no leads. You have no leads. There is nothing."

"Nothing."

"And the girl?" Elizabeth asked, speaking for the first time since her father appeared.

"Nothing more than before. There's nothing to connect her to . . . anyone else."

"Including my husband," Elizabeth said, finishing my thought.

"You're barking up the wrong tree, there. My son-in-law managed to maintain his integrity despite being swallowed up by the Industry and the city. If not, that WASP nest downtown wouldn't have given him a second look. You can rest assured that they would have known more about Richard than his own mother before boosting his ego with talk of politics."

Of course Ryan was right. The politicos wouldn't have touched Wheeler with a fork if there had been the slightest hint of a crime connection. Ryan continued to stare at me smugly.

I said, "Perhaps you have a theory." Knowing he did.

"Isn't it obvious?" the old man shot back immediately. "Our culture killed Richard; that city down there killed him. Richard was a victim of the random nightly violence I spoke of. No one set out to kill *Richard*—for some reason we'll probably never understand he was chosen from a city of three million by someone who wanted merely to *kill,* someone who *enjoys* killing. But he didn't set out to get *Richard;* that was kismet, unfortunate fate."

"You've heard about the film?" I asked.

"The 'death film,' as they call it on TV? I have indeed. That explains that unfortunate girl's death but not Richard's. He was killed by someone who wants us to believe that the murders are connected. But they aren't. I'm certain of that."

"Two different killers," I said. "Two different crucifiers."

Ryan said, "I suggest that it's difficult for you as well as the police to accept since it implies that there is no motive and nothing to base an investigation on. Much better for the public to see the authorities barking up the wrong trees with needless inquiries than admit that they have nothing else to do."

Elizabeth came to her feet. "I think I'd better get my father upstairs for a while for his afternoon rest. He's staying with me for a few days, and this has all been trying for him."

"Of course." I stood and shook hands with the old man, who repeated his invitation to view his film collection. Then Elizabeth said she'd walk me to my car. Outside she laid a hand on my arm. "My father is quite aware of being a Hollywood legend," she said with an understanding smile. "Sometimes I think he's concerned about being colorful enough to be included in the later histories."

"T. S. Eliot and the horrors of modern-day life."

She nodded and smiled and the sunlight filtering through the tall trees lightly touched the soft contours of her face. "Hollywood as Sodom and Gomorrah. That was another of his films, you know. He was a great director. A master of illusion."

It was two-thirty when I left the Wheelers', and my appointment with Scali was not until four o'clock. I drove over to Rodeo anyway and deposited my car in a valet parking lot just off Wilshire and joined the Japanese tour groups and Iowa farmers and Iranians—the ones who had gotten out before Khomeini and were living off hoarded gold—ogling merchandise along the half dozen blocks of glitz, glitter, and superficial elegance, and wondered who was the richest. Probably the farmers. The ones in ostrich-skin work boots.

After a while I began to feel foolish pressing my face against shop windows and gawking at goodies I'd never be able to afford and probably wouldn't know what to do with if I could. It was pleasure too far removed from reality, the same sort of vicarious not-quite-real enjoyment you get from reading *National Geographic,* I thought. Or *Playboy.* Looking at all those sights you'll never enjoy in person.

At exactly four o'clock I rang the buzzer at Scali's locked

front entrance. Almost immediately the door was opened by a very chic, very bejeweled, and *very* attractive young woman whose manner and accent were distinctly French.

"Meester Eton, *of course!*" she said, and clapped her hands and beckoned me inside with a look of pleasure too long delayed. Meester Scali, he ees waiting; please I would follow. Which I did, wandering behind her wiggling round ass, past stylized mannequins and circular clothes racks and up the open stairway set down in the rear of the store. We came to a sort of landing where there was a low lacquered coffee table with a large Chinese vase and off to the side a long glass-topped serving table with trays of prepared foods: canapés and sandwiches and such. My young guide saw me glance wantonly in its direction.

"A reception." She smiled. "For the Saudi chargé d'affaires. Please—" She indicated that I was to wait while she checked with Meester Scali, so I wandered over to the table and began to munch on exotic finger foods, while she knocked on Scali's door and then stuck her head inside the office.

A moment later she returned, still swinging her tight little ass.

"What are these?" I asked, holding up a grayish blob impaled by a toothpick.

She dazzled me with a brilliant smile. "Crab balls."

"I didn't know they had any," I said as I carefully put it back.

A momentary shadow crossed her lovely face as she led me to the door and said, "Meester Scali will see you now." But then a tiny grin seemed to materialize as she turned and disappeared behind me.

As I came in Scali was standing at the far end of the large room, a smallish good-looking man in his fifties, holding a heavy ocean-fishing rod by the handle. He looked up and smiled, immediately resting the rod against the wall and coming toward me, walking quickly and holding out an elegant hand.

"Vincente Scali. And you must be Mr. Eton. Come in, please, sit—"

Affable and energetic, he waved me to an upholstered chair and then seated himself behind a large antique desk that was obviously designed more for looks than work and completely bare on top except for an enameled cigarette case and marble ashtray.

"I'm getting ready for a trip to Mexico," he said with obvious relish, and nodded at his rod. "With my two boys. We're going down to Cabo San Lucas, see if we can tease the wily marlin from the depths of the sea. Do you fish? It's a marvelous recreation. Very calming."

"I hate fishing," I decided as I sat down. "Every time I plan a trip something comes up. I used to have a small ocean boat, though; just an eighteen-footer, but it was fun for a while. Then I figured I couldn't afford both it and my daughter."

Scali settled back in his chair and laughed with genuine amusement. "You know the old joke: A boat is a hole you pour money into."

"So's a Morgan."

He looked at me.

"It's a car," I explained.

"Ah!" He laughed again. "Well, my boys would probably know, then. They're 'into' cars, as they say. Especially fast cars: Ferraris, Maseratis. The insurance alone is unbelievable." He blinked suddenly as if rousing himself and came quickly to his feet. "Excuse my rudeness. Can I get you a drink? Perhaps some sherry? It's not too early, is it?"

I told him no thanks, but he walked over to a portable bar and poured himself a drink from a decanter while I took the opportunity to have a look around the office. It was more or less standard Beverly Hills opulent: antique furniture, probably reproductions, but expensive still. Two large oil paintings, landscapes, obviously old and varnish-darkened and cracked, not at all like Allison's. An antique mirror in an ornate gold frame over a credenza. And the bar he was standing at, very tasteful and understated. Scali himself was trimly aristocratic, like an Italian count: smooth olive-colored skin, dark wavy hair just going gray at the temples, a clear, soft, faintly accented voice. He brought his glass back to the desk and smiled with pleasure.

"One before dinner and one after dinner. Doctor's orders. I don't look like the sort of person with heart trouble, do I? Not an ounce of fat, weigh exactly the same as I did in high school. But the inside's a mess. Stress, the docs say—too much worry. You'd think the booze would help you *stop* worrying, but that's not the way it works. So! How can I help you, Mr. Eton? Something to do with one of my customers, I understand. I didn't quite grasp it all from your call."

"Richard Wheeler."

"Yes, of course." His face turned serious. "Terrible how these things happen. Especially to someone here in Beverly Hills. You'd think we'd be protected from random violence like this."

"It's not random violence. You must have heard about the other victim."

"The young girl, yes. This is what they call a serial killer, one, two, three. . . . Who knows where it will stop?"

"I think it has stopped."

"Yes?"

"The girl was killed for a movie. A snuff film."

"I believe I heard that on the television." Scali took a sip of sherry and smiled at its taste. A handsome man, I was thinking as I watched his face: a lover of fine wine, a patrician, goes fishing with his boys. The new-style hood. Probably signs petitions against killing whales and supports stricter enforcement of the Clean Air Act. He put his glass down and looked at me without expression. "And Richard was involved in a film of this sort also? This is what you think?"

"I'm not sure. But somehow the deaths are linked."

Scali's face clouded just slightly, and he began to fiddle with the lighter on the desktop. "Maybe we should back up a little. I find myself confused. You are working for who? Richard's wife?"

"The family of the first victim."

"And by coming to me you hope to . . . what?"

"Learn a little about Richard Wheeler. Find out what kind of man he was. Look for a connection between him and the girl. Did you know him well?"

Scali stared at the ceiling for a moment. "Well? As well as I know most of my customers, I suppose. We were not what you would call friends. Richard would come in here three or four times a year, get some nice suits, a coat for winter." He made a deprecating gesture with his hands.

"Did you ever have any business dealings with him?"

His dark eyes stared benignly at me across the desk. Like a papal ambassador: all smiles and secrets with a just-tangible hint of menace beneath the surface. "All my dealings with Richard were business dealings."

"I was referring to his company, Westway Records."

"Ah! Westway Records. I begin to see where this is going. Richard was a record company executive, and as everyone knows they are all corrupt. And I am Italian and therefore in the Mafia. How very sinister this all sounds."

I waited.

Scali pressed his lips together; he was getting a little impatient now, beginning to wonder if it was a good idea to talk to me at all. Somewhat brusquely he said, "Richard Wheeler and I had no business arrangements other than that he purchased some of his wardrobe here. Period."

"Did you know his wife?"

He shook his head impatiently. "I'm afraid not. I was never at his house."

I felt an odd satisfaction at his indifferent denial. Elizabeth Wheeler had not seemed the type to associate with a man like Vincente Scali. I handed him a picture of Rosa, a full-length shot, with the holes through her wrists and the bullet holes in her torso and her face frozen in a scream.

Scali grimaced and handed it back. "Disgusting."

"Have you ever seen her?"

"Of course not."

"With Wheeler, perhaps."

"Again, no. Why would Richard know a common prostitute like this?"

"The newspapers did not identify her as a prostitute," I said as I put the pictures back in my pocket.

He leaned back in his chair and regarded me stonily. "No, perhaps they did not, Mr. Eton. But they did devote a good deal of attention to the rather odd tattoo of hers, didn't they? It was pathetically obvious that she made her living on the streets. Or am I to conclude she spent her time tending to the halt and the lame, like Mother Teresa? You are being silly, my friend. Richard was just not the sort to cavort with a cheap hooker like that. Do you forget where he worked?"

Richard Wheeler, the big-time studio executive. And the fifteen-year-old streetwalker who could hardly speak English.

It didn't make sense to me, either. Unless . . . I had an idea and took a chance:

"Did Wheeler ever tell you about his interest in pornography?"

Unexpectedly Scali began to chuckle, the soft sound bubbling up from his throat like oil rising to the ground. "Oh, my, yes. Richard was what you would call a connoisseur of pornography, I suppose. He would tell me of an interesting book he had acquired; sometimes he would carry these exotic magazines in his briefcase—filthy stuff, really. I wasn't interested."

"What about films?" I asked, keeping my voice steady; but I had stumbled onto something, an opening, and I began to squirm into it. "Did Wheeler like to go to porno films, too?"

"I couldn't tell you," Scali replied, sitting forward in his chair now as if suddenly aware of a vague threat somewhere nearby. He twisted uncomfortably. "It was not a topic of conversation that I encouraged."

"Parties, maybe?" I put just a hint of insistence in my voice as if I wasn't fishing but already knew the answer to the question, and smiled at him. "Parties up in the hills with girls?"

Scali was becoming flustered. "No! Of course not."

I saw it suddenly in front of me now: tiny cracks in Scali's elegant façade; his face hardening, his hands involuntarily clenching into fists.

*Make something happen. . . .*

"I understand you're the owner of a recording studio in Hollywood." I repeated the address on Edgemont.

Scali was definitely irritated now, but he struggled to regain a hold on his composure. His voice suddenly cold, he said, "I would very much like to know where you got that information, because it happens not to be true. I don't even know the area in question; I am never *in* Hollywood. It depresses me. Does my name appear on the records in the county recorder's office?"

"I had a long and fascinating talk with the LAPD intelligence unit. The building's registered in another name, of course." I held Scali's dark eyes. "But you own it."

Scali's face hardened; the suave businessman suddenly vanished, and his hand shot out to the enameled case on his desk as he seized a cigarette, quickly lighting it and letting loose a stream of smoke. *Back off a minute. Let him relax.*

"What kind of customers do you get in here?" I asked, looking appreciatively around the office.

Scali puffed on his cigarette. "Gentlemen." He dragged the word out slowly, in case I was not familiar with it. "Wealthy gentlemen, important people, people with taste to whom money is no object."

"Business pretty good?" *Give him a little smile.*

"Excellent," Scali said, relaxing a little, sitting back in his chair.

"You get a lot of South American or Mexican customers?"

He seemed momentarily taken aback by the question, a breach of good taste his Beverly Hills customers would never make. "I don't really know. . . . We do have customers from Latin America, of course. Several, in fact. Businessmen. It takes thirty thousand to open an account with us, so—"

"Drug dealers," I said. "You buy from them, they buy from you, money crosses borders and gets lost in banks."

Scali was suddenly livid, his whole body seemingly drawn up like a spring. "Now, see here! You've got no right to talk to me like this. I'll—"

"I'm having trouble understanding your attitude. A fifteen-year-old girl was tortured to death. Very slowly, very painfully. A friend of yours was killed the same way. And you don't seem interested."

"I'm telling you that I don't *know* anything about it. I don't *know* anything about a building on Edgemont, I don't *know* anything about pornography. What the hell are you doing?"

"The problem I've been having is with the connection. What is there to tie a knocked-around teenage hooker to a millionaire record company executive? Where's the tie, Rosa to Wheeler?"

Scali sat back and looked at me with eyes as dark as olives, eyes that had contemplated a hundred deaths and now began to contemplate mine. "Obviously there is none."

"It's there; you told me about it yourself: Richard Wheeler was a 'connoisseur' of pornography. He liked that sort of thing—maybe even snuff films. So there *is* a link—if a little tenuous—between Wheeler and Rosa. And I know that the film was shot in your studio on Edgemont and I know that you knew Richard Wheeler quite well. Now I'm beginning to wonder who owns that cement factory out in the Valley.

"It's like the hub of a wheel," I went on. "The spokes might go off in a dozen different directions, but they all come back to the same place, and that's where you are. They all come back to you. Interesting, isn't it? You're the hub."

Scali came suddenly to his feet. His fine Italian face had gone red, the veins in his neck and head popping out like dozens of tiny snakes. Discarding any pretense of self-control, he glared at me, his voice trembling with rage. "Who the hell do you think you're dealing with? I'm not some fucking hick you can scare with your goddamn accusations." He stared at me while he struggled to regain some control over himself, finally seating himself again behind the desk, his breath coming slower as he smothered his anger. "Do you know how much I lost at the track last week? I took my oldest boy, we gotta box out at Hollywood Park. I lost thirty-three thousand last week."

I stared at Scali in fascination. His voice had lost that smooth milky tenor and begun almost imperceptibly to slip back into a nasal twang. He snatched at his lighter and lit another cigarette, regarding me angrily from across the desk and repeating his earlier point. "Thirty-three thousand in one week. In one damn week I dropped more than you probably make in a year. Jesus Christ, you think you can come in here and accuse me of being mixed up in some murder and you don't even have a shred of evidence. Not even a shred, and you come in here and start talking about *hubs.*" His eyes blazed angrily. "You think I'm a fuckin' asshole hick you can scare into saying something stupid? You don't even live in the same damn world I live in and you think you can talk to me like that?" He waved angrily around the room. "No one comes in my store without spending thirty thousand cash. That's the rules. Thirty thousand *cash* every time you step through the fuckin' door. Look at you—buy your clothes off the fuckin' rack at Sears. I wouldn't wipe my fuckin' ass with your clothes and you're sitting here in a fuckin' chair you couldn't afford if you saved all your crummy life and you think you can tie me into some murder without a goddamn piece of evidence? You're something. You're really something. You gotta be real dumb—brain damage, maybe. Bad brain damage, you come around here talkin' like that, talkin' about fuckin' *hubs.* You just don't know what you're doing. That's it, isn't it? You don't know what you're doing. You better watch your fuckin' step, pal, or you're going to fall off the fuckin' world."

I came to my feet and dropped one of my business cards on the polished desktop. "Call me if you remember something I ought to know."

Scali looked at me as if burning my face into his memory. "You just fell off the edge of the fuckin' world."

Now we wait," I said.

"Shouldn't be too long," Rudy replied. "He's not going to let you lean on him like that. You want to see if I can get you some protection, put a couple of guys out in front in a black and white?"

I shook my head. "I want to see what he does next. I hit a nerve."

"How'd you know Richard Wheeler was into porno?"

"I didn't. But I was sitting there, looking at Scali and asking myself what tied Rosa to Wheeler and this scumbag Mafiosi. It was either prostitution or porno. So I took a chance, and he started coming unglued."

"You never had a real soft touch with interrogation. Sometimes you lean on them like that, it works, sometimes it doesn't. You gotta watch their eyes and hands, look for the tension, see how they take it. They start getting wild, you back off a bit."

"You always wanted to be the good cop," I reminded him. "So we'll wait awhile now, see what happens."

Rudy thought about it a minute. "I guess I still don't see where it's going. All I see is you've made a few moves, stirred up the pot. But you don't *know* anything, you don't have anything you can go to the D.A. with."

I went to the kitchen, got two Buds, and brought them back with some chips and salsa. "I'm looking for connections, and suddenly it starts coming together. Rosa was killed in a porno film. Wheeler was a porno freak, or so Scali claims. The way he said it, I've got to believe him. Wheeler's wife didn't mention anything about it but maybe she didn't know. Anyway, her husband has just been killed, why dig up any unpleasantness? We know Scali controls porno, Scali owns the studio on Edgemont, Scali knows Wheeler—"

"The *hub,*" Rudy said, and shook his head, just a hint of disapproval in his eyes.

"Making something happen," I reminded him as I went over to a living room window and pushed it up a foot. Rock music came floating in from the courtyard below on the flow of warm air: the Nazi Joy Boys.

Rudy said, "I'm still having trouble trying to see how you're going to fit this all together. Rosa was killed for a film. Scali controls the films. All right, I see that. Scali knows Wheeler. I see *that.* So why was Wheeler killed? Someone crucified him, drove nails through his wrists. Dropped him at the sign. Vice went through all the films they picked up at the cement factory. They got warrants and went through the files at *all* the porno producers in Hollywood. Nothing. No films of a man being tortured like that, no evidence of such a film ever being made."

"Then maybe we're going about it from the wrong direction," I said. "Maybe we should look at Wheeler's work instead of his recreation. He was an Industry executive, a big-shot at one of the biggest studios. So he gets antsy and decides to move out of the music side and into films. Pornography was a hobby with him, maybe more than a hobby, an obsession. So he decides to film a few of his fantasies—"

"Wheeler *died,* Vic. Does that sound like one of his fantasies?"

I sank back on the couch. I didn't believe it, anyway. Like Allison had said: Why would someone like Wheeler risk everything for a snuff film? It just didn't wash. I said, "I don't suppose one of those naked bodies in the snuff film could have been Wheeler's?"

Rudy shook his head. "Vice checked. No go."

"All right, then, try this: Wheeler works for T-I Studios. He's in the commissary or the john or somewhere and he hears some scuttlebutt about a snuff film making the rounds, hears it was made at the studio on Edgemont, puts two and two together, and comes up with his friend Scali. Now he's got a little leverage, decides to see what it's worth, and he leans on Scali a bit."

Rudy's head swung slowly back and forth. "Blackmail the Mafia? You're stretching, Vic. You're trying to *make* the pieces fit."

I finished off the beer, trying not to show my impatience. Maybe he was right: I was trying to force it. *Give it up for now and let your subconscious work on it for a while.* I said, "So I wait. Let Scali make the next move."

"What did you learn out at Wheeler's this morning?"

I relaxed back on the couch and closed my eyes and tried to think. What the hell had I learned out there? It seemed like weeks ago now. Weird day. "I guess I don't know what to make of it," I said finally. I told him about Elizabeth Wheeler and Ivan Ryan. "It was all a little bizarre. Old Ivan talking about

Hollywood, his daughter staring off into space, the attendant acting like he didn't hear a word. That damn old mansion of theirs. Real Hollywood Gothic. Ivan told me I was dredging through the murk of Richard Wheeler's background. That was the word he used: *murk.*"

"Funny thing to say about his dead son-in-law."

"I get a strange feeling up there. Like there's no real grief about Richard's death. Regret, maybe, but not grief."

"But Elizabeth Wheeler looked pretty good to you." No expression on his face. Just staring at me.

I glared at him. "What the hell does that mean?"

"I've known you eight years. I see it in your face, the way you talk about her. You're hooked on the lady. You're planning to take Tracy up there, aren't you?"

"I hadn't thought about it."

"You've thought about it."

Just then the door opened, and Tracy came in and collapsed theatrically in a chair. "Hot."

"Hang on a few days," I told her. "When I get the Morgan back from the paint shop we'll drive up to Santa Barbara for a couple of days, lie on the beach in front of the Biltmore and pretend we're rich."

Tracy smiled. "Nice . . ."

Rudy said, "How's the boys, kiddo?"

"Boys!" She said the word in the tone she normally reserved for snakes or worms or other slimy creatures.

Rudy looked at me, his large, dark, mustachioed face without emotion. "I have no sympathy for you."

"I know."

"I have five children."

"Three."

"Whatever."

Tracy said, "I think I'll get something to eat." Then,

suddenly remembering, she said, "There wasn't any earthquake damage here, was there? I forgot to check."

"Just a vase, I guess. I didn't look around. I've had other things on my mind the last few days."

"Like Elizabeth Wheeler," Rudy explained.

Tracy sat up. "Who's Elizabeth Wheeler?"

"A lady in Beverly Hills that caught your daddy's eye. You're not the only one with those strange pangs in the heart, kiddo."

I gave Rudy a look, then tried to change the subject. "What's new at school?"

"Next Thursday is Back to School Night. You gonna come? Sister Cindi says you haven't been to the school since the day you signed me up. There's some doubt that you actually exist."

Rudy said, "Always has been."

"There can't possibly be a Sister Cindi," I said to her.

"I guess you'll have to come to find out. I'll introduce you to Rabbit MacPhearson. And you'll get to see the career plan we each drew up. Mine's on fashion design. You coming?"

"I'll see how busy I am. What's Rabbit's career plan? Or dare I ask?"

"Secretary of Defense. Or a shepherd. He's not sure."

Rudy said, "You better go."

Tracy said, "We had to go through an emergency drill when the quake hit: line up and march outside. Just like a fire drill. Some of the boys hid in the boys' bathroom to sneak cigarettes. Sister Urbana caught them."

"In the boys' bathroom?" Rudy asked. Parochial school had evidently changed more than he'd realized.

Tracy was unaffected. "Sister Urbana said she'd walk into the devil's chamber itself if she smelled tobacco smoke.

Unfortunately for the boys, it wasn't tobacco."

"Wonderful," I said.

"They're jerks," Tracy said as she stood and made her way to the kitchen. "They think pot makes them macho. Most of the kids think they're creeps. Anyway," she cried from the kitchen, "they'll be suspended for a couple of weeks. And the earthquake knocked over the big globe in the science lab and smashed it to bits. Sister Maxima said it was *symbolic.*"

"Sister Maxima?" Rudy said to me.

Tracy came back with a Diet 7-Up and a box of Chee·tos. "First the globe, then the earth. It's a sign, a warning. Sister Maxima is convinced of it. Vampires, earthquakes, kids on dope, crucifixions. What more proof do you need?"

In the morning before I shaved or had breakfast I got a call from a Sergeant Donavon at Parker Center.

"They're holding a reception for you at four o'clock today. Very impressive. *Two* captains, believe it or not, some lifers in three-piece suits from the D.A.'s, a guy from Sacramento from the PI licensing bureau who wears a bow tie. I think they're talking about pulling your ticket. Better not to be late."

I sighed and told him I'd be there.

"You used to be with Hollywood dicks, didn't you? You musta really screwed up, all the weight they're going to throw at you. Probably ought to wear a suit and tie and real shoes. Make a good impression, just like your mom told you."

I waited until after one o'clock, when the stock market back east closed, and called a broker I knew. Only once had I actually purchased stock but several times I'd been given studio stock as a year-end bonus. I didn't like having to worry about it, checking the price every day in the paper and feeling my pulse race up and down, so I finally sold everything and put the money in the bank. And the Morgan. After a moment the broker came on the line, full of salesmanship and bonhomie. After I told him what I wanted his voice cooled, and he said he'd get back to me.

Twenty minutes later the phone rang, and Allison said, "It's been a while."

"Been busy," I said carefully, trying to gauge her emotion from her voice. I added, "Chasing bad guys. Remember?"

"Well, it's time for an accounting, my friend. Come by tonight and tell me what I've got to show for paying your exorbitant rates."

*Back on an up mood,* I thought with relief but aware that it could change in a minute. We agreed on seven o'clock. When I hung up the phone immediately rang again. The stockbroker.

"Trans-International Studios does not have sufficient stockholders to be listed on the Big Board, but it's on the Pacific and other regional boards. Seventy percent of the stock is held by East-West Securities, Ltd., which is itself a wholly owned subsidiary of Westmoreland Investments of the Cayman Islands. Why do you want to know this?"

"Who owns Westmoreland?"

"I thought you were a cop. Ask your white-collar guys downtown."

"I'm not in the department anymore."

"Yeah, all right, but what I'm telling you, you didn't hear it from me. Okay?"

"I don't even know you."

"Our research people tell me Westmoreland's a holding company, a shell, a magic place where people turn dirty money into clean profits. Most of the dirty money comes out of Vegas, L.A., New York, Miami, places like that. It's owned by guys who wear dark glasses inside and whose last names end in vowels. Paying attention?"

"All right. Thanks."

"Thanks, nothing. Don't ask me to do favors. I'm in business."

As I was getting ready to drive down to Parker Center the manager of the paint shop called.

"I did Redford's Ferrari, I did Reggie Jackson's Porsche. This is better. It's a jewel. I don't wanna let it outta here. It's just too damn beautiful to drive."

"When can I pick it up?"

"Tomorrow. Bring a closed trailer, you hear? I don't want you getting a speck on it driving it home."

"It's a car," I said. "I bought it to drive it."

"A crime!" He was almost crying. "A real crime. It's so *beautiful*! Be here at noon."

I stood there for a minute with the phone in my hand. I couldn't believe it. I was done. I was going to be able to *drive* the damn thing.

They chose one of the smaller conference rooms at Parker Center. No windows. No air. Residue of day-old cigar smoke floating about our heads like tear gas. A blond-colored table with me on one side and all of them on the other.

They wanted me to see the odds, feel the walls closing in when they went to work.

There were six of them:

Captain Oscar Reddig.

Captain James Blalock, in charge of the Hollywood Sign Task Force. A heavyset, square-shouldered man with a flat, unexceptional face to go with his flat, unexceptional mind.

Two attorneys from the D.A.'s office: Haskins, who was running the case, and a bland young fellow called Selkirk who kept squinting at me from behind thick tortoise-shell glasses as if I were some exotic form of animal he might never get to see again. *Seize the day,* I thought.

A sixtyish robust-looking man from the state licensing bureau. Tanned face, balding, relaxed, comfortable with his sense of authority. Wearing a yellow bow tie.

A youngish man with glasses on a leather leash around his neck, sitting stiffly at the end of the table with a machine like court reporters use.

They were wearing suits, long-sleeved shirts with ties, shined shoes. I had on blue Levi's, a yellow knit pullover, and blue running shoes.

Captain Blalock hunched his heavy shoulders over the table. "There've been complaints."

"Be specific."

"Vincente Scali. He says you barged into his place and accused him of being in the rackets, being in the drug business."

"Which part of this is confusing to you? Perhaps I can help."

The note-taker glanced up at me quickly as he pounded silently on his machine and then stared down at his fingers again.

"You're a real smart-ass, aren't you?" Blalock said as he glared at me.

"More or less."

He seized a notebook from his coat pocket and began to read. "You accused Scali of laundering money. You accused him of racketeering. You accused him of being involved in pornography."

"We talked about it," I said. "I don't recall any accusations."

The man from the licensing bureau cleared his throat and said, "There's the question of *professionalism* here—"

Blalock didn't like the interruption; his face went as red as a string of Mexican chilies as he glared at me. "You accused Scali of being involved in the Hollywood sign killings! What the hell do you think you're doing? This is a police matter, Eton, and you're not a cop, goddamn it! Stay the fuck out of police business. This is *my* investigation. Do you understand that? *My goddamn investigation!* I'm in charge of the task force. What the hell do you think you're doing?"

"Your job. And I agree, you should be doing it. But you're not."

"Look, goddamn it, you stay outta my way! You stay away from this case before you fuck up everything we've done."

Haskins from the D.A.'s office tried to be conciliatory. "We think we're making some progress on this, Mr. Eton, the sort of progress we can't discuss with the public, of course. But your interference can only muddy the waters. We're narrowing it down, honing in on it, as it were, and I think we see the light at the end of the tunnel. It's merely a matter of time now. Just tie up a few loose ends."

I had lost track but I was almost certain Haskins had set an indoor record for the most clichés without taking a breath. And in my presence! When he began to breathe normally again I asked, "Is Scali a suspect, then?"

Haskins gave me a friendly smile, as he might to a child selling Kool-Aid on the sidewalk, and shook his head. "Mr. Scali, as you've already implied, is known by us to be involved in the pornography business, as well as several other lucrative but unsavory areas of commerce. Rosa Luzon, however, was killed as part of a very, very amateurish production. You saw the film and will agree, I'm sure. To answer your question, no, we do not suspect Mr. Scali of this particular crime. We are, however, continuing to monitor other areas of his business, particularly his alleged drug dealings, and your involvement with him just confuses matters. We simply can't have it."

"We also got a complaint from Ivan Ryan," Oscar Reddig said in a calm voice.

*Even Oscar,* I thought with a sigh.

Blalock was boiling again, sweat beginning to glisten on his size-seventeen neck. "Fucking old Ivan Ryan calls up the chief and says who's this asshole harassing my daughter a few days after she buries her husband? Holy fucking Christ!"

"Jimmy—" Oscar tried to calm Blalock, then said to me, "Ryan wasn't exactly complaining, just wanted to know who you were. For all he knew you were some kind of nut."

*"Christ!"* Blalock threw a ballpoint pen he had been holding at the tabletop, and it skidded off onto the floor, where the young notetaker quickly retrieved it. Blalock snatched it out of his hand without a word.

Haskins glanced at some notes in front of him. "You were involved in a bit of a contretemps at a recording studio on Edgemont also. It all sounds very odd. You seem to have accused the management there of murder." His voice took on a tone of amused surprise, and his eyebrows arched upward as he stared at me.

"Do you want to know who owns the studio?" I asked.

Again Haskins slowly shook his head. "It's all irrelevant, I'm afraid. Why should it be of any interest to us in the absence of any evidence that a crime occurred there?"

The man from Sacramento shifted in his chair and touched his bow tie. "Your license is not up for renewal until two more years. A mechanism does exist, however, for holding a special relicensing hearing should the facts so warrant, and I am beginning to lean in that direction now. There seem to be so many unusual circumstances—" He glanced at the others.

Oscar Reddig said, "You've always been a little bit eccentric, haven't you, Vic? Just a little bit off center in how you approach an investigation?"

I had the feeling he was saying it for my benefit, trying to take a little heat off me. Victor Eton, the oddball, a little out of whack, a little bizarre, but not really someone to worry about.

But Blalock immediately went through the roof. "*Eccentric?* I had his file brought up from Personnel. How the hell did you ever get on the force in the first place? You've always been a troublemaker, not following orders, fucking insubordinate to your superiors—"

Haskins smiled around the room. "I'm sure we can wrap this up without any unpleasantness. We'll consider this an unofficial get-together to share our perceptions vis-à-vis the progress of this case and what can be done to ensure its successful completion. The bottom line is that there is an official investigation of utmost importance continuing, one that requires the complete noninvolvement of all unofficial parties. Mr. Eton certainly understands our position, and I'm sure he'll see the wisdom of staying away—very far away—from our efforts. I think that's pretty clear, don't you?"

I was still boiling when I arrived at Allison's at six-thirty. She was wearing skimpy white shorts and a halter top and had just finished putting two steaks on the balcony barbecue; I could smell the enticing aroma of sizzling beef and see the smoke through the sliding glass door. She handed me a bottled beer and sat me on the couch. "You look like someone stole your cape and magnifying glass."

Briefly I told her about the meeting downtown.

She thought about it for a minute. "You must have pushed some wrong buttons. Especially for the D.A. to get involved. It doesn't sound right. Don't they usually stay out of something like this until an arrest is made?"

"Some of it I can understand," I said. "Scali, the two apes at the recording studio. I wanted to lean on them, see what happens. But Ivan Ryan I don't understand at all. Why would he invite Tracy and me out there and then complain about me harassing him?"

"Maybe he's going senile," Allison guessed. She stood up a minute to glance at the steaks through the glass door and then came back and sat next to me on the couch.

"Ivan Ryan's no more senile than I am," I told her. "He did it for a reason. Did you know Trans-International was largely owned by the Mafia?"

She looked up at me. "No. Should I have?"

"I thought you might have heard something."

"I don't have friends in *all* the studios. Or the Mafia."

"That was overkill, this afternoon. Blalock, the 'A Team' from the D.A.'s office, someone from Licensing in Sacramento. I must have stumbled onto something without knowing it."

I stood up and began to prowl around the room, still brooding on it. "Why should Scali have any pull with Blalock?"

Allison stared at me from the couch. "Do I really have to tell you?"

"No, it's not that. Blalock's not on the take. Nobody in that room was. I'd bet on it."

"Then maybe Blalock's just afraid you'll break the case. From what you said he sounds like the type that likes the glory. He doesn't want an ex-cop getting any credit. Especially a smart-ass ex-cop."

I let out a sigh and flopped down on a chair. "I'm getting a headache."

She walked out to the balcony and flipped the steaks. When she came back she sat on the floor in front of me, drawing her knees up to her chest and giving me a little-girl look. "Don't be so hangdog, Victor Eton. You did what I hired you to do—you found out who killed Rosa."

"The *police* found out," I reminded her. "Just like I told you they would. The police turned up the film; they've got it sewn up if they can identify the actors. Which they will."

"But *they* didn't turn up Scali. You did."

"Yeah. Now all I gotta do is show the bastards how Scali is really behind it. They just don't want to believe it—or believe anyone will prove it. Where's your aspirin?"

She rested her chin on my knee and looked up at me. "In the bedroom. Let me show you."

I looked into her face, all the doubts from before, all the resolutions I had made to myself, rising up in my mind and dissolving in seconds. When she got to her feet and crossed into the bedroom, I pushed out of the chair and followed dumbly.

When I got home at ten-thirty Tracy was already asleep. I stood in her bedroom doorway and watched her turning uncomfortably in the heat for a moment and then went to my bedroom, leaving the door open. For an hour I lay in the warm, stuffy darkness, thinking not about Allison this time but about the Morgan. *Ten years,* I kept thinking stupidly. Ten years. It's like seeing your kid grow up and get married and move away. Are you happy or sad? Ten years. *It's just a damn car,* I told myself as I finally slipped into sleep. *Just a damn car!*

*

At two o'clock in the morning a ten-year-old brown Toyota with primer spots on the fenders double-parked on Rossmore, and a heavyset man lumbered out of the passenger seat. He stood on the sidewalk with a twelve-gauge double-barreled shotgun and yelled my name. Then with both barrels he blew out my bedroom windows.

First there was screaming and then sirens and then people in bathrobes on the sidewalk standing in nervous little groups or talking to uniformed policemen. After a while a fire truck and ambulance showed up, their horns and sirens audible in the distance for at least five minutes; they waited in the street, blocking traffic, and then left quietly and with an air of disappointment.

No, I told the skeptical young patrolman, I couldn't imagine *why* someone had done this. Maybe it was a mistake, maybe he was after someone else.

He yelled your *name,* the policeman said in a calm voice. "Half a dozen people saw it: He got out of a Toyota, shouted your name, and *aimed.*"

I just shook my head.

Rudy came by before going in to the station. We sat at the kitchen table with coffee, a woman reporter keeping us company on TV, interviewing an Egyptian diplomat.

"He's trying to make an impression," Rudy said. "Scali. He's giving you a message."

I sipped my coffee.

"Now you back off, show him you're not dumb. It's just a message. If he wanted you dead you'd be in a body bag by now. It's how he works."

"Not very subtle."

"He doesn't have to be, does he? How's Tracy?"

"She left for school already. When the windows blew out she screamed once, and that was it. She's a tough kid."

Rudy said, "So now what do you do?"

I put down the coffee cup. "Get the Morgan out of the shop, I guess, and drive around in my goggles and scarf and impress the ladies."

Rudy nodded. "That's probably what I'd do, too, if someone tried to kill me."

"I called Ivan Ryan this morning and took him up on his offer. Tomorrow Tracy and I are going out to the Wheelers', have lunch, and watch some old films. She's looking forward to it; she said she never met a legend before. Later she wants to find his star on Hollywood Boulevard."

Rudy sat back in the chair and regarded me, the ends of his long black mustache twitching slightly. "You want me to believe you're going to drive forty minutes in the heat to watch old black and white flicks with an eighty-five-year-old man?"

I nodded; that was what we were planning.

Still watching me, he said, "I hope this means you're going to let Scali see you're backing off. How come I'm not too confident about that?"

The next morning before leaving for Wheeler's I called Holgrin at Organized Crime with a few more questions about T-I Studios and Scali. He said, "Hey, I heard about you on the news. You're getting famous. I don't think I want to know you." But a few minutes later he called back with what I wanted. Then at noon Tracy and I left in the Morgan for the Wheelers' fantasyland in the hills. I already had one hundred miles on the car. Damn, it was nice! At the corner of Sunset and Crescent Heights two girls in a silver Porsche pulled up next to us and whistled. Tracy gave them a look from behind her dark glasses and said, "Forget it, he's getting married tomorrow."

"We were whistling at the *car*!" one of them said, stung by the thought they'd be interested in an old duck like me. When the light turned green they left us in a cloud of exhaust and burning rubber and I thought I heard Tracy mumble, "Bitches."

When we arrived at the Wheelers' even Ryan was fascinated by the car. He stared at it from the narrow library windows, still in his wheelchair. "Haven't seen one of those since I was in England after the war. It was a classic design. Even then."

"I've already been contacted by a prop company. They want to list it in their inventory, rent it out for 1940s-era films."

"Beautiful," Ryan reflected. "An honest piece of workmanship." He abruptly spun his chair around and looked at me, his bony monk's head held erect and steady. "I admit to some small surprise that you took me up on my offer."

"But we're glad you did," Elizabeth added pleasantly. "We don't have many visitors up here. And Dad seldom gets an opportunity to show off his films anymore." She smiled warmly at her father and then at me. "He's always been a bit of a ham."

"Bit of a ham!" Ryan harrumphed loudly. "A massive mountain of a ham is more like it. Trained as an actor, you know. That's why I was so blasted good as a director. I knew how to direct to the *actors'* advantage. They loved me." He chuckled loudly. "That's one thing that hasn't changed in this town in sixty years: The modest and timid, poor souls, find themselves trampled underfoot by the loudmouths like me. Hollywood has never been the place for the quiet intellect."

"My dad's always taking me to those thirties and forties revivals," Tracy told him. "Randolph Scott and John Wayne and Rory Calhoun. All that old leather and dust and guns. But my favorites are the musicals."

Ryan chuckled and pointed a bony finger at her. "*MGM!* I knew it, by God! I've got one on the projector downstairs. You'll see," he added with a wink. "I know what the ladies like. And it's on *film,* damn it, and a projector and a *screen*! Not that hideous *videotape* of the present generation."

I was amazed at the way Tracy and Ivan Ryan had instantly taken to each other, one of those inexplicable pairings of age and youth that happen so often and yet seem so odd. And the old man appeared to be genuinely enjoying himself today, not trying to impress anyone with his eccentricity.

Elizabeth rose and crossed over to the den windows to draw the heavy drapes against the early afternoon sun. She moved slowly, with a fatigued weariness, the strain of the past few days still evident in the lines and shadows of her face. She desperately needed a rest, I thought as I watched her, and I recalled the fog of my own existence after Laurie had died. Elizabeth's eyes had the same deadened look of uncomprehended tragedy, her gestures the same wooden acceptance of the inevitability of grief that I had felt. She needed to get away from the police and the reporters and the constant reminders of these last dreadful days; it was wearying her, dragging her down, and she seemed to be aging in front of my eyes. As she reached up for the cord the sunlight slanting through the high arched windows fell on her face and shoulder-length hair, the firm rise of her breasts visible through her blouse, and I thought: She's still beautiful; even with everything she's been through—the questioning, the innuendos about Rosa and her husband, the horrible reminders of death, the sleepless nights mirrored in the red-lined eyes—she was still a beautiful woman. She noticed me staring and smiled faintly as she pulled the drapes shut.

"I'm sorry your daughter couldn't be here, Mrs. Wheeler," I said as she sat down.

She smiled at Tracy and me. "Since you're here at our invitation, why don't we just be Ivan and Vic and Tracy and Liz?"

"Ivan Denesovich!" Ryan boomed and winked at Tracy. "I'm reclaiming my heritage."

"My daughter's still not feeling well," Liz explained. "But perhaps if you and Tracy come back in a week or two, we could play tennis or go swimming. I'm sure Megan would enjoy that."

The maid came in to announce lunch. "We're just having cheeseburgers and salad if that's okay with everyone," Elizabeth said. She looked at us both, as if to apologize for the less-than-luxurious lunch.

I said fine, cheeseburgers were great.

"I think I'll just have a salad," Tracy said, and then, feeling she may have committed an unforgivable social blunder, added, "If no one minds."

Elizabeth, evidently recalling her own daughter's eating habits, threw me a quick smile. "Of course."

After lunch we descended to the basement projection room. His male attendant didn't work weekends, Ryan explained, so I wheeled the old man down the special ramp that had been built to the basement from outside. The underground room was smaller than I expected, with space for maybe a dozen people on couches and upholstered chairs. A tiny projection booth was hidden in the rear behind a thin gypsum wall.

An old-fashioned popcorn machine like I remembered from years past sat lit up like a shrine in a corner, and Liz cooked up a batch, handing it out in long paper bags before turning on the projector. The popcorn was warm and salty, and I suddenly felt like I was eight years old, paying fifty cents at the Tower or Wiltern on Saturdays and eating popcorn and Milk Duds and Jujubes. *Jujubes!* I could still remember how they stuck to my teeth and how I would pop one into my mouth in the dark of the theater and try to guess what flavor it was. I wondered if they even made them anymore.

The films were from Ryan's private collection: a 1950s musical and two episodes of a G-men serial that he had directed in the forties when he was still relatively unknown—shootouts, bank robbings, cars racing around corners on two wheels while tommy guns ripped up storefronts, cliff-hanging endings to bring you back the next week.

There was a gritty journeyman professionalism to these old black and white prints, a sense of seeing real people doing real things rather than the glossy overbudgeted superficialities coming out of the studios today. It was more than nostalgia, I thought: They were good films. "And real *stories,*" Ryan said with gusto. "With a beginning, a middle, and an end. An *end*! Today's movies start and stop, but there's no real beginning or end: It's all middle.

"Today," the old man continued, his gravelly voice dismissive of the current Industry, "no one's interested in *stories;* they deal in 'concepts.' But not until after 'research' and 'market testing.' And no one gives a tinker's dam anymore about the *story*. That's what happens when the video-game generation takes charge. *Concepts*!"

Ryan was enjoying himself immensely, directing his remarks primarily to Tracy. During the film he had interrupted constantly, booming out recollections of the actors or studio executives or others he had known; never maliciously or cruelly, though. That he saved for the modern Industry.

Tracy and I enjoyed it all tremendously, enjoyed even Ryan's odd interruptions and editorial addendums. It gave us a sense of being whisked back in time to the wellhead, of having the opportunity to meet those who made history: Here we were, actually *talking* with Ivan Ryan, one of the half dozen or so legendary men who made Hollywood what it was near the end of its Golden Age. Ryan enjoyed it, too, looking pleased with himself as he talked about his accomplishments. Only Elizabeth seemed uninvolved. Sitting stiffly next to me on the couch, she stared at the screen and from time to time joined in the conversation, but it seemed forced. Her mind was elsewhere, her eyes gazing straight ahead. As I watched her in profile, silhouetted in the flickering light from the projector, I had a sudden vision of Laurie—the same tiny hands and small tapered fingers, the same almost weightless fall of brown hair around her shoulders—and I felt a chill along my spine and involuntarily shivered. And once again I found myself wondering what sort of person Elizabeth Wheeler was, what kind of marriage she had had, and how happy she really had been. She and her husband seemed so odd a couple—her loyal and loving Richard with his pornography and punk rock singers and mob friends. It just didn't fit with what I thought I knew of Elizabeth Wheeler. What the hell did these two people have in common? She had never really spoken of her marriage except in banalities, always picking her words carefully so as not to admit an outsider to the private sanctity of her family, her face betraying no emotion other than exhaustion. But again I felt with absolute certainty that something was wrong up here, that something was being kept from me. Ivan Ryan's booming bass broke in on my thoughts.

"I hate to say it, Victor, but those really *were* the days. We had to get people into the theaters *without* sex. A remarkable notion, eh? Now it's the only thing movies offer. Sex! No plot, no characterization, no finesse. No *class*!"

"Save it for your memoirs, Pop," Elizabeth said, flicking on the lights. She smiled weakly but affectionately at her father, blinking in the sudden light and slipping quickly around the side of his wheelchair to the projection room.

"I'm dictating into a tape recorder," Ryan told me with a chuckle. "Can't write anymore, can't hold a pencil. But I can *talk*. Then I'll give the whole mess to some professional at one of the studios to scribble up for me."

"I've heard some of your dictating," his daughter said from the projection room. She came out and gave him a disappointed stare. "Something about your mother, a cousin of Czar Nicholas, fleeing for her life through the frozen Siberian wilderness in 1918."

"A little drama never hurt a story." Ryan chuckled. "It's the *story*, after all, that counts, the entertainment. Victor!" He fixed a Methuselahlike stare at me. "You can wheel me back to the den, dear boy, and we'll have a cold drink before you take off for the long journey down the hill to what you are pleased to call civilization. Perhaps Elizabeth can show Tracy around the grounds, point out some of the more exotic flora and fauna of *alta* Beverly Hills."

Back in the den I fixed a bourbon and water for Ryan and myself and sat back in the soft leather couch. Ryan's cat sulked in a corner, eyeing me warily from translucent eyes.

"Rather bad taste of me, wasn't it?" Ryan suddenly asked in his guttural voice. "Calling the department and complaining about your questioning. Shouldn't have done it. Don't know what got into me."

"You're right," I agreed, and looked at his weathered face. "You shouldn't have done it." I wasn't going to give the old man the satisfaction of forgiveness.

Ryan scowled and fumbled with his drink for a moment, finally painfully bringing it to his lips. He took a long sip and put it down and held me in his gaze. "I didn't want Elizabeth going through any more questioning. Her husband had just tragically died, and you come up here asking about prostitutes and crime. Damned insensitive, I'd say."

I held his gaze without responding.

The old man dropped his eyes, and his voice lost its edge of defensiveness. "The funeral was Thursday. Private. Just Elizabeth and myself there. Cremated."

"And Megan?"

Ryan's eyes flashed angrily and he glared at me. "My granddaughter is too ill to attend a funeral."

I watched as the eyes settled again into an uneasy calm as he took another drink from the glass, setting it down with a clatter. "I'm glad you and Tracy liked the films. Unlike some modern directors I could name, I'm not ashamed of any of the films I made. Maybe they weren't all exactly classics, but they did entertain. People left my movies feeling good, not cheap and dirty like today."

With deliberate provocation I asked, "Your son-in-law disagreed with you, I take it."

Ryan's gnarled white hands clenched into weak fists and he stared at me. His voice rose slightly. "Is that so?" The cat in the corner came to its feet and began padding silently toward Ryan, its back arched.

"Wheeler was a fan of pornography," I went on evenly. "A collector. He had quite a reputation." Maybe that was what the old man meant a few days ago by "the murk of his background."

"My son-in-law was not a perfect human being, Victor," Ryan said as the cat leapt into his lap. He clasped his arthritic fingers around the glass on his wheelchair table and took a drink before continuing. "But his sins were venial; not the sort of thing a man dies for."

I stood and crossed over to the tall windows and spread the drapes so that I could see the side yard. The shadows from the pines were lengthening and stretching out toward the house as the sun began to settle behind the hills. Liz and Tracy were nowhere to be seen. I disliked what I was about to do but I wanted to get it over with before Liz got back. Turning back to the old man, my voice flat, I said, "Let's stop playing games, Mr. Ryan. Your son-in-law was not some sort of pure and innocent lamb tragically trapped in the Sodom and Gomorrah of Hollywood. Richard Wheeler was a shit."

The fiery eyes held my gaze. "Indeed?" He wasn't going to give an inch. He waved me back to my seat. "They were not the sort of sins one dies for," he repeated, and added, "His sins were only those of his times."

I sympathized with the old man's desire to protect his daughter's reputation, but I wasn't going to be bullied into silence. "Richard Wheeler was up to his armpits in organized crime, Mr. Ryan. *Organized crime.* Mafia. Real life."

A sudden movement of Ryan's arm overturned his glass, and it flew to the floor. I rose out of my chair with the intention of picking it up, but the old man snapped at me loudly. "Sit down, damn it!" He stared at me angrily. "Mafia? You're being rather melodramatic, aren't you?"

"I picked up some information from the LAPD intelligence unit and the FBI. Do you want to hear it?"

His body stiffened. "I appear to have no choice. Continue!"

I leaned back on the soft couch. "You've heard the name Vincente Scali?"

"It rings a distant bell," Ryan said with what sounded like sarcasm.

"He owns a men's boutique on Rodeo."

Ryan brushed the comment away with disdain. "Trendy purveyors to the nouveau riche."

"And a perfect front, as well as being the sort of cash-rich business the Mafia needs to launder the massive sums of money it deals in. According to the LAPD, Scali is third-generation mob and running the entertainment side of things in L.A. for the families in New York. He is also listed with the Securities and Exchange Commission as sole owner of Westmoreland Investments, Ltd., a dummy holding company incorporated in the Cayman Islands. Westmoreland Investments in turn owns a handful of other 'investment' firms which in total own most of—"

"Trans-International Studios," Ryan answered coldly.

"Which owns, among other things, Westway Records."

Ryan's lips compressed and his expression turned from contempt to disgust. "A tangled web, Victor. I had no idea that the police were so well informed."

"There are no laws being broken in this chain of ownership. Of course, the FBI and police and SEC are curious about the *use* all these companies are being put to."

"I'm sure they don't need our help in trying to imagine what's going on in those concerns," Ryan said. "But I can assure you that Vincente Scali and the scum he associates with aren't the least interested in the movie business.

Trans-International was merely an investment, one of many, and highly profitable, at that."

"And the police don't even have a file on you," I said.

Ryan laughed heartily but with little warmth. "You checked, did you? Never can be too sure. Perhaps I run the Russian side of the Mafia: sable and minks and black-market caviar."

"We're talking about Wheeler," I reminded him.

Ryan sighed heavily and looked down at his pale arthritic hands. "Ah, yes. Perhaps, Victor, you'd be so kind as to fix me another drink."

When I handed him the glass the old man looked haggard and drawn; even his eyes were tired now. He sipped at the drink for a minute and then gazed at me. "Richard was not always involved, you know. Just lately, the last five years, maybe six. He founded Westway, as you're aware, and made it into a phenomenal success." There was a trace of pride in his voice as he smiled slightly at the pictures from the past he was drawing up from his memory. "He was a millionaire on his own by the time he was twenty-five. Quite an achievement. Then he sold the company to Trans-International about six years ago."

Ryan's voice ground down to a husky whisper, and I waited silently, suddenly feeling oppressed by the large, high-ceilinged room. The old man seemed to be arranging his thoughts, wondering how to proceed. Finally he looked up and continued with an effort.

"Soon after he sold the company to T-I, I began hearing things. Friends in the Industry let things drop. Nothing blatant, just comments here and there. Mr. Scali, it seems, was not universally admired, and it didn't take much time to discover that it was he who actually owned the record company now and, as it turned out, Richard."

Ryan fixed me with a stare. "They've always been fascinated with the entertainment industry, haven't they? Maybe they just like having America's heroes at their beck and call. I imagine so. But it's been like that for sixty years—movies, records, nightclubs, jukeboxes. Everything but the opera, I suppose.

"Richard could simply have sold out and gone into something else, of course. But he didn't. They seduced him. I'm not sure how, but I imagine it was nothing more exotic than money and power. It all sounds rather trite and tawdry, doesn't it? But there never seems to be enough of either for people in this town. They always want *more.* Richard was free to walk away at any time but he chose not to, not until he had more, more of everything. It was all downhill for him from then on, even if he did manage to stay above the seamier aspects of his newfound associates."

Ryan let out a sigh and sank back in his wheelchair, staring past me. Both of his large weakened hands lay on the little metal wheelchair table, wrapped around the tall glass. He seemed suddenly shrunken in the large room and I wished I could leave him in peace but couldn't. So far the old man had told me nothing I hadn't already known. I took a sip of my drink and waited until Ryan's eyes came back to me, two candles burning down now to nothingness. "Did your son-in-law ever mention a snuff film?"

"It wasn't the sort of thing we would have discussed."

"How did you happen to know about his interest in pornography, then?"

"I came across his collection one day. I have since had it burned, every filthy piece." His hands tightened on the glass and his face colored.

"I realize that this is difficult for you to talk about, Mr.

Ryan, but I thought it would be better to ask you than your daughter."

The old man nodded. "I appreciate that."

"But," I continued, "you both could have volunteered this information when I first talked to you."

I could see him bristle again, as if the adrenaline were suddenly pumping through his veins. "Be realistic! You came up here to investigate Richard's death, not his life. I still don't see what all this has to do with his death and I don't think you do, either."

Before I could answer, the door swung open, and Elizabeth and Tracy came in, laughing. Tracy ran up to me. "I've decided what I'm going to be when I grow up," she said breathlessly. *"Rich!"*

"You liked the pool," Ryan boomed out to her. He was delighted to see her again.

"You've got to see it, Dad. It's got three different *levels* and two waterfalls and a fountain and all these Greek columns—"

"Some other time," I said.

"Nap time for Czar Nicholas's nephew," Elizabeth said, and walked to her father's wheelchair. "But we hope you both can make it back again."

As she smiled my heart speeded up a notch, and I could feel an odd light-headedness I hadn't felt in years.

I dropped Tracy off at the apartment so she could shower and then drove around back and stored the Morgan in the garage. There were splatter marks on the rear fenders from a puddle out front, and I started to wipe them off with a shop rag and then suddenly stopped, feeling like an idiot. *It's a car, for Christ's sake, not the Mona Lisa. It'll get dirty.*

I locked up and walked to the other garage (another two hundred a month) and collected the Buick and set off for El Cholo's to pick up two take-out Mexican dinners: enchiladas, tamales, beans, a bag of chips with salsa. On the way back I switched off the radio and tried to put my thoughts in order.

Exactly what had I learned from my long afternoon with Ivan Ryan and Elizabeth Wheeler? That Richard Wheeler was a Hollywood lowlife? That wasn't exactly news to me now. That Wheeler had friends with mob ties? Again, so what? Half the Industry bigwigs had their seamier relationships. Like Ryan said, the mob liked to associate with the entertainment industry; it made them feel important, perhaps even vaguely human.

But these were all things I had already known or suspected. Things Ryan hadn't confirmed, however, until he was certain I was already aware of them.

So what had I actually learned?

Old Ivan, I thought with a sigh: dispensing information like a mother handing out sweets to a child, a little bit at a time, to make sure he behaves.

Yeah, Ivan was really something.

And another day wasted.

I parked on Rossmore and took the ornate old gilt elevator up to the second floor, listening to my stomach growl and balancing the two dinners in my arms. But the minute I stepped into the hallway I stopped cold. For a long moment I stood stupidly without moving, holding the two covered plates, and stared at the partially open apartment door. My breathing halted, and I began to feel a pounding in the back of my head, as if someone were drilling into my skull. Then I pushed on the door and went in.

In the living room the television was switched to MTV, bleary images jumping and flickering on the screen. I switched it off and called Tracy's name, but there was no response. Rousing myself, I put the dinners down and quickly checked the bathroom and bedrooms. Nothing. In the kitchen the refrigerator door stood ajar, a small pool of water forming on the tile floor. I stared at it dumbly for a long moment, then my knees began to feel weak and my mind reeled: It couldn't be. It must be some kind of mistake, I told myself. *It couldn't be!* But Tracy would never have gone off like this.

A timid knock at the door almost panicked me, and I wheeled around. "Yoo-hoo, Mr. Eton—" An elderly voice, becoming more insistent. "*. . . Mr. Eton, are you there?*"

Mrs. MacDonald from next door stood propped with her cane in the open doorway staring uncertainly into the unlighted living room. She adjusted her glasses and smiled weakly when she recognized me.

"Oh, *there* you are, Mr. Eton. I saw you drive up and I said to myself that I should come right over and tell you. Not that it's necessarily anything important, of course, but you just can't tell anymore, can you? Not with all the strange things happening in this neighborhood. Absolute insanity is what I call it. Why, just yesterday somebody stole the garden hose from the yard out front. The garden hose! Can you imagine? Young fellow walked right up, brazen as all get-out, and commenced to unhook the hose and *walked* right off down the street with it. Now, what do you suppose he did that for? Couldn't be worth more than a dollar or two."

I was feeling weak. Trying desperately to keep my voice calm, I said, "Mrs. MacDonald—"

"Oh, my, yes." She looked suddenly concerned and focused her eyes on me. "Well, I was sitting by my window like I do in the afternoons, you know, just watching the street. Usually there's not much to watch, a quiet street like this not much happens until after dark. Except stealing hoses! Never thought that would happen living on Rossmore. Not in the daytime like that. Anyway, I was watching out the window and listening to that psychologist that's on the radio every day, the one that talks to crazy people who phone in. I knew you weren't home because I saw you drive off earlier." She shifted her weight on the cane and looked at me plaintively. "Do you mind if I sit down, Mr. Eton? My legs aren't all that strong anymore, and all that standing—"

"Please, Mrs. MacDonald." I could feel myself losing my grip but realized that trying to hurry the elderly woman along would only confuse her. Holding her by the elbow, I escorted her to the couch, where she slowly lowered herself and stretched out her weakened varicose-veined legs.

"My, that's better." She smiled limply and began to fan herself with a magazine. "These legs are the oldest things on this block, Mr. Eton. Can't expect perfect service out of them, can we? Now, where were we?"

"The window—"

"Oh, my, yes. Well, a car drove up and parked in the red zone there where it says no parking, and these two men, nice-looking gentlemen in gray suits, got out and came up the walk. Nice-looking men, not the ragamuffin sort you usually see in Hollywood these days. Well, I watched them real close in case they were thinking of stealing the hose. I should have known better, such clean-looking men in nice expensive suits like doctors. But then they walked right into the building and not more than a minute later they came out with that nice little girl of yours, one on each side of her like the police on the TV when they arrest someone, but I knew they weren't arresting her, of course. But they each had her by the arms, little Tracy between those two big men. It didn't seem right to me. But they were all very quiet and dignified. I mean, she wasn't crying or screaming and they didn't say anything, not anything I could hear, anyway." She suddenly stopped and fixed me with an appealing glance. "They weren't friends of yours, were they, Mr. Eton? I *was* right to tell you, wasn't I?"

An awful weakness came over me, and I began to feel the throbbing of my pulse. "No, Mrs. MacDonald, they weren't friends."

"I thought so!" she announced triumphantly, and leaned forward on her cane. "Because she *looked* at me. Tracy! She looked right at me. She knows I sit at that window, of course, and just before those men put her in that car she twisted her pretty little head back and looked at me, just looked right at me like she wanted to say something. But she didn't say a word. Then one of the men saw her and he looked over and saw me staring at them out the window and right away he gives me a big smile like he's telling me everything's on the up and up, but I didn't believe it for one minute. He was play-acting, he was, just like most everyone else in this town. Smiling at me like that, as if we were old friends. . . ."

I was on the edge of panic now but I tried desperately to keep the hysteria from my voice. "Please, Mrs. MacDonald, this is very important. What did those two men look like?"

"Such nice-looking men," she said earnestly, and relaxed back in the couch. "Nice gray suits, looked *very* expensive. Young men, about your age, I should imagine. Very *neat*-looking, not like most of the riffraff here in Hollywood, hair all over their face and down their backs, looking like they never wash. No, those boys were very *neat,* Mr. Eton, hair all in place just like gentlemen used to do. Of course it was longer than I like, but I do accept the fact that fashions change.

"Let me see, now—" She concentrated, eyes closed and both hands grasping the curved handle of her cane. "One of the men was bigger than the other and older, I suppose. He was the one who smiled at me; bigger, strong-looking, *thick*-looking with a very neat little mustache. He reminded me of a policeman or maybe a soldier. Authoritative, you know."

She searched her mind, eyes tightly shut behind thick spectacles. "They both were . . . ah, dark-looking, if you know what I mean. Not black but dark. Like Mexicans. *Swarthy,* we used to call it." She gave me an embarrassed little smile.

"*Think,* Mrs. MacDonald. Was there anything else about them you remember? Anything! The car, maybe."

She opened her eyes into the gloom of the hot, unlighted room. "Yes, indeed; it was one of those fancy foreign cars, the one named after that actress."

"Mercedes?" I guessed quickly.

Mrs. MacDonald beamed. "*That's it!* A light blue Mercedes. They got in after that heavyset man smiled at me and then they zoomed off down the street. *Zoomed* off like they were in a race. Of course, I knew then they wanted to get out—"

"The license, Mrs. MacDonald, did you get the license?"

"Land sake's no." She looked at me sternly. "My eyes, Mr. Eton. Can't expect a body my age to see little bitty numbers like that. Goodness, I do hope everything's going to be okay. Those men kidnapped Tracy, didn't they? They kidnapped her, just like the Lindbergh baby."

"Yes, Mrs. MacDonald, they kidnapped her."

Using the cane, she struggled to her feet, looking both confused and alarmed; her eyes seemed to lose their focus as she stared around the room. "Well, you won't be wanting me around. I'd just be getting under your feet. I'll go back to my window, but if I remember anything else I'll come right over. I do so hope everything turns out all right for you and Tracy. As soon as I saw those men I *knew* they were up to no good."

I came out of my chair, my legs weak and my head spinning. In a haze I helped Mrs. MacDonald through the door and back to her apartment before collapsing again onto the couch. My mind reeled back to the day Laurie was killed, and a horrible sickness came over me, and I thought: *It can't be! I can't be losing Tracy, too.* And for the second time in my life I was totally lost, immobilized by fear, not knowing what to do, knowing only I needed help. In a panic I grabbed the phone and dialed Rudy at home. But the phone rang and rang and rang. "*Answer it!*" I screamed out loud. "*Goddamn it! Answer it!*" Finally the ringing stopped and I heard Rudy's voice. Haltingly, I stammered out what had happened.

*"My God,"* he whispered. "You've gotta call in, Vic, get an APB on the car—"

"No," I said, "I've got to think. Rudy, I need your help."

I paced the living room, going again and again over Mrs. MacDonald's story and trying desperately to force my mind to focus on the details she had been able to remember. "It had to be the two men from the recording studio," I said. "The description—"

Rudy nodded from the couch. "Scali's punks."

"This was no snatch. They walked in during broad daylight and walked out holding her. They *want* me to know who has her."

Rudy agreed, but it didn't make any sense. "What's the point? Unless he just wants to put a little more muscle on you."

I stopped suddenly and grabbed at the phone, dialing directory assistance and scrawling the number for "Scali" on a magazine cover. Immediately I punched out the number and listened while it rang. I felt helpless and alone and my self-control started dissolving again as the phone rang endlessly on the other end. Suddenly it stopped and a pleasant female voice said, "Scali," her voice going softly up and down as if singing.

"This is Eton," I shot out instantly. "I want Scali."

Before she could respond, Scali was on the line, sounding buoyant. "Mr. Eton. I thought perhaps we had heard the last of you."

With a mighty effort I kept my voice calm. "Let her go, Scali."

The other man gave no indication of hearing. "Perhaps you forgot our conversation earlier. You were most unpleasant, and I suggested at the time that it would be to your benefit if you stopped intruding into my affairs. For some reason I'll never comprehend, you chose to ignore my advice. The only conclusion I could come to was that you were either a complete fool or you just did not hear me. My colleagues have concluded that you are a fool or worse, Mr. Eton. I, however, have given you the benefit of the doubt and assumed that you merely didn't hear me before. Do you hear me now?"

My fingers tightened on the receiver. "You touch her, Scali, and I'll kill you myself. I promise you: I'll kill you myself."

"Now, as I understand it," Scali went on evenly, "when that horrible film turned up you fulfilled your contract with the person who hired you. In fact, if you talk to the young lady I am sure she will tell you that your services are no longer desired. There is nothing left for you to do. Even the district attorney's office has told you to back off. And yet you persist in nosing around. This morning you inquired again about me with the police department downtown and this afternoon you even spent several hours at Mrs. Wheeler's.

"Really, Mr. Eton, you surprise me. What can you expect to gain from such interference? You are causing me a great deal of annoyance and confusion, and for what? All because of some stupid notion that I am responsible for that pitiful young girl's death." Scali's voice rose a notch. "Are you listening to me now, Mr. Eton? *I had nothing to do with that girl's death. Nothing!* Now get the hell out of my life."

"*Scali—*" I screamed.

But there was only the monotonous drone of the dial tone. I slammed the phone down and yanked it up and frantically punched out the number again, but the phone rang without interruption. I was sick with panic, my body trembling and drenched with perspiration. Quickly I dialed Allison's number. She answered on the first ring.

"Scali got to you," I said.

"It's over, Vic. Just drop it. I don't care about Rosa anymore. I'll send you a check."

"Where's Tracy?" I demanded. I could hear her breathing on the other end of the line and she paused momentarily before answering.

"Vic, I don't *know* anything. I don't *want* to know anything. Believe me when I tell you: I don't *know* any of these people. But don't ask me anything else. Tracy will be okay."

"Allison, goddamn it," I screamed at her. "I want my daughter back." But she had hung up. When I redialed, the phone was off the hook. *Damn her! Goddamn her!*

"He'll let her go now," Rudy said. "He wanted to get your attention. Blowing out your windows didn't work, so he tried this. This time you'll listen."

I jerked out of the couch and began pacing the room. I checked my watch: It seemed as if hours had passed since I had gotten home, but it was only six forty-five and the two take-out dinners sat unopened in the kitchen. *If those bastards touched her I'd kill them.* The thought pounded at me like a hammer in my mind; but I knew it was true. I'd do it personally. I'd kill them.

"We've got to call Oscar," Rudy said, watching me pace.

"No, not yet. Scali's not an idiot. He's not going to hold her where anyone's going to be able to dig her out. Besides, it's obvious now he's got someone inside the department. He knew about my call to Organized Crime today and the meeting with the D.A. He even knew I'd been out at the Wheelers'."

Rudy closed his eyes, rubbing his temples. "No wonder he's so clean. He probably knows everything that goes on inside the Department. Christ. . . ."

I sank onto the couch. "We wait. I've got no choice. Scali's calling the shots. We wait."

Together we waited.

And shortly before ten the call came. I lunged at the phone.

Tracy was crying hysterically. "Dad, I'm at the harbor in San Pedro . . . I'm okay . . . I . . ."

I could hardly hear her; her breath was coming hard and she was sobbing and there was a horrible cacophony of noise in the background. "Dad," she managed through the sobs. "Dad, they blew up the Morgan."

With Rudy in the passenger seat, I drove, frantically pushing through the congested weekend traffic on the Hollywood and Harbor freeways and finally racing along the moist, dark, industrial streets of the harbor area, past bars and warehouses and condemned apartment buildings rotting silently in the night. My mind swarmed with uncontrolled emotion, thinking of Tracy, filling with relief, then remembering Scali and feeling a surge of hatred and revenge that made my whole body shake. But as I drew near the docks I sensed only the tremendous exhilaration of relief as my thoughts settled on Tracy.

The excitement was obvious from two blocks away, police cars and fire engines with their lights flashing red and blue in the night, two-way radios blaring, a Harbor Patrol helicopter hovering noisily overhead, directing a powerful searchlight on the scene. I eased up on the accelerator and felt the pain in my hands as I released my grip on the steering wheel.

A police barricade had been erected on the cement dock a hundred yards from the sea. The explosion had been heard for blocks, and the curious and the sick had crawled from their holes and slinked out onto the dockside, where they crowded by the hundreds behind yellow sawhorses, hoping to catch a glimpse of human tragedy. I found Tracy trembling in the back of a patrol car. She burst suddenly into tears, climbing unsteadily out of the car and rushing into my arms.

After a moment the shaking ceased, and her crying subsided sufficiently for her to pull away and point toward a group of men fifty yards away poking through the rubble of what had been the Morgan. "When they . . . took me from the apartment"—her voice was quivering and her face pale and frightened when she turned back to me—"another man was in the back taking the car. After they brought me down here they made me watch as they blew it up. They made me watch! They said next time we'd be *in* the car. . . ."

I stared down the pier at the burned-out hulk without emotion. Newspaper photographers were snapping pictures, their bulbs making excited, tiny flashes in the damp night air.

"Rudy—"

Rudy nodded and came over. "Henning from Harbor Division's in charge. I'll talk to him. Take her home." He put a hand on Tracy's shoulder. "I'll see you tomorrow, kiddo."

I wanted Tracy to sleep, but she couldn't, she was too pumped up. She surprised me by saying she wanted to eat. But the Mexican dinners I had left on the counter had congealed into a thick rubbery mess, and there wasn't much else in the kitchen. So I fried some eggs and bacon and watched as she devoured her meal. *God,* I thought, *if I had lost her. . . .* And I could feel my hands begin to tremble again.

Tracy finished her meal with a sigh and glanced up at me with a weary half smile on her thirteen-year-old face. "Quite a night."

"Ready for bed?"

She shook her head. She was still too keyed up. On the drive back from the harbor she had been surprised to hear an account of the explosion on the radio: Tracy Eton, daughter of the car's owner, had been nearby at the time of the explosion but had not been injured. There were no other details available.

Tracy poured herself a glass of milk. "I never heard my name on the radio before. I guess I'm a celebrity."

"Your fifteen minutes of fame." I smiled. "Now you'll get your own star on Hollywood Boulevard. Rabbit McPhearson will want your autograph."

Her voice suddenly small, Tracy said, "They never spoke to me. Except to say, 'Shut up.' Not another word; just drove around for hours and then down to the harbor. Then they held me and made me watch as they blew up the car. I felt so horrible. . . ." Her eyes began to water again.

"We can talk about it tomorrow," I said. "Time for sleep."

Tracy started to protest, but the phone cut her off.

It was Elizabeth Wheeler, her voice tense with emotion. "I was watching the eleven o'clock news. I couldn't believe it. Is she all right? Is everything okay?"

I let Tracy talk to her for a while, then came back on the line and assured Elizabeth that Tracy was okay, just a little shaken up; mostly she needed sleep, I said.

"It had something to do with . . . the killings, didn't it?"

Not in the mood for long explanations, I briefly told her

about Scali and the hoods from the recording studio.

"My God," she muttered. "I'll call her again in the morning, Vic. It must have been horrible, those terrible people. . . ." Her voice trailed off as she thought of her own tragedy.

After she hung up I put Tracy to bed. I was entering the kitchen when the phone rang again. The voice on the other end sounded anguished. "That you, Victor? Ivan Ryan. Elizabeth told me what you said about that filth Scali. Look, Vic, I'm calling from the back hall, I don't want Elizabeth to hear, but I had to talk to you. I really am sorry about what happened to Tracy, Vic. I like that girl and it makes me sick, really makes me sick.

"I want you to drive out here tomorrow. I want to show you something. And I want to talk to you. I feel somehow responsible for what happened to Tracy. You see, Vic, I know who killed Richard."

Sometime after five I realized I wasn't going to get any sleep. Why fight it? I propped myself up in bed and began to rub my neck. I felt like hell. I had gone into Tracy's room half a dozen times during the night, telling myself that I was checking on her sleep but more to reassure myself that she was still with me. The final time I sat on a chair and watched for twenty minutes as she lay on top of the bed, the covers thrown to the floor because of the heat, and I wondered what I would do without her. But my mind just formed a blank; without Tracy there was nothing.

I stared toward the ceiling. What the hell was Ryan up to with that phone call last night? The old man wouldn't talk further about it, but his voice had been clear and held the weight of truth: He knew who killed his son-in-law. "I'd appreciate it if you could come before ten, Vic. I'd like to have this taken care of while Elizabeth's out of the house. And just you, Vic; no one else."

Crazy old Ivan.

After breakfast I drove out to the Valley, taking the long way through the canyons, making sure I wasn't being followed. I dropped Tracy at a friend's from the Department, then drove toward Elizabeth Wheeler's. It was early and I met little traffic. The air was clean and fresh but already hot; it was going to be miserable again.

The Asian houseman was waiting at the front door, emotionless as always, standing with clasped hands. Mr. Ryan was already in the screening room, he said, waiting for me.

I let him lead me through the long central hall to a rear stairway that descended to the basement. The massive house seemed dead and austere. I asked after Mrs. Wheeler. The houseman shook his lean, dark head; Mrs. Wheeler was at church, she'd probably be back by noon.

The door closed behind me, and I descended the stairs alone, finding myself in the short hallway. Ivan Ryan was sitting in his wheelchair waiting. His face was expressionless, but he sounded alert and well. "Good morning, Victor. Push me in here, please." He indicated the screening room with a jerk of his head. "It promises to be an unpleasant day for all, but I will be as expeditious as is humanly possible."

I maneuvered the chair around and pushed Ryan into the small room. The old man pointed a hand toward the projection area. "Through there. You'll find another door." He handed me a key.

I wheeled him into the tiny dark space, no larger than a closet; at the far end there was a door with a dead bolt. I unlocked it and flicked on a light to discover a large room, perhaps thirty by thirty, that had been left unfinished: bare concrete walls, cheap carpeting, a few pieces of unmatched furniture here and there. A storage room, not meant for visitors, dozens of cardboard cartons stacked neatly along one wall as if someone were in the process of moving out.

"Every family has a skeleton, they say," Ryan rasped as I stared around the room. "Shut the door. I don't want to be interrupted as I unearth ours."

As I turned the lock the old man nodded his leathery bald head at the boxes. "Richard's avocation; if it had remained such, perhaps it would never have become a problem. Unfortunately, it became the focal point of his life. Take a look."

I rummaged inside an open carton on the floor marked PRINTED MATTER. Inside were two dozen neatly packed film cans. I held one up and read the label: *Dallas Delights.* I pulled open another box: two dozen copies of *Oriental Hot Spots.* I checked three more of the hundred or so cartons; each contained two dozen pornographic films.

The old man stared up at me with tired, saddened eyes and motioned toward a chair. "When Vincente Scali and his 'associates' took over the studio several years ago they did so with the understanding that it was an investment only and that they would not become involved in day-to-day studio decisions. To my great surprise they've kept their word, at least as far as Trans-International is concerned. At the time, everyone felt that they were merely seeking 'legitimacy' and that the studio was to be their entrée to straight society. It was even argued by some of the more naive in this city that they were so well off now that they could afford to eschew illegal activities altogether. Why risk long prison sentences on drug or prostitution or gambling arrests when a single movie could make a profit of a hundred million dollars? What that rather dubious argument ignored, of course, was the fact that none of the high-ranking members of Signor Scali's rather extended family *ever* went to prison. It also ignored the fact that legitimate filmmaking is an extremely risky business: Perhaps only one out of five films ever makes a real profit, and the *Star Wars* and *E.T.*'s are few and far between. The little niches that Scali's family have carved out in the business world are, on the contrary, both remarkably profitable *and* recession-proof. Indeed, most of them may even do better in recessions. And of course at the wholesale level where Scali operates there is little competition."

The old man stopped and leaned back in his wheelchair, his head thrown back and his gaze on the ceiling as if experiencing a pain. After a moment his dark eyes again came to rest on me. "I should have asked if you would like some coffee. I could call upstairs."

I said no, I wasn't interested.

"I let my attendant go yesterday," Ryan went on, apropos of nothing. "Did I tell you that he was a Guatemalan? Pure Mayan, from the Yucatán. Fascinating, isn't it? I didn't know any Mayans had survived the Spanish talent for extermination but there are several hundred thousand in Guatemala and southern Mexico. Most of them don't even speak Spanish, but José knew a little, enough to carry on a conversation with me and my several dozen phrases of guidebook Spanish. I wired him some money to an account I had set up in Guatemala City. He'll disappear into the jungle now, set for life, and live like Indian royalty."

I shifted uneasily, uncertain where the old man was going with his rambling conversation. But I wasn't going to push him: It was Ivan Ryan's story.

Ryan noticed my discomfort and smiled thinly. "Be patient, Victor. This is a tale that requires some explanation. As

I told you before, my stories all have a beginning, a middle, and an end. We must take them in order." As he continued, his voice began to grow tired.

"There was an element of truth in Scali's contention about the studio: It *was* an investment and certainly not the sort of thing they typically get involved in. Too public, you know. It would be like the Mafia buying the New York Yankees or ABC television; they bought the stock legally through a holding company and then just left it alone. But not so with Westway Records. Westway was precisely the sort of business these people covet: a small number of employees selling millions of copies of dozens of different titles every year through a half dozen different labels that exist legally, but only on paper. And the sales were ultimately to tens of thousands of different retailers. Imagine the bookkeeping possibilities! Scali set up dozens, maybe hundreds, of dummy companies to funnel dirty money into and out of Westway. In a sense Westway became the most important part of Scali's empire of filth because it legitimized the large sums he dealt with. The scum had to have some rationale for the enormous amounts of cash that flowed like water through their filthy hands. *That* was what he needed Westway—and God knows how many other firms—for.

"Richard didn't know this at first, of course. He had convinced himself that friend Scali wouldn't be interfering in Westway, just as he'd left the parent company alone. And Scali was too adroit to put any muscle on Richard. So he romanced him, he played him like a fish, Victor: a classic case of monumental Hollywood ego blinding poor Richard to what was patent to everyone else.

"Friend Scali was a *master* of the fine art of angling. He played out his line slowly, telling Richard what a 'genius' he was. That's *the* operative word in Hollywood, of course. You're not anyone here if you're not a genius. So Richard became the town's newest genius, and you would have sworn that his body began to glow from an inner fire from that moment on. By God"—Ryan slapped his little wheelchair table—"we had a certified Industry *genius* in the family.

"And then Scali let out a tad more line: He began to invite Richard to his parties. At first he invited both Richard and Elizabeth as well as dozens of other Industry and political names. Richard loved it, especially the politicians. That was something new for him: names he'd read about in the papers for years, senators, governors, and the like.

"But then Scali started inviting Richard alone. Special parties, small parties where the new genius was the guest of honor, so to speak. Richard told me about it last year in an unusual moment of anguished introspection brought on by a half bottle of twelve-year-old Scotch. Scali's house was 'stocked,' he said, with the typical Hollywood assortment of winsome young beauties. Choose your type: black, white, brown, and yellow. And choose your age. My dear son-in-law's rather odd preference was for the very, very young."

Ryan stopped, a disgusted look growing on his face, but quickly pushed on as if afraid to stop now that he had begun to roll out the family's secrets.

"And cocaine, of course. Richard's first encounter, believe it or not. Or so he told me." He shook his head. "It became quite a habit. A thousand a week, he told me proudly. Can you begin to envision that, Victor? I'm afraid I can't. A thousand dollars a week. It cost him nothing, of course. Friend Scali provided it all without cost.

"It was meant to tie Richard to Scali but it wasn't really needed. Remember what I told you earlier: Richard wanted *more.* The cocaine was an unnecessary emolument. Richard was addicted to the trite but classic Hollywood exaltation of *more.* More money, more sex, more power. More of everything. When he met those politicians and they slapped him on the back and called him by his first name . . . well, you had to know Richard.

"The cocaine wasn't necessary but it was a little added tie to keep Richard in line if necessary. Scali *understood* Richard; he knew what made Richard tick and he knew what Richard wanted. I'm sure Scali had dealt with any number of Richards over the years. All you have to do is trot out the politicians and the girls and great gobs of money and people like Richard fall into line just like toy soldiers."

Ryan suddenly stopped still. "I think I better have a bite to eat, Victor. I skipped breakfast, and it was a mistake. I'm beginning to feel a trifle wheezy. Will you please wheel me over to the phone?"

I took a breath to calm myself; I was feeling the first stirrings of excitement as Ryan slowly zigzagged toward whatever point he was aiming at. But there was no doubt that he was unveiling the most hidden of his family's secrets. I still had no idea where he was going, but it wouldn't be long now. I pushed his wheelchair to the far table and handed him the phone. The old man's grip was firm as he seized the receiver and punched a single button. I took the opportunity to wander around the room, breathing deeply, trying to relax. The room suddenly looked dank and depressing, not at all like the fantasy make-believe world one floor above.

"It'll only be a minute," Ryan announced loudly as he replaced the phone.

I waited until a knock came at the door, then unlocked it, and the houseman entered holding a silver tray with fresh croissants and two glasses of grapefruit juice. Without a word or a glance he placed one glass and a single croissant on Ryan's wheelchair tray, leaving the remainder on the table.

"Sit," Ryan rasped, and pointed to the food. "And eat. I cannot abide to look up at people."

I dropped into the chair and took a sip of the juice.

"I wonder where I was," Ryan mused as he took a bite of his croissant. "Ah, yes. Richard's long descent into hell, act two.

"Well, then, I pretty well knew of Richard's depredations two years ago. By then the cocaine was an open secret, and his behavior at times could be quite bizarre, particularly when he had been drinking and taking cocaine together. Most of the time, however, he was, shall we say, *decent.* Not a model husband and father, perhaps, but decent, passable in a place like Beverly Hills, where most children need both hands to count all their parents.

"This marvelous little room I didn't discover until Richard was once again in his cups and going through another bout of trauma and guilt." The old man snorted his disgust. "Look at this—box upon box of human depravity." Ivan Ryan's eyes drifted lazily around the room and then came back to me.

"You know something, Victor? I'm not convinced that I totally disagree with pornography. It serves some useful social purposes, I imagine. We had 'blue films' in my day, too, you know. Nothing like today, though; just a few of the guys and gals getting together for a little fun. You'd be surprised at some of the big names involved. But it wasn't commercial. Just one print, usually, to travel around the screening rooms of Beverly Hills. And none of the depravity you see today, none of the utter filth: animals, kids, torture." Ryan shuddered and finished off his grapefruit juice.

And suddenly I knew. "Wheeler was involved in the snuff film."

The old man nodded his great head slowly up and down,

the revelation painful to him. "Richard . . . told me about it last month. Drunk again, of course, and stuffed to the gills with cocaine and feeling the need to expiate his guilt by talking about it to me. The whole disgusting story vomited out, and with it why he was so damn important to Scali.

"Hard to believe, isn't it? My own daughter, my own flesh and blood, married to someone like that!"

I looked at him without speaking. Since learning about Wheeler I had been bothered by the question of why Elizabeth stayed with him. Why didn't she just pack up and leave?

Ryan seemed to sense my thoughts. "I begged her to leave him, Vic. I *begged* her. But she wouldn't do it. Elizabeth's a rather old-fashioned girl, which perhaps is my fault. Living here in the birthplace of revolving parents, I always stressed the sanctity of the family, the importance of staying together and providing a stable life for the children. Elizabeth grew up feeling very strongly about family and she believed that Megan needed a father, a *real father.*" Ryan's aged face darkened. "A monster like Richard, he was *worse* than no father, but Elizabeth couldn't see it. Not then. Richard's outlandish behavior had always been restricted to late nights or to Scali's house, with only occasional outbursts of depravity here. So Elizabeth chose to live with it. At least for now, she said. . . ." The old man's voice trailed off; he didn't like thinking about his daughter's involvement with Wheeler. After a moment, he gathered his strength and continued, his voice weary and exhausted now.

"The film, the snuff film, was shot here. In this room."

I looked at him, stunned. It had never occurred to me.

"I thought you had guessed as much," Ryan continued, glancing about. He pointed a gnarled hand at a bare wall. "They hung a couple of pieces of cheap paneling on that wall, put a bed in front of it. And later . . . used the wall. The paneling has been burned. But you can see where they patched up the nail holes. No bullet holes, of course; the bullets lodged in that poor girl. Or in the wood."

I stood up and inspected the walls, running my finger along the smooth surface. The patches were there and they looked fresh.

The old man said, "Circumstantial evidence, of course. Doesn't prove a thing in court. But it is true."

The monstrousness of what Ivan Ryan was saying was just coming to me from behind the fog of the old man's tale; it took a moment before the full impact hit. I turned around and faced him. "Wheeler killed that girl. *Wheeler!*"

Ivan Ryan's face was unspeakably miserable. His eyes watered, and he looked at me without speaking.

For a long moment we stared at each other without speaking, and then I walked back to my chair, sinking down dumbly. Finally, Ryan's mouth forced itself open, his voice hollow in the horribly silent room.

"There had been others. This was the third, according to Richard. Three girls. These films are sold by mail all over the world. Or as Richard rather disingenuously put it, the 'civilized' world. And only by personal courier in this country to escape problems with the postal authorities. The profits were incredible and all in cash. All sales were in cash. Suitcases full of cash, trunks full of cash.

"That's what is in those film cans, Vic. Snuff films, animal films, torture, bestiality. All of them. This was not just a studio; it was the warehouse, a private storehouse of human misery. Friend Scali takes no chances, you see. None of his companies is connected in any way, there's nothing to tie Scali to anything. The risk was *all* Richard's. And Richard knew it. But it was worth it to him, Vic, because it gave the *more* he so desperately needed to stand out in this town."

I was dazed, the words reaching me faintly as my mind grappled with what the old man was saying: Wheeler had been responsible. *Wheeler had killed Rosa!* And right here. Right here in this room. And there had been others. My stomach ached in revulsion. I looked at Ryan almost pleadingly. "Elizabeth—"

"Elizabeth knows nothing of this," Ryan snapped. "Richard made sure she was out of the house during the filming. She knew about Scali, the drugs, the girls. But not this."

I felt a spasm of relief at the old man's words. It was inconceivable that Elizabeth Wheeler could have known what her husband had become. But Ryan was giving me no time to reflect on any of this; as he stared blankly at his small wheelchair table, his voice continued.

"You can see that Richard was quite useful to Scali. Westway became a key part of his machinery to launder massive sums of cash, more than you can ever imagine, money coming in daily from drugs, prostitution, his other 'businesses.' And Richard had his own more personal value to Scali in this potentially risky but profitable film operation; Richard was to be the sacrificial lamb in case the authorities ever got close. But of course they never did.

"Richard was also in charge of the filming. He didn't do the actual camera work, but he decided when and how it would be done. He was the director, you might say, carrying on the fine family tradition. He managed both of the cameras, set the angles and so forth, and even shot a little film and did some editing. Most of the actual filming was done by two of Scali's associates. . . ."

Ryan's voice trailed off again, as if he were unwilling to go on. His eyes squeezed shut and the aged, leathery face contorted in silent pain. It had to have been horrible for him,

I thought, watching, helpless and confined to that chair, as Wheeler sank deeper and deeper into filth, bringing disgrace to his family. I felt miserable for him and for Elizabeth and Megan and the horror their life must have been.

"What about the actors?" I asked finally. Richard Wheeler wasn't enough. I wanted everybody even remotely connected to Rosa's death—actors, production people, workers at the film lab. And Scali, most of all Scali.

The old man waved a contemptuous hand, and his head came up suddenly, his voice angry. "*Actors!* Who knows? Their heads were covered. It took little skill, Vic. The ability to achieve an erection, to force themselves on someone weaker. They weren't actors, they were animals, rabid dogs. You couldn't convince me that they were thinking, feeling human beings."

Ryan fell silent again, worn out. After a moment I pushed myself from my chair and crossed to the far wall. I needed time to think this through; it was still too difficult to fit together. *Wheeler* . . . all the time it had been Wheeler who was responsible for Rosa's death. But then who killed Wheeler?

"A beginning and middle," the old man said as I sat down again. "And now the end, the satisfying conclusion. So we can all go home feeling better.

"As I told you, when Richard gratuitously offered me this final scintilla of information concerning his role in that young girl's death, he was quite drunk. It was several nights following the filming, and her body had already been discovered, of course. One of Scali's people had been entrusted with the task of disposing of the body and had thought it amusing to dump her under the Hollywood sign, a little joke on our town: throw the locals into a frenzy. Friend Scali, I was given to understand, failed to see the humor.

"Richard, at any rate, was trying to face his conscience and fortifying his soul with prodigious amounts of our finest scotch. That's when he told me about his directorial talents. Then he brought me down here to show me a remarkable little piece of film."

The old man stopped for a moment, the lines on his face seeming to deepen. He was tiring. He breathed heavily for a moment and then looked up slowly again at me. His voice was weak as he continued. "As in all movies, much more footage was shot than was actually used. There must have been three hours of film for what turned out to be a forty-minute movie. Much of what was not used was merely repetitious, of course, some of it poorly lit or the 'actors' out of place, a camera not pointing in the proper direction, a bystander accidentally caught on film. The standard sort of mishap.

"But Richard, whatever we may say of him, was not entirely stupid. It was one of these outtakes he wanted to show me. It was his 'insurance policy,' he said. It would keep him alive forever. You'll find a film can next to the projector. Take a look. I'll wait for you here. I couldn't stand to see it again."

The film was in an open can in the projection room. I threaded it carefully and flipped on the projector and watched as pictures flickered suddenly on the screen. The film was unedited, evidently a backup copy of the original, a long series of brief, disconnected scenes often not more than several seconds in length, followed by a second or two of blankness. The portion of the film I was looking at showed Rosa already nailed to the wall, screaming and passing out. Several times the filming was stopped to revive her, once catching a man I didn't recognize slapping her awake. Five minutes into the film I saw what I was looking for: The camera had been left running for several seconds longer than necessary as it swung swiftly past the small paneled set to two men standing alone off to the side. They were in shadows, and the shot was quick, but there was no mistaking them: Scali's lieutenants, the two "executives" from the recording studio—the men who had taken Tracy—standing passively with their hands in their pockets, watching the actors going through their motions. Punks. *Scali's* punks!

I flicked off the projector and came back into the large room.

"Richard was responsible for that, of course," Ivan Ryan said as I took my chair again. "He was inordinately proud. Scali's two closest aides, caught in the act. It shouldn't be difficult to show Scali's involvement, he thought. And Scali would never touch him now, Richard said. The moment Scali lost interest in him or considered him a liability, Richard would send him a copy of that film. It would keep him alive forever."

"But it didn't, did it?"

"No, Vic, it did not."

Ivan Ryan's hard ascetic face showed each of its eight decades as he stared at me with defiance. "My son-in-law was a monster whose final years had become a hell of his own devising." Speaking very slowly he added, "He was a thoughtless animal who destroyed the happiness and well-being of both my daughter and granddaughter as well as making my own life miserable. God only knows how many deaths he was responsible for. He should never have lived."

I felt sick as I suddenly realized what Ryan was leading up to. "You killed him. You killed Wheeler."

The ancient monk's head nodded and the eyes were clear as he stared at me. "I rectified nature's error. Richard Wheeler had become a subhuman creature, a horrible aberration. I merely corrected that."

I could scarcely believe what I was hearing: The old man was *proud,* he was practically bragging about having murdered his son-in-law.

"Richard's advanced paranoia necessitated his keeping a variety of guns around the house, including a new .38 in that cabinet by the wall," Ryan went on. "A pimp's gun, all chrome plate and shiny; quite appropriate, I remember thinking at the time. As he boasted to me how that film clip had made him invincible to Scali I made the only decision that any civilized being could: Richard had forfeited the right to live. As he sat here, drinking and bragging and crying like a baby, I wheeled over to the cabinet and removed the gun. And then I put him out of his misery. José was kind enough to dispose of the carcass up at the sign. I thought it only fitting that Richard be treated in the same manner as his final victim. It was my perhaps feeble attempt to throw the police off the track: mad-dog killer loose, and all that. José drove nails through the wrists after Richard was quite dead, of course. Then we cleaned the body and dear José dumped it."

Ryan stopped for a minute, breathing heavily as if catching his breath, and then continued in an even tone. "That, of course, is why José can now afford his luxurious new Guatemalan lifestyle." His eyes flashed at me. "I'm afraid that there's no record of my attendant ever having been in this country; he was an illegal, naturally. I doubt that his name was even José. But now that he's disappeared, he never *existed.*"

I finished the thought: "And he'll never be found again."

Ryan made a deprecating gesture. "I'm not at all certain why I've told you all this. Except perhaps to show you that you're wasting your time. That young girl's killer has already been brought to justice, something that happens all too rarely in California. And Richard's death must remain unsolved, because I certainly do not intend to go to jail for ridding society of his continued disgusting existence."

"You expect me to keep this to myself?" I stared at Ryan

in a sort of fog of disbelief. Patches of perspiration had formed under my arms and dripped along my ribs.

The old man's tone was dismissive. "Surely you don't expect me to confess to premeditated murder. Dear me, no, Victor. I'm far too old to spend the rest of my days in jail. As an ex–law enforcement officer you must, at least in your heart if not your conscious mind, applaud what I have done. What we so humorously call the criminal justice system would not have been so successful. No, my dear Victor, I shall not confess. And if you reconstruct what I have told you it will become apparent that you have no evidence at all of my involvement. None! José is gone, the gun is gone, the backdrop is gone; you have nothing."

Ryan put his hands on the wheels of his chair and spun around to face the projection room. "Be thankful for what you do have. I have given you Scali's hoods—perhaps Vincente Scali himself, a coup: this *Mafiosi,* considered untouchable, and I hand him to you." He shot me a quick look. "The man who kidnapped your daughter, Vic. Be thankful."

"And now"—he leaned forward, directing the full force of his personality at me—"let us go on with the business of living. Let Elizabeth and Megan try to put their lives together and leave me alone to die in peace."

I sat in the chair, staring at the blank cement wall. After a long moment I asked, "Does Elizabeth know anything about this?"

"Of course not," Ryan snapped. "And you won't tell her. There's absolutely no way for you to prove anything I've told you about Richard's death. So what would you possibly gain by telling her that her *father* killed her husband? She's been through quite enough, Victor. She knows what her husband had become. Let us leave it at that."

I came to my feet and looked at the old man's remorseless face; there wasn't a trace of guilt or shame.

"Don't forget to take the film off of the projector," Ryan snapped at me loudly.

Without a glance at him I went into the projection room, where I rewound the film and dropped it into a film can. Leaving Ryan brooding by himself in the storage room, I found my way back up the stairs to the main floor, where the houseman was waiting for me. "Mrs. Wheeler would like a word with you in the library before you leave, Mr. Eton."

Surprised, I glanced at my watch. I hadn't expected her back yet. But it was almost noon now; I had spent two hours with Ivan Ryan.

Elizabeth Wheeler put down a china cup and forced a smile as I came into the large room. I stared at her blankly, for once unaware of the slight, attractive body and beautiful/sad face, unaware of anything outside of my own thoughts as my mind clouded over with the story I had just heard.

"Can I get you something?" she asked, sensing my discomfort. "Some coffee?"

I blinked and shook my head, clearing my mind, seeing her and again experiencing the familiar attraction but still shaken by Ryan's story and unsure of myself. "What I'd really like is a drink." My eyes came to rest on hers and I smiled feebly: "Or two."

She nodded understandingly and pointed toward the bar. "Ivan can have that effect on people. Feel free—"

I poured a small crystal tumbler half full of scotch, added a splash of water, and then carried it over to the couch, seating myself directly across from Elizabeth. She was wearing a tan and white suit that seemed created expressly for perfect Beverly Hills Sunday mornings. The drapes behind her had been pulled open, filling the large, comfortable room with light. Everything seemed so right here, a reminder of what life might have been like before Richard Wheeler's slow disintegration. As I sat she leaned forward, her voice concerned. "Tracy really is all right, isn't she? I felt so horrible when I heard about it last night. Those men—"

"They didn't hurt her. Scali thought I was getting close, and this was his way of telling me to back off. She's all right now."

Elizabeth shuddered. "Why would anyone attempt to harm a child? I can't understand people like that." She was clearly affected; she blinked back tears and tried a smile. "I hope you can bring her out here again. After Megan is back home."

"She's feeling better?" I asked.

Elizabeth nodded. "Much. Thank God!" Her expression eased but she still looked troubled. "Maybe next week."

"I've had quite a talk with your father."

She took a sip of coffee, then put the cup down. Her voice was soft and without tension. "I saw your car out front. I'm sure it was quite an experience. Ivan was quite a success in Hollywood for fifty years, of course. I don't know why he should be so worried about his reputation. He was not only a great director but also a masterful storyteller."

"A beginning, a middle, and an end," I remembered out loud.

"And credibility. No matter how strange the story may sound, the audience must think that it is *possible.*"

"My head's still spinning. Ivan can be a little overwhelming. But I can think of at least two reasons why he didn't shoot your husband." My hands were damp and I could feel my heart thudding dully as I watched her. I wished to heaven that I could stop right now, that I could get up and walk out. But it had gone too far; we had to play it through to the end.

Elizabeth stared up at the ceiling for a long moment,

and I could see her breasts move as she took a deep breath. "So that was it: Ivan the Terrible. He always liked that part. But he didn't have much time to prepare for you—only since he heard about Tracy last night. No matter what you may think about him, he adores her, Vic. I'm sure that's when he made up his mind to try to get you to drop the case."

"He had me believing it," I admitted. "In fact, I'm still trying to sort it all out. It all made some sort of sense when he was saying it but the longer I'm away from that presence of his and able to think it out by myself the more it starts to fall apart. The bullet holes, for instance—"

She gave me a questioning look.

"They were clean, no traces of fabric. That means that your husband wasn't wearing a shirt at the time he was shot. But according to Ivan, Richard was in the basement with him, getting drunk and fighting off his recurrent guilt. As bizarre as he might have been, I don't see the elegant Richard Wheeler sitting around bare-chested drinking with your father.

"And then there's the angle of the bullets—they entered his body from a horizontal position. If Ryan had shot him from his wheelchair the bullets would have entered at an upward angle. Unless Richard was seated when he was shot; again unlikely but not impossible."

"Credibility," Elizabeth Wheeler repeated as if to herself. "It has to sound as if it *could* be possible."

"The part about his attendant added a nice exotic touch to the story: the colorful supporting player. I believed it for a moment." I told her what Ryan had said about his mysterious Mayan.

"A bit too melodramatic," Elizabeth agreed. "José's real name is Thomas Escobar. He's a registered nurse and a member of the Screen Extras Guild and lives in the Valley."

I took a sip of my drink, still trying to make sense of all the bits and pieces in my mind and having difficulty because of where it led me. "The thing is," I said after a moment, "you follow this out, you wonder why he's doing it, who he's covering up for. If he is covering for someone—"

She finished my thought. ". . . he must be covering up for me."

With an effort Elizabeth came to her feet. She grabbed a Kleenex and walked to the tall windows, keeping her back to me. She seemed determined to keep her composure. After a moment she tossed the crumpled Kleenex on the floor and turned around. In a voice edged with emotion she asked, "What did my father tell you about Richard?"

I repeated what Ryan had revealed to me about Wheeler's involvement with Scali, the cocaine and pornography and finally the snuff film. Throughout, Elizabeth listened stoically.

"Richard wasn't always like that," she said hoarsely when I was finished. "We were married for fourteen years, Vic. Most of that time, believe it or not, he was a wonderful man. It was only after Scali—" She hesitated, choking on the emotion.

I waited while she struggled to continue.

After a long moment she said, "The drugs did it. It wasn't just cocaine: heroin, quaaludes, uppers, alcohol. It ruined his mind. It ate away at him and finally killed him. Mentally, emotionally, it killed him."

She sighed and grabbed another Kleenex from the box on the table and dabbed at her eyes. "They . . . Scali and the others . . . they used him; for years they used him. They turned him into a monster; they destroyed his mind and his body. But Richard was too far gone to realize it. He thought he'd finally become a real somebody in Hollywood. Not just one more Industry executive, but a real somebody, with hundreds of millions of dollars at his fingertips and about to become a political force."

"Did the politicians downtown know about Scali?"

"No. I don't think so. They were fools; they thought they were making Richard into their own little puppet. Scali knew what they were planning, of course. He must have thought it hilarious.

"The last two years have been a horror. Richard drunk or on drugs, disappearing for days, violent, hitting me. And then the pornography, the sex. Filthy books around the house all the time. And with Megan here . . . I pleaded with him, but it didn't do any good. Then two months ago I took Megan and left. I didn't even tell my father where I was going. We drove to San Diego and checked into a motel, and after a week I called Richard and told him I was going to get a divorce. He broke down, Vic. He broke down and cried for the first time in his life."

She fell silent. I knew what was coming. "He talked you into coming back."

She nodded, holding back tears. "He promised to change. He promised to see a psychologist. I *made* him promise. And to give up Scali, the drugs, the filth. I knew he couldn't do it alone and I knew he'd never be able to do it if I left. He *promised,* Vic, and he needed me, and I couldn't turn him down. After fourteen years I couldn't turn him down. And Megan needed him."

I sighed inwardly. I had heard this sort of promise too many times before, the appeal to pity, the practiced attempt to get others to throw aside common sense for "one more chance." How sincere it always sounds; and how superficial it usually is. Quietly, I asked, "How long did he stay straight?"

She kept her voice steady, but her hands clutched at the wadded-up Kleenex. "A week, maybe less, I don't know. I was out of the house when that . . . film was made downstairs. Megan and I were visiting friends. By the time we got home everyone was gone. We didn't know a thing about it.

"Then the next weekend he started drinking as soon as he got up. He was horrible all day, drinking, insulting me, telling me about all the young girls at Scali's, how they'd do anything for him. After dinner he was worse. He stopped insulting me and hit me; then he grabbed me and dragged me down into the basement to show me that horrible film, the unedited film he was so *proud* of, the one with Scali's people. I couldn't believe that human beings could sink so low, to kill someone for a *movie.*

"Watching that film again, watching that girl die, *excited* him, Vic. It excited him, made him want to have sex. I was sick, I started to vomit. He got undressed and when I tried to run he grabbed me and hit me in the face but I still couldn't do it. I couldn't get over seeing that girl—

"He kept hitting me and hitting me until I fell to the floor and almost passed out. He was crazy, screaming and hitting me and yelling.

"When he saw me on the floor crying, bleeding, he said if I wouldn't cooperate there was still Megan."

She looked at me in disbelief and horror. "His own *daughter,* Vic. His own daughter! He left me on the floor and started for the projection room. He was going upstairs. All I could think of was Megan. I grabbed the gun out of that drawer and ran after him. I caught up to him out by the stairs. He turned around to hit me and I shot him. I shot him three times and he stood still and looked at me as if he wanted to crush me and then he dropped, right there. And then Megan opened the door and saw him and saw me with the gun—"

I swallowed hard, and Elizabeth subsided into sobbing, her entire body trembling. I waited a moment, not wanting to make her live through it again but having to know. Keeping my voice gentle, I asked, "Did Megan know what he was going to do?"

"I don't know," Elizabeth sobbed. "Maybe. She knew what he'd become, she'd seen him drunk and she'd seen him hit me." Her eyes, red with tears, opened wide as she stared at me. "She *saw* me, Vic! She saw her mother with the gun and her father dead and she started screaming and screaming—"

Her voice cracked and she looked away. "She's in a private psychiatric hospital in Bel Air. She wakes up in the middle of the night screaming."

I could feel my body tense, the muscles in my stomach contract as if I were going to be sick. For several seconds I was silent.

"Why didn't you just call the police?" I finally asked, feeling helpless and angry. Why had they covered it up like this, creating this elaborate fantasy that merely dragged them both deeper in a hole of their own making? "You could have been spared all this—the investigation, the rumors—"

She looked at me with pleading eyes. "I called my *father*! He told me not to do anything. Then he had Thomas Escobar drive him over here. When Dad saw the body he was afraid I'd be arrested for manslaughter or even murder. Richard wasn't armed, there was no proof he was going to harm me or Megan . . . her bedroom's in the other wing on the second floor."

She buried her face in her hands. After a moment she said, "Dad said we'd be better off just getting rid of him; nobody would know what had happened. Megan wouldn't be dragged into it, made a spectacle of in the papers. I wouldn't have to worry about a trial. We'd all be better off. He told me to get Ton—that's our houseman. He was asleep in his room on the third floor. I don't know how Dad convinced him—

money, I imagine. But Dad made me take Megan over to his house and stay there. Then he arranged about the body. I guess the rest of what he told you was true—the holes in the wrists . . ."

I stood slowly and walked over to the bar and refilled my glass while Elizabeth continued to sob on the couch. I took a sip, felt the liquid warm my body. My mind was numb, and I felt like hell.

Elizabeth looked at me, her face distorted with fear and shock and living it all over again. "Vic, he was going to *rape* her!"

I put my glass down on the small bar. *Take a breath,* I told myself. *Relax. Think. But slowly. Don't move too fast.*

After a moment, I said, "Don't do anything right now. I'll call you in the morning."

I walked back to the chair and picked up the film can. "Take care of Megan. No one should have to go through what she has."

As I left, the houseman wheeled Ivan Ryan into the room, and up to his daughter.

*What to do about Elizabeth?* I wondered as I lay awake all night.

And what to do about Scali?

That one was easier. Scali's hoods were on film. *Scali doesn't do jail,* the cop at Organized Crime insisted.

We'll see. It's one thing to buy off punks taking a drug rap for you, another when they're facing what California calls "special circumstances" in a murder case. The special circumstances leading to a newly resurgent Death Row. No, Scali was going to be history.

But Elizabeth . . . Elizabeth killed her husband. . . .

I thought about it all night. Then decided.

I did nothing.

The police were right. Whoever killed Rosa must have killed Wheeler. It made sense. Same M.O., same location of the bodies. Hell, let a jury worry about it. Let Scali worry about it. No reason to go beyond that.

In the morning I took Tracy over to a girl friend's house in West L.A. and told her I'd pick her up after I took care of a few things with Oscar Reddig and the LAPD. She leaned through the car window and said, "Safety first, Dad—put your seat belt on. And drive carefully; this is the only car we have now." Then she laughed lightly and kissed me on the cheek.

On the way back to the apartment I debated with myself about calling Allison. I thought about last night and Scali getting to her, and what she had said when I asked about Tracy, and what she had said about not caring about Rosa. I thought about it all the way home. And then I didn't want to think about it anymore.

I killed an hour back in the apartment straightening up. Then I called a guy I know who restores cars and asked him what I should do about the Morgan. Push the pieces into the sea, he said. I told him I didn't think so; I thought I'd save them. Maybe something was salvageable. I wanted to try, anyway. A little later I was standing at the sink, washing out the coffeepot and beginning to mentally prepare my story for Oscar Redding, when the phone rang.

Allison.

"Vic? Everything's all right, isn't it? Tracy's okay?"

Yeah, sure, I told her as I sat down at the kitchen table. Everything was fine. How was she?

"Okay." Her voice had gone suddenly distant, the mood change beginning already as surely as if a switch had been thrown. Where was she drifting? I wondered. Into Allison the artist or Allison the entrepreneur? Or Allison the hooker? Manic Allison or dejected Allison?

"Vic—" she said at length, and let out a deep breath. I

could almost see her as she tried to work it out—not what she was going to do but how to say it. For someone whose life was focused on human relationships of one sort or another, she was surprisingly inept at talking about them. I remained silent, held the phone in a tightened fist, and listened.

"I'm sorry about what happened, Vic. I really am. But *please* try to understand. These men came to my apartment—they didn't have to tell me who they were. I knew! They told me to drop it, to stop worrying about Rosa." She paused and I could hear the sound of the clock on the stove five feet away from me ticking loudly. My hand tightened on the receiver. With a little burst of energy she added, "They made me promise to forget about all of it. And to stay away from you. I'm not even supposed to be *talking* to you. . . ."

"And you agreed."

Her tone hardened, became accusatory. "*They had a bottle of acid!* They held my head and jabbed it in front of my face and made me smell it. They were going to *blind* me if I didn't do what they said. What the hell did you want me to do?"

I thought, *I never knew* what *I wanted you to do, Allison.* And I thought, *I should learn to trust my instincts: When that little voice comes alive in the back of my mind I should know enough by now to pay attention to it.*

Her voice went suddenly soft and a spasm of anger went through me as I felt myself being dragged along on the arc of her emotions: "I know it sounds corny, Vic, but it was different with you. I mean it. It'd been a long time since I cared. Maybe never, maybe I've never cared before. . . ." A pause, short, a shift of gears again, her voice going up an octave. "I can't fight these people, Vic. I've got to watch out for myself. Allison's plan for financial independence, right? How many years do I have? Two? Three? I'm not going to lose everything now. I'm not going to end up on the street like Rosa. I should have listened to you when Davey brought me to your office. What the hell was I trying to do, looking for her killer? It was stupid, a schoolgirl's dream, and I'm no schoolgirl. I should have listened. Then none of this would have happened."

Despite herself she started crying softly. "Those stupid men, *those goddamn stupid men. . . .*"

"They're going to jail," I told her. "Scali's men, Scali. They're going to jail. It's over for you. You can relax."

"Don't fool yourself, Vic. It'll *never* be over. Do you think it *matters* that Scali goes to jail? Does it matter?"

"It matters," I said. "It matters to me."

"Does it make *me* any safer? Do his friends disappear? Does his organization disappear? It doesn't make any difference at all, Vic. None! Not one damn bit. Not to Hollywood, not to me. Nothing. They're *not* going away. Ever!"

She paused long enough to take a breath. "I mailed you a check this morning. We're even now." The words raced along, as if she had allocated herself only so much time to get it all out. "Vic, I'm sorry, I'm really sorry it ended like this. But I *know* those men, I've dealt with them before. Not those two exactly, but like them. I know what they can do—and they'll do it, without a second's thought. I'm not going to let that happen."

I started to say something but she bulled ahead. "It wouldn't have been any good, anyway. We're too different. And neither of us is going to change. . . ."

*What am I feeling?* I wondered silently as I listened to the erratic words, the roller-coaster emotion. But I couldn't isolate it. Anger at Allison's self-absorption, at her inability to see beyond her own self-interest. Anger at Allison, and at myself, for risking Tracy's life. Anger, and maybe a little wounded ego, at the way she was able to cut me—and Rosa—

out of her life without much more than a blink of an eye. At her goddamn plans for the future.

But it had all been as inevitable as the sunrise, I knew. Even though she would never admit it to herself, Rosa and I had served our purpose for Allison, whatever that might have been: a little boost to her self-esteem, perhaps; a half-hearted attempt at loyalty to a dead friend; or even a sudden surge of civic responsibility—helping the police find a killer. But it was over. Scali's men or not. What pain there was for her would be short-lived: Rosa and I were already slipping from her consciousness. Her voice cracked a bit, then began to race again as she hurried to bring it to an end. "We both work in Hollywood—maybe we'll run into one another someday. . . ."

"Sure," I said. Maybe we will. And she said good-bye and I said good-bye and we hung up and I realized my hand was wet with perspiration. Then with a sudden twist of anger I imagined her going back to her painting, a Beethoven quartet playing softly in the background—and almost immediately cursed myself for not being fair: Allison was doing what she had to, what was best for Allison. Like she said, what did you want her to do? Maybe she actually had cared, maybe she *was* capable of a spark of real emotion. Then I thought again of last night: Allison's *Just drop it, I'll send you a check,* and Tracy shaking in the backseat of the police car. And Tracy joking with me this morning and kissing me good-bye: *Drive carefully* . . . And I closed my eyes and let the images slip away. *Stop probing it,* I told myself. *Let it be.* And thought: *You're right, Allison. We're too different.*

And maybe we will run into one another.

In the afternoon I took the film downtown and spent a few hours with Captain Oscar Reddig and the team handling the case. It couldn't be any simpler than this, I told them: It's all right there in front of you—Scali's people caught in the act. It won't be difficult implicating the man who paid them.

Yeah, well, where'd the film *come from*? they kept asking, as if something about it bothered them.

"Someone gave it to me," I said. "Anonymously. It was sitting on my desk when I got into the office today. Someone must have slipped the lock on the door this weekend and left it there. Probably someone in Scali's organization, maybe someone who wanted his job: number-two capo, trying to move up the hierarchy. Everyone wants to be a success."

"You'll testify to that?" Oscar asked blankly.

"Of course. But if you folks get a warrant and poke around all the properties that Scali and his various business firms own you'll probably turn up quite a few interesting films. Might even find one with the second victim."

"That'd be nice," Oscar said. "But we probably don't need it. Same M.O., same location of the bodies."

I said that made sense to me.

Rudy came by after work with a six-pack and a container of homemade guacamole. Tracy pulled a bag of tortilla chips from the cupboard and said, "I'm off my diet until the dip's gone."

Rudy said, "Scali's being booked right now. It's taking a while because he showed up with half a dozen lawyers and his own bail bondsman. He'll be out in twenty-four hours but only temporarily. Oscar was able to get warrants on eight properties Scali controls and they're going through them now. He has high expectations for turning up something dirty—drugs, if not more films. How's the widow Wheeler, by the way?"

"Great!" Tracy said through a mouthful of guacamole.

"We're going up there next week. Ivan's going to show us the *Pickwick Papers* he made at MGM in the fifties. They did it as a musical."

Rudy looked over at me. "I guess you've become friends."

"I like them," I said. "I like all three of them: Elizabeth, Megan, Ivan. They're nice people."

Rudy lifted his feet one at a time and stretched them out on the coffee table and sighed. "Funny how things work out sometimes, isn't it? Like you folks becoming friends. Or you turning up that film; that was pretty lucky."

Yep, I agreed. Pretty lucky.

"We're out of chips," Tracy announced. Nobody moved, so she got up and went in the kitchen, returning a moment later to put another bag on the table. "Sometimes you've just got to make things happen," she said as she sat down.

Rudy looked over at me. "Yeah, that's what I figure."

Tracy ripped open the bag. "Dad and I are going up to Santa Barbara for a week and lay on the beach, catch some rays and mellow out. I can't wait. It sure beats fishing."

"Santa Barbara," Rudy said wistfully, and dipped a chip into the guacamole. "I like that." He thought about it some more, to make sure, then smiled to himself. "Yeah. I like it."